MOONSTRUCK

NECESSARY EVILS

MOONSTRUCK

ONLEY JAMES

MOONSTRUCK

NECESSARY EVILS BOOK THREE

Cover and Interior Design by We Got You Covered Book Design
WWW.WEGOTYOUCOVEREDBOOKDESIGN.COM

ISBN: 978-1-68489-143-6

TRIGGER WARNING

This book contains graphic violence and very dark humor.

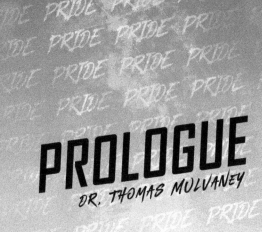

PROLOGUE

DR. THOMAS MULVANEY

Thomas shook off his umbrella, looking back at the storm raging outside the children's home. It was almost apocalyptic out there—lightning chasing across the sky, thunder shaking the ground with each boom. The streetlights gave the sheets of rain an eerie glow, or maybe that was just Thomas's imagination. His head was a mess tonight.

This was it. The beginning of his plan. A culmination of everything he'd planned for the last year...if the boy worked out. Allen seemed sure that this boy—this orphaned eight-year-old child—was the perfect subject for Thomas's project.

He wiped the rain from his brow as he walked towards an elderly security guard hunched over the front desk. Just as he was about to announce himself, Allen came sweeping out from a doorway on the left. "Thomas, just in time. Come with me."

Allen clapped him on the back and turned him around just as the security guard noticed him. Allen gave the man a wave. He dipped his head, returning to whatever had his

1

attention on the desk.

Allen gave him a reassuring smile, running a hand through his dark hair. He was in his late forties, handsome in a distinguished way, graying only at the temples. He was almost the same age as his father would have been had he lived. It made sense given he was one of Thomas's father's closest friends. All these years later, their friendship still baffled Thomas. His father was a nightmare of a human, rotten to his core.

Allen on the other hand was…solid. Not overly friendly or ingratiating. Not too cold or distant. He was the definition of steadfast. When people said somebody had a good head on their shoulders, they were often talking about somebody like Allen. He was respected, connected, and beyond reproach. How had Allen tolerated his father all those years?

It didn't matter. Thomas was grateful to have Allen as an ally, somebody to easily navigate the system, cut through red tape, facilitate transfers, and run interference.

The building was deceptively small outside, but inside was a sea of closed doors and tunneling hallways. They'd painted the walls a nauseating mint green that had faded to an even dingier yellowish green over time. The linoleum tiles were starting to peel up from the concrete floor beneath, and the lights flickered like something out of an old horror movie. When they reached a crossroads, they took a hallway on the left.

Thomas gave a nervous laugh. "There's no end to this place."

Allen chuckled. "It seems that way."

Thomas darted a glance in the older man's direction. "Where are we going?"

"Trust me, just…just trust me," Allen said, increasing his pace.

They made a right turn and came to a dead end where there were four closed doors. Allen nodded to a woman wearing jeans, a baggy sweatshirt, and a ponytail. "Is he in there already?"

She nodded.

"Alone?"

She shook her head, eyeing Thomas curiously. "No sir, with Frankie."

"Excellent."

He led Thomas to the first door on the left. An observation room of sorts, with a two-way mirror dividing them and two young boys. One of the boys had a shock of red hair, eyes so blue Thomas could see them from across the room, and a smattering of freckles across his cheeks. He might have been the most wholesome looking child he'd ever seen. He sat at a table with a small blond boy, much younger than himself. He was showing the little boy something in the book. The little boy made a face like he thought something was gross and then began to giggle. The red-headed boy followed suit.

He and Allen observed their play for roughly five minutes before Thomas asked, "What am I looking at here?"

"Just wait for it."

Thomas shifted restlessly, crossing his arms over his chest.

Another minute or two passed, and then the woman with the ponytail entered, calling the smaller boy to come with her. He stood and waved. The red-headed child eagerly waved back. Thomas gave one more puzzled look at Allen before the man pointed back to the room.

When Thomas looked back, the red-headed boy was now methodically tearing out the pages of the book, taking those pages and shredding them into smaller and smaller strips, a blank expression on his face. The rapid shift in his demeanor was bone-chilling given his liveliness just moments ago.

Before he could enquire further, another woman entered. This woman was wearing a skirt and blouse, dressed as if she were about to go to a function or maybe on a date. The boy turned to the woman, looking her up and down with slow, methodical precision. She smiled warmly. He did as well. She extended her hand and he took it, shaking it. When she sat beside him, she crossed her legs at the ankles, keeping her hands in her lap. The boy did the same. When she leaned in, he did the same.

"He's...mimicking her."

"Yes."

"Why?"

"We're not quite sure."

"What's his backstory?" Thomas asked, unable to tear his eyes away from the seamless way the boy mirrored the woman.

"They raided a property down south after they'd heard rumors it was a grow farm. And it was. Everything from

weed to poppies. There were several people living on the property. None of them related, all of them indigent. They still haven't sorted who's who. The ones who can speak with any coherency aren't talking and the rest have had their brains strangled from huffing paint and gasoline."

"Jesus."

"This boy is one of thirteen children they detained, ranging from six months to eight years. He was caring for all of them. Feeding them, dressing them, creating makeshift diapers out of old bedsheets, doing the best he could to keep them clean considering there was no running water and the trailer the children were kept in had a floor that was sagging straight into the dirt."

"And nobody knows who he belongs to?"

Allen shrugged. "Nobody is claiming him. We haven't sent DNA swabs yet. Even if he does belong to one of those tweakers, they're not going to see the light of day for years. The others are young, easy to place. But this one... I saw him and I knew."

"Knew what?" Thomas asked, riveted by the boy on the other side of the window.

"They had him evaluated by a psychiatrist. He's intelligent, well-spoken, fastidious, very particular about his things. Shows a surprising level of education given his living conditions and even speaks fluent Spanish, though that likely has to do with the migrant workers on the farm. The psychiatrist gave him a glowing report other than a diagnosis of obsessive compulsive disorder."

"So, why am I here, Allen?"

"Because he fooled a board certified psychiatrist, Thomas. When he's not interacting with another person, he's observing. He watches them, mirrors them, does what they do. He's teaching himself to fake emotions he doesn't have. And he's learning very quickly."

"You're saying…"

"He has no sense of fear, no anxiety, no guilt. He steals from the other kids, hoards food, money, clothes. Admits guilt when caught but feels morally righteous about his crimes. He's not violent. At least, that we've witnessed. But if he's placed in the wrong hands, imagine what he'll pick up. The behaviors he would mirror. Make no mistake. That boy is a psychopath."

The gears in Thomas's head were already turning. Allen was right. The boy was perfect for his purposes. A gifted mimic who could blend seamlessly into polite society, while also lacking the remorse or guilt others might have at committing violent acts, no matter how deserved they might be. Nobody knew how to train this child better than Thomas. It would almost be a crime not to take him.

"And nobody knows about him?" Thomas asked sharply.

"Nobody but those of us who have worked with him. It would be easy enough to fabricate a transfer to another facility on paper. Nobody would question his disappearance."

Was he truly doing this? This was the point of no return. If he took this child, he had to put his money where his mouth was, literally. He'd have to forge documents, bribe officials, and raise a child under rigorous moral guidelines. He was barely more than a child himself.

Still, he knew this was the right thing. It had to be. If he could prove that psychopaths weren't a plague on society but a gift, an evolutionary tool that could be harnessed to cull the monsters of their society, he'd change the world.

Dr. Molly Shepherd had proven it could be done once. She'd raised a sociopath, had turned him into a productive member of society. But she did it as a mother, not as a scientist. No peer review board would approve a study with children as lab rats, but science required proof via replication. And that started with study subjects like the boy in there.

"Does he have a name?" Thomas asked.

Allen nodded. "He says his name is Christian."

Thomas nodded. "We'll have to change that. We'll have to make him disappear and reappear as somebody else entirely. New name, new birthday, new birth certificate."

Allen nodded. "We've been putting these things into place for months now, Thomas. This one is your first. I know it."

Thomas swallowed audibly, feeling like there was dust in his throat. "May I speak to him?"

"Of course."

Allen led him around to the room's entrance and beckoned the woman within. "That's all, Nancy. Thanks for humoring me."

"No problem, Allen. What a sweet boy. This was probably more fun than the dinner I'm being forced to sit through tonight."

She was gone with a wave and a nod.

Once more, the boy sat quietly, picking at something

beneath his fingernails.

Thomas approached him slowly. "Mind if I sit with you?"

The boy looked up at him with solemn blue eyes and shook his head. Thomas took a seat.

"I'm Thomas."

"I'm Christian."

"Do you like it here, Christian?" Thomas asked.

The boy looked him in the eye and said, "It's nice. I'm very happy here."

Thomas tilted his head. "Are you *really*?"

The boy tilted his as well, studying Thomas's expression for a long moment. "No?"

"Is that a question?" Thomas asked.

"I'm not sure what I'm supposed to say," Christian finally admitted.

Fascinating. "I imagine this place isn't a lot of fun."

The boy shrugged tiny shoulders. "It's clean. Nobody beats me or touches me where they're not supposed to. I wish people would stop touching my stuff, though."

Thomas's stomach churned at the casual comment. How much had the child endured that he would make a statement like that offhand? "People touched you where they weren't supposed to?"

The look the boy gave him sent a shiver down his spine. "Only once."

The malice in those two words was the very reason people like this boy needed Thomas and his program. "I am looking to adopt a boy just like you."

The boy's brows knitted together. "No offense, mister,

but you don't look much older than me."

Thomas grinned. "I'm older than I look." When the boy shrugged again, Thomas said, "I have this big old house and nobody to share it with. I want to fill it with kids just like you. But there are rules. A lot of them. But it's very clean and nobody will touch you without your permission. Ever. I can't promise that when you have brothers they won't mess with your stuff. But you'll be my first. My eldest. You'll look out for them. How does that sound?"

"What do I have to do for it?" he asked suspiciously.

"Just abide by my rules."

He seemed to think on it for a long moment before giving a singular nod. "Yeah, I guess I can do that."

"There is one more thing. In order for you to come with me, we'll have to give you a new name. Would that be alright?"

"Okay."

"What name would you like?" Thomas asked.

"What name would *you* like?" the boy countered.

Thomas could have pushed the issue, tried to make the boy choose a new name for himself, but it seemed a ridiculous hill to die on given the battles he was sure would come as he aged. "Me? I've always liked the name Atticus."

Again, the boy tilted his head the way Thomas had. "Atticus? Why?"

"Because Atticus Finch from *To Kill a Mockingbird* was my favorite book character."

"Why?"

Thomas chuckled. "Because he believed in personal

responsibility and in doing what was right. Because he was brave in the face of opposition. Because he didn't need to throw his weight around and get violent or defend himself against people who talked badly about him. He let his actions speak for themselves. But mostly, I guess he's my favorite character because he was a good father and my father... My father wasn't."

Thomas hadn't really meant to get that deep with his answer, but the boy looked him in the eye, nodding. "It's a good name. I like it. I don't know if I can be all those things."

"You don't have to be all of those things. You just have to live a life where you leave the world better than you found it," Thomas said.

"Okay."

Allen entered the room, looking between the two of them. "Are you ready to go, Atticus?"

Of course, he'd been eavesdropping.

The boy nodded, pushing his hair from his eyes. "Yeah." He looked to Thomas. "What's our last name?"

"Mulvaney."

"Mulvaney," the boy parroted. "Cool. I've never had one of those before."

Thomas put a hand on the boy's head briefly before removing it. He'd promised the boy no touching without his permission. He didn't want to damage his trust in him before they left the building. "Well, it's yours now. From now on, you're Atticus Mulvaney, eldest son of Thomas Mulvaney, and that's all anybody ever needs to know."

Atticus looked him in the eye. "Okay."

ONE
ATTICUS

Atticus cursed as his three hundred dollar hiking boots sank into a muddy rut in the ground. It was the closest thing to a path in the heavy underbrush. It had rained hours ago, making the trek through the woods far more treacherous than he'd imagined. He'd dressed for the occasion in a black long-sleeved shirt and waterproof tactical pants. Even the small bag slung over his shoulder was made for hiking. He just hadn't expected it to be this hot…and dirty. He hated getting dirty.

His boot made an obscene sucking sound as he pulled it free of the muck with a disgusted grunt. He was going to have to find a way to clean that off before he left. He'd never get the filth out of his car if he didn't. The smell of rain and rotting vegetation was permanently imprinted in his nostrils.

His target, Trevor Maynard, was a sniveling little wannabe gangbanger who got off taking advantage of the immigrant women his parents employed at their dry cleaners. He wore his shirts too tight and his pants too low

and thought tying a bandana around his forehead made him some kind of thug.

Trevor liked to abuse his power, threatening the jobs of his victims to lure them out into the woods where nobody would hear them scream. While Atticus's father's insistence on taking the man out in the middle of nowhere to kill him was karmically just, it was also unnecessarily dramatic in Atticus's opinion.

Guys like Trevor rarely put up a fight in the face of danger. If anything, he would beg and plead, attempt to use his perceived status—of which he had none—and offer money as a last resort. It would all end the same, with Atticus Jackson Pollacking his brains against the back wall of his shitty cabin. This could have all been done closer to the city.

Still, he didn't argue with his father—just followed orders like the dutiful eldest son he was. The faster he finished the job, the faster he could go home and shower. He had an early day at the office tomorrow. Luckily, the full moon overhead cut a wide beam, allowing him to see without much trouble, even if the clear path was hardly a path at all. He stepped free of the grove of trees, finally finding himself outside the small cabin. Why did these creeps always go for cabins in the woods? Atticus found torturing people in the city was just as effective. People had very little problem ignoring the distress of strangers. Sad but helpful in his particular line of work.

An ear-shattering scream pierced the silence, sending a shock of adrenaline through Atticus and spurring him into motion without thought. He pulled his gun, making sure

he was locked and loaded, silencer in place, advancing on the flimsy cabin door. Why hadn't it occurred to him the man wouldn't be alone?

It took two hard kicks before the door flew in on its hinges, startling the two occupants. His victim was tied to a sturdy wooden chair in the center of the room, bleeding from several oozing wounds and missing no less than three fingers and an earlobe. There was no woman in the room so the scream must have come from Trevor.

Beside him, a man in his late twenties stood holding a wicked-looking serrated blade. He wore faded blue jeans and a black v-neck t-shirt that revealed an intricate tattoo down his entire left arm. Atticus found himself riveted in place as he took in thick black hair and serious eyebrows set over dark brown eyes. The stranger looked equal parts irritated and surprised, but it was clear he was weighing his options.

"I heard screaming," Atticus heard himself say lamely.

The man blinked in confusion, holding up his knife. "They do that when you poke them with this."

Atticus gave him a pissy look. "Yes, I've connected the dots, thank you."

Realizing that he'd brought a knife to a gun fight, the stranger dropped his hand to his side. "Listen, man. This is a really bad guy. I know he looks like a harmless nerd—"

"Wow," Trevor muttered.

"But he's really a huge piece of shit. Why don't you just turn around and walk away? No harm, no foul, you know?"

"How do you know I'm not a cop?" Atticus asked.

The stranger scoffed. "Yeah, you're not a cop. That gun

isn't police issue. Hell, no cop could afford that gun."

Atticus wasn't sure why the man's smug assessment annoyed him, but it did, just like the man's sweeping gaze made him feel like he stood there naked. What the fuck was happening right now?

It didn't matter. If he fucked this up, he'd never hear the end of it. Adam still hadn't let go of the meat cleaver incident and that was a year ago.

Atticus pinched the bridge of his nose with his gloved fingers. "Unfortunately, I can't do that. He's on my list. I have to kill him. I have…people to answer to."

Once more, that gaze raked over him, this time with a lot more heat. "Yeah, you don't look like a pro either."

Atticus bristled. "Well I assure you, I'm no amateur."

Trevor snickered, then yelped when the man jabbed him with the knife, the blade barely sinking in half an inch just above his nipple. "What the fuck, man!"

"Pro or not, this kill is mine. I promise you, he'll never see the light of day. So, you can just go."

"Yeah, I can't do that. I need to see him dead. And I don't know you, so your promises don't mean a whole helluva lot. No offense," Atticus said, making sure his tone implied full offense.

"This is such bullshit," Trevor grumbled.

"Shut the fuck up, Trevor," the man snapped.

"Hey, fuck you, Jet Li," Trevor fired back, seemingly realizing the error of his ways when the stranger flicked his gaze towards him.

"Jet Li is Chinese, you racist fuck. Do I look Chinese to

you, man?"

Atticus fought the urge to smile at the loaded question.

"How the fuck should I know?" Trevor wailed. "You all—"

"Jesus, please, don't say all Asians look the same," Atticus begged. "Die with some fucking dignity."

The stranger gave Atticus another appraising look that left him feeling hot all over. He wondered if his face was turning bright red. One of many drawbacks of being a fair-skinned redhead. After a moment, the stranger slapped the flat part of the blade against the space between Trevor's eyes.

"Let's play a game."

"No thanks, asshole," Trevor said, eyelids fluttering like he might actually succumb to his obvious blood loss.

The stranger paced around Trevor's chair. "Oh, come on. If you can guess where I'm from, I'll let you live."

Trevor scoffed. "And then what? This dude fucking shoots me? I'm still dead, man."

Atticus sized up the man. "What the hell. If you can guess where he's from, you can walk out of here alive."

Trevor's gaze swiveled between the two of them. "Really?"

Atticus shrugged. "Sure. Why not."

"See, you got nothing to lose and your life to gain," the stranger said.

Atticus hopped up on the sturdy wooden table, fishing through his bag until he found what he was looking for, making a satisfied sound as he pulled out a granola bar. He tore into it, suddenly ravenous, taking a bite and chewing it slowly while they watched. "What? It was a long walk from the road."

Trevor quickly lost interest in Atticus. "How many guesses do I get?"

The man tossed the knife in the air, then caught the blade between two fingers, considering the question. "Three."

"Oh, come on. There's like a thousand Asian cities."

"Asia is a continent, you dumb fuck. You only need to guess the country."

"You know what I mean. Asia has a bunch of countries," Trevor whined.

"Just forty-eight," Atticus offered around a bite of peanut butter and dark chocolate, earning a smirk from the stranger.

"Hey, you know I'm not Chinese, right? So, now, you only have to guess from forty-seven countries. Come on, Trevor. Put that big racist brain to work."

"Fuck. Okay. Um, Korean?"

The stranger mimicked a buzzer noise. "Strike one."

There was another scream as Trevor lost a finger for his trouble. Atticus swung his feet, looking down at his granola bar. It wasn't his usual brand. He usually preferred the ones his housekeeper picked up from Whole Foods, but they'd been out, so she'd substituted them with a different, slightly less expensive option. These were far superior.

The scent of urine and blood was cloying, competing in Atticus's nostrils with the fetid dirt and vegetation from moments ago.

Trevor was whimpering and crying now. "Fuck... Fuck. You didn't say there was a penalty for wrong answers!"

"You put Jenny Tran in the hospital for six weeks from her injuries, and then you had her fucking deported. You're

lucky I started with your fucking fingers. Now, guess or die."

Trevor whined, his head lolling on his shoulders. "Japanese?" he said weakly.

The stranger's handsome face contorted into one of fake remorse. "Afraid not, Trevor."

Trevor screamed like a topless girl in a seventies horror movie as another finger fell to his stupidity. His frantic gaze found Atticus. "I'm serious. I have money. A lot of it. Shoot him in the head, and I'll give you fifty grand. Help me out here, man. My parents will be hella grateful."

Atticus snorted, pushing up the sleeve on his shirt. "Do you see this watch? It's a Patek Philippe. It's worth a hundred grand, and it's my backup casual watch. Offer declined."

The stranger shrugged. "Guess it's just you and me, Trevor. Last chance. What do you think? Feeling lucky?"

Trever made a whining sound. "This isn't fair…"

"No, not fair is you raping and abusing powerless women who were just trying to make a living. What's not fair is using fear and intimidation to hide your crimes. What's not fair is forcing girls to have unwanted abortions to keep your sick fucking fetishes to yourself. That wasn't fair. This… This is fucking karma. You taking your last guess or not?"

Heavy breathing filled the room, and Trevor's eyes darted around as if the answer might magically appear on the wall.

"Tick-tock," the stranger teased.

"Uh…Thailand? The Philippines? Madagascar?" Trevor blurted.

"Madagascar's in Africa, you dumb fuck," Atticus said, taking another bite of his granola bar.

The man dropped to sit on Trevor's knees, causing the man's face to contort in horror. "Wrong answer."

Atticus didn't see the knife blade sink in, but he saw the way Trevor's eyes went wide and heard the wet rattle of his last breath as blood bubbled from his lips. He watched as the stranger stood and used Trevor's shoulder to wipe the mess off his blade as red bloomed across the dead man's chest.

"What are you going to do with him?" Atticus finally asked, crumpling his wrapper and carefully putting it back in his bag.

The stranger shrugged. "Leave him here with the doors open and let the animals clean up for me."

Atticus nodded. It wasn't what he would have done, but it wasn't his kill so, technically, it wasn't his problem. Not that he was planning on telling anybody but his father any of this. "So, just out of curiosity, what was the right answer? Where are you from?"

The stranger grinned, revealing perfect teeth and a smile that went straight to Atticus's dick. "Me? San Diego."

Atticus snorted. "He was way off."

The man floated closer until there was only a few feet between them. "Not really. I'm half Chinese. I'm also half Mexican. But I wasn't about to give that racist prick the satisfaction. Besides, it added a little something, don't you think?"

"It was fun. Like killing with my brothers." The moment the words slipped free, Atticus closed his eyes, irritated with himself.

"Like, your literal brothers, or are you in a gang of beefy

gingers, who look like they moonlight as insurance salesmen?"

Atticus didn't know if he was supposed to be flattered or offended. The stranger's words were mocking, but his tone was borderline salacious. "Are you... Are you flirting with me?"

The stranger shrugged, closing the distance between them. "I mean, how often do you meet somebody who you don't have to lie to about what you do?"

"I'm not gay," Atticus managed, sounding unsure even to himself.

The stranger grinned, and Atticus's stomach did somersaults. "Yeah, but you're not straight either, are you?"

"I'm a psychopath," Atticus blurted.

The stranger leaned forward, his whisper conspiratorial. "I'm a Scorpio. I still like banging dudes."

"I—" Atticus stopped then. "I don't know what to do with that information."

The man's brow hooked upwards suggestively. "I can think of a few things?"

Atticus floundered, hoping they could both ignore his obvious erection. "I don't even know your name."

"Jericho."

"That's not a real name," Atticus scoffed.

Jericho snorted. "My mother would beg to differ. What's your name?"

"Atticus," he managed, clearly giving up all attempts at self-preservation.

"That's not a real name," Jericho countered, tone somewhere between teasing and seductive, advancing until

he stood between Atticus's splayed knees. His gaze dropped pointedly to his dick straining against his zipper. "Need some help with that?" What Atticus needed was to just open his mouth and say no and then get the hell out of there, but then Jericho said, "I always wanted to suck off a ginger. Do you taste different?"

"That's offensive," Atticus managed, earning another grin from Jericho. That fucking smile.

Atticus didn't remember curling his fingers into the other man's shirt and dragging him forward, but he must have because their mouths were crashing together in a kiss that was more teeth than tongue. The minute they touched, Atticus's sense of reason flew out the window, his need consuming him. There was nothing soft or slow or restrained about it. It was rough and borderline painful, teeth dragging and biting over tender skin, tongues fighting for dominance.

When hands caught at the hem of Atticus's shirt, he didn't resist, just raised his arms. Jericho tossed it aside, then went to work opening Atticus's pants. He didn't stop him. Hell, he lifted up when the man dragged his pants and underwear down just enough to close his mouth over his aching cock.

"Jesus Christ," he muttered, hips spasming as this stranger attempted to suck the soul from his body. He fell back on his forearms, stomach muscles clenching as each sucking draw of his lips sent sparks of electricity along his spine. Fuck. The tight heat of his mouth was perfect. Atticus couldn't stop himself from tangling his hands in the silky strands of his hair and fucking up into his mouth.

Had he ever had anybody suck him like this? He'd fooled around with a man a time or two but his experiences were limited with either sex. Other than his icy, long-term now-ex girlfriend, Kendra, he could count his partners on one hand and have two fingers left. But this… Holy shit. Atticus couldn't stop the sounds he was making or the way his fingers twisted punishingly in the other man's hair.

"I'm close," he muttered.

Jericho didn't stop. If anything, he doubled down on his efforts. Atticus couldn't tear his eyes away, almost as turned on watching the head bobbing between his legs as he was by his talented lips and tongue. When brown eyes cast upwards, catching his gaze, that was it. Atticus gave a harsh shout, flooding Jericho's mouth.

He swallowed every drop, sucking until Atticus's abs contracted and he hissed, pulling him off his oversensitive cock. He yanked Jericho close, capturing his mouth, sucking the taste of himself off the other man's tongue as he plunged his hand into his jeans. He wrapped his fist around the other man's thick, leaking cock, unable to stop his low hum of approval. That definitely didn't help sell his 'not gay' statement, but he was too far gone to care. Atticus worked him with the same level of enthusiasm Jericho had given him, swallowing every panting moan, using them as a guide.

It didn't take long. Atticus used his precum to ease the firm catch and slide of his movements. Soon, Jericho was fucking up into his fist, hips snapping faster. They were no longer kissing, but their mouths were close enough for him to hear each shuddering breath, every throaty moan. It was

hot enough to make Atticus wish he hadn't come already.

Jericho's hips suddenly stuttered, and his breath punched from him as he spilled over Atticus's fist until he shivered with the aftershock of his intense release. Jericho rested his forehead against Atticus's before he pulled his hand free and wiped it clean on his pants.

Once they separated, they each busied themselves with righting their clothing. Atticus was flustered. He had no idea what had just happened or how things had gone so wrong, but he'd just given a hand job to a man three feet away from a fingerless corpse. There was no way he was telling his father that.

He cleared his throat. "Well, this has been..." He drifted off. What was he going to say?

"Yeah," Jericho acknowledged.

"Are you sure you don't need help with..." He pointed to Trevor.

Jericho gave a small cough. "Nah, I'm good."

Atticus slung his backpack over his shoulder once more. "Okay, then. Bye...I guess," he managed, making for the door, turning back, then turning once more when he saw Jericho no longer faced him.

He supposed that meant he was dismissed.

It was all for the best, he supposed. He wasn't gay. Even if he was, what was he going to do? Ask Jericho on a date? They weren't even living on the same planet. Besides, Atticus had to keep up appearances. As the oldest, Thomas expected more from him. That was just how it was. His father wouldn't care if Atticus was gay. Hell, Thomas was gay. His brothers were gay, some were bi. It was just… He couldn't be. He couldn't. Being straight was just…easier. Girls were fine. They were soft and smelled nice. He had a plan for his life and it didn't involve jerking off beautiful murderers in creepy cabins. No matter how intense his orgasm had been.

Once he made it back to his car, he tossed his backpack in the passenger seat and pushed the ignition button before realizing he still wore his muddy boots. Goddammit. He smacked his head on the steering wheel then flung himself back against the driver's seat dramatically.

What the fuck?

TWO

JERICHO

Jericho entered his shop through the front office. From there, he could see the counter where he helped his customers and his work space with the hydraulic lift. He could also see the large space he kept available for friends. It had a massive television and a tattered, comfy wrap around sofa where more than one of them had camped on bad nights. He and his brother, Felix, had small rooms upstairs.

He was unsurprised to see Felix and Arseny sitting on the couch, screaming at each other around gales of laughter as they played some game on the PlayStation. Arsen was easy to spot with his aqua-colored hair. As Jericho watched, his brother launched to his feet before crashing back onto the couch, as if that could encourage the character on the screen to do what he wanted. The action had his brother's strangely flowy printed top falling off one slender shoulder.

He ignored them, leaving his office to walk to the sink, unable to wipe the stupid smile off his face.

He had no idea what happened back in that cabin, but

he couldn't remember a time when he'd ever come so hard from a fumbling handjob. But it wasn't the act that had gotten him, it was the man behind it. There had been something so goddamn hot about that man, red hair and big blue eyes and freckles that disappeared when he flushed with embarrassment...or from an orgasm. It had been so easy.

All Jericho had done was put the offer on the table; it was Atticus who made the first move, drawing him in, kissing him hard. He'd been so tightly wound, so conflicted. It was like something snapped and all that repression and conflict had just exploded out of him, becoming this wildly desperate act. Jericho was just grateful he'd been on the other end of it.

He smiled a little wider. It was always the buttoned up ones that were freaks in bed, and the whole way home, Jericho couldn't stop picturing himself taking the man apart a piece at a time until he was shivering and begging to be fucked. He bet, with just the right amount of pressure, his little ginger psychopath would do dirty, dirty things for him.

Jericho snorted when he realized he was getting hard all over again. Shit. It was a shame he couldn't see him again. He splashed water on his face, pulling a clean paper towel from the dispenser above and blotting it dry. He realized too late that the noises of the game had stopped. He turned to find the boys standing directly behind him, like something out of a horror movie, their expressions quizzical.

"What's up?" he asked hesitantly, leaning against the dirty wooden countertop, crossing his arms over his chest.

"You good?" Arsen asked, his Russian accent seeping into

his words.

Jericho frowned at the blue-haired boy. "Yeah, why?"

Once more, Felix and Arsen exchanged glances. He was used to his brother's judgey face. He'd come out of the womb looking at everybody like they were beneath him. But it was odd seeing the look on Arsen. His father had been an enforcer for the Russian mob and he was a twenty-two-year-old murderer. Glass houses and all that.

Felix cocked his hip, gaze flicking over him from head to toe, suspicious. Jericho rolled his eyes. He was such a fucking diva. "What?"

"You're covered in blood," Felix noted.

Jericho snorted. "Yeah, kind of a hazard of the job."

Felix scoffed. "Yeah, but you're also wearing that weird smug, smirky look you only get whenever you get laid, and since you were in an abandoned cabin with Trevor the perv, we're...alarmed." He flicked his hand dramatically.

"Alarmed," Jericho echoed.

Arsen leaned in, his tone conspiratorial. "Did you fuck Trevor the perv, Coe?

Felix pulled a face. "I'm just hoping he fucked him before he killed him, not after. Once you cross that line, you don't come back."

Jericho tried to follow their dizzying thought process, but before he could formulate a response, Nico and Levi arrived. Fuck. Levi looked like a wanted poster had fucked a tattoo model. His inky dark hair fell in his face, and he sucked on a Dum-Dum lollipop. Nico's springy blond curls hung in his face. He looked surprisingly angelic for

somebody who was such a little monster.

"What's up? Why's everybody looking so constipated?" Levi asked.

"Coe fucked Trevor the perv," Arsen said, as if this was fact and not their wild speculation.

Levi wrinkled his nose. "That dude was gay? Or was he, like"—he mimed a blowjob—"trying to bribe his way out of it?"

Jericho's face contorted at the idea of a blowjob from greasy ass Trevor, but they paid him no mind.

Nico also looked disgusted. "What the fuck, man? Like, I get it. Who hasn't wanted to fuck somebody they killed or kill somebody they fucked? But it's a slippery slope, man."

"This is what I told him," Arsen said, shaking his head. "Once you cross that line…"

"Jesus Christ. I didn't fuck Trevor the perv. I killed Trevor the perv," Jericho said, walking around the four of them to head to his office, attempting to close the door behind him. His brother caught it and swung it back open.

"If you didn't fuck Trevor, then who was it? And don't lie and say it didn't happen. Your after orgasm glow never lies," Arsen said, flopping down into a chair hard enough to rock it back dangerously far before it righted itself.

"I—" Jericho shook his head. "I ran into a guy."

"With your dick?" Levi asked.

Nico's brows knitted together. "In the middle of the woods?"

"Like, a homeless man in the woods? A… What's the word? A hobo?" Arsen asked.

Levi elbowed him. "We don't call them that anymore. Show some respect."

Arsen shrugged. "Sorry. What do you call a man roaming the woods looking for sex?"

"A lie," Felix said, his mouth set in a hard line. "No way my brother banged some hot, sweaty lumberjack in the woods. That's not his type." His long, elegant fingers trailed over his collarbones, a slow smile spreading along his face as his brother seemed to get lost in his own lumberjack fantasy.

"I—"

"There's nothing in the woods but animals and Sasquatch," Nico said.

"Sasquatch?" Levi parroted.

Nico nodded. "Yeah, you know. Bigfoot."

"Did you fuck Bigfoot?" Levi asked, pulling the lollipop from his mouth with a pop.

"Yeah, who was it? The not hobo, the lumberjack, or Bigfoot?" Arsen asked.

Jericho made an exasperated sound, falling into his stuffed leather office chair. "D. None of the above. I ran into a guy at the cabin. He was there to dispatch Trevor as well. One thing led to another and we kind of hooked up."

Levi's eyes bulged, chair rocketing upright. "In front of Trevor?"

"You'd rather I fucked Trevor?" Jericho asked, distracted by his friend's pearl-clutching.

"Kinky," Arsen said, nodding his approval.

"No," Jericho said. "Listen. Trevor got dead first. I was kind of keyed up. He was…there. And willing. He was a

redhead. You know I always wanted one of those."

"Wow." Only Felix could put that much condemnation in a single word.

"Was he hot?" Levi asked, once more rocking the chair back on its hind legs.

Jericho couldn't stop the smile that spread across his face. "Yeah. He was. And kind of like…I don't know. He was dressed like any other pro, but there was something so… subdued? Inhibited? It was like getting a handjob from a bible salesman."

"You're a cretin," Felix muttered, flouncing into the chair beside Levi, crossing his legs primly. "So, are you going to see him again?"

Levi grinned around his lollipop. "Yeah, are we getting a stepdad?"

Jericho lobbed a pen at his head. "Fuck off. It was a blowjob, not a marriage proposal."

"You got a blowjob from a bible salesman?" Arsen said, admiration leaking into his tone.

"No, I gave a blowjob to a bible—You know what? This is none of your business," Jericho snapped.

How did he let these kids run him around like this? He was the adult. They were all adults, really, but still. He was the adultiest of the adults at thirty. He paid the bills, he kept them fed when they couldn't take care of themselves, and in exchange, they helped him clean up their neighborhood by taking out trash like Trevor. And around there, there was no shortage of trash.

"So, are you going to see bible boy again?" Arsen asked.

Jericho's first instinct was to say hell no, but what came out was, "I'd have to find him first."

Arsen snorted, jumping to his feet and shooing Jericho away from his desk. He plopped down into Jericho's desk chair and opened his laptop. He rolled his eyes when the boy typed in his password without asking. Not one ounce of respect out of these little monsters. Not a drop.

"What do you know about him?"

"His name is Atticus. A little over six foot, kind of bulky, definitely worked out, insanely blue eyes. Like, swimming pool blue. Had a snake tattoo curling over his right shoulder. He said he was a pro."

"A pro? Like a hooker?" Nico asked.

"Sex worker, dude. Come on," Levi said, disgusted.

"No, you idiot. A pro like a hired killer. He didn't look like any hired gun, but he was wearing a watch that would probably buy this entire block and he called it his backup watch so…who else has that kind of money?"

"Atticus Mulvaney, eldest son of billionaire Thomas Mulvaney," Arsen said, as if reading from a cue card.

"Son of a billionaire. Definitely not—"

Arsen swung the computer around to face Jericho. "Is this not your bible salesman?"

Jericho was almost positive his brain had short-circuited. That was definitely him. He was standing on a stage in the world's most boring tuxedo, receiving an award of some kind. "Holy shit."

"What's it say about him?" Felix asked, leaning forward to prop his elbow on the corner of the desk and resting his jaw

on his palm. Of course, Felix wanted to follow the money.

Arsen squinted at the screen. Jericho wished he'd just wear his glasses. "He's a doctor and a science doctor. He heads a research company where they study gene therapy for orphan diseases."

"Orphan diseases?" Levi echoed.

"Rare diseases," Jericho clarified absently.

"Oh, that's nice," Felix said. "What else does it say?"

"He's adopted. Has six brothers. Used to be engaged to a woman."

The three other boys seemed to all lean in at once, like vultures. "Is there a pic?"

Arsen typed furiously. "This is her Instagram."

He showed the screen to the others. "She's pretty enough," Felix said. "But that's a gold digger if I've ever seen one."

Jericho didn't know if he'd call her pretty. She was conventionally attractive, if somebody liked that sort of thing, but she had a pointy face and a cold, calculating look in her eye that made Jericho think she spent a lot of time asking to speak to somebody's manager. He couldn't picture Atticus—his Atticus—cozying up to that ice cube with boobs.

"You said ex, though, right? So, he's free and clear."

Jericho sighed. "Except, he's a total closet case. Said he's 'not gay' right before he shoved his hand in my pants."

"One of his brothers is married to a man and the other is engaged to one. So, clearly they are not homophobic, right?" Arsen asked.

Jericho scooted Arsen out of his seat and closed the laptop. "It doesn't matter. It was just a hookup. You guys go find something else to do. I have to work on the books for a bit before bed."

The looks on their faces said they didn't believe him, but they all trudged from the office as ordered, closing the door behind them. A minute later, the television was blasting and they'd all moved on.

Jericho opened the laptop, but not his bookkeeping app. He just stared at the pic of Atticus. His eyes really were so blue. He had a strong jaw, a roman nose, full lips that Jericho knew from experience were soft and supple and parted so easily for him.

He slammed the laptop closed and rubbed his hands over his face. He needed to move on. This was what happened when he didn't get laid enough. He started to hyper-fixate. He couldn't obsess over this completely unattainable man. He couldn't. He just had to deal with the fact that they were like ships passing in the night or whatever that expression was.

Fuck.

Jericho cleared his throat, drawing attention to a small blonde with a headset. She gave him the 'one moment' finger.

After a second, she flicked her gaze up at him, a smile coming alive on her face as if he'd triggered some kind of sequence. "Hi, how can I help you?"

"I'm here to see Atticus Mulvaney."

"Oh," she said, surprised. "Is Dr. Mulvaney expecting you?"

Definitely fucking not. Jericho wasn't even expecting to be there. "No, but if you could tell him Jericho Navarro is here. I think he'll make time to see me."

She frowned at that but gave a stilted nod, clicking a button. "Hi, Dr. Mulvaney—yes, sir. I know you said you didn't want to be disturbed but there's a man here to see you." She paused as she listened. "Yes, sir, but he said you'd make an exception. His name is Jericho."

Her eyes went comically wide. "Yes. Okay." She looked at Jericho with a newfound interest. "Once I buzz you back, make a left, and then another left. Look for the large office at the dead end. Dr. Mulvaney said he'll be right with you."

Jericho followed the woman's instructions, letting himself into the modest sized office. The size was where that modesty stopped. The entire wall behind Atticus's desk was covered in degrees and accolades. There must have been a hundred of them. Jericho couldn't help but smile. He certainly had a psychopath's ego. Normally, Jericho would say he was overcompensating for something, but having seen the man pantless, it wasn't that.

Before he could fall too deeply down that rabbit hole, the door flew open. Atticus entered, closing the door firmly behind him and then locking it. Interesting. Seeing him up close again was a shock to Jericho's senses, his body instantly aware.

He watched as the older man shucked off his lab coat,

hanging it beside a tweed blazer. He wore a crisp white button down and tailored houndstooth dress pants that clung to his thighs and cupped his ass. Tortoiseshell frames highlighted his pool blue eyes. Jericho caught a whiff of expensive cologne as he passed.

Atticus didn't sit at his desk, just perched on the corner, crossing his arms. "How did you find me?"

Jericho smirked. "I have my ways. So, you're a doctor and a doctor, huh?"

"What is this? You figured out my father's rich and you're here to blackmail me?"

Jericho chuckled, floating closer, enjoying the way the other man bristled when he entered his personal space. "Blackmail you for what? I'm the one who killed Trevor. You just ate a granola bar. How would my turning you in benefit me?"

"So, why are you here?" he asked in a prissy tone that went straight to Jericho's dick.

"Honestly," Jericho said, stepping between Atticus's splayed knees, "I have no idea. You're kind of under my skin. I think it's the freckles. I'm a sucker for freckles."

"Sounds like you need a doctor," Atticus said, trying for cold but seeming to dead end at unnerved.

Fuck, Jericho liked ruffling his feathers. He leaned forward to murmur in his ear. "Aren't you a doctor?"

"Not that kind of doctor," Atticus said.

Jericho inhaled the scent of his cologne, dick hard enough that he was sure he'd have a permanent indentation from his zipper. He ran his nose along Atticus's cheek. "Then tell me to leave," he challenged.

"Leave," Atticus managed, voice a raw whisper.

Jericho brushed his lips across his. "What was that? I couldn't hear you."

Atticus swallowed audibly. "You should leave," he said weakly.

Jericho ran his tongue along the seam of Atticus's lips teasingly. "Open up for me, Freckles. You know you want to."

There was a brief hesitation, then his lips parted, letting Jericho take what he wanted. "That's good. Really good. Give me your tongue."

Atticus slipped his tongue into Jericho's mouth. God, he was so good at following orders. Fuck. He took his time, finding he really liked the slick slide of his mouth on Atticus and the hesitant way his tongue caressed his own.

When he slid his fingers upwards to knot his hands in Atticus's hair, he made this sound at the back of his throat, this sort of breathless *hnf* that made Jericho want to do very bad things to him. When he broke off to trail biting kisses along his jaw, Atticus tilted his head to give him more access. He bit and sucked at his earlobe.

"You're killing me. All I can think about is your mouth on my cock. Can you do that for me? Hmm?"

Atticus heaved a shuddering breath. His indecision was palpable.

"Nobody ever has to know, if that's what you're afraid of."

When Atticus went rigid against him, Jericho sighed,

leaning back enough to cup Atticus's jaw, giving him a chaste kiss.

"Okay, Freckles. I get it. Message received."

Jericho had no idea why he was pushing the issue. They had nothing in common, except they both sometimes murdered people. Not exactly something to build a life on. He shook his head at his own ridiculousness. His hand was on the door knob when he was spun around and slammed up against the door hard enough to rattle the window blinds.

Before he could process what was happening, Atticus was sinking to his knees, freeing Jericho's cock and swallowing him down, taking him deep enough to gag. His head thudded against the door, and when Atticus's lips retreated, Jericho's hips followed of their own volition, not ready to give up the perfect heat and suction of those spit-slick lips.

He hissed as one of Atticus's hands crawled beneath his shirt and the other slipped into his own pants. "Oh, fuck yes."

Once they found a rhythm, there was only the sound of Jericho's rapid breaths and the wet sounds of Atticus's very enthusiastic blowjob. Whenever Jericho's hands would clench in his hair, he'd moan like a whore, sending an electric hum along his shaft and through his balls. His movements seemed fast and slow in equal measure.

"Fuck, I'm close. I'm gonna come," he warned, giving Atticus the chance to pull off.

He didn't. He not only redoubled his efforts but he groaned, his body shaking as he found his orgasm. Christ. That was enough for Jericho to lose it, flooding Atticus's

mouth, eyes rolling with pleasure as he tried to milk every drop from him.

When he slipped free of Atticus's lips, the man didn't rise but dropped his head to Jericho's hips, drawing in shaky breaths. It was such an oddly submissive gesture that he found himself petting his hands through his hair to soothe him. The touch seemed to jar something loose in the other man. He jerked to his feet, righting his clothing and wiping at his mouth with the back of his hand.

Jericho zipped up, waiting to see if Atticus would acknowledge he stood there, but he just stared at the wall of awards like he couldn't bear to look at him. Once more, Jericho sighed. "Ball's in your court, Freckles. If you want more, you're going to have to find me this time."

His only indication Atticus had heard him was the stiffening of his posture. Jericho shook his head, making his way out of the building. He didn't know why he'd done it. Why he'd sought him out, toyed with him. He was just prolonging the inevitable, but it was so hard not to poke at him when he reacted so easily.

His phone rang. He frowned when he saw the name. Detective Vélez. The name was like a punch to the gut. It had to be about Mercy. Her face flashed in his vision, and part of him was relieved he still remembered what she looked like from memory. It had been eight years since she went missing.

Jericho mentally geared himself up for whatever was coming next before he swiped to answer. "Detective."

The man on the other end of the line cleared his throat.

"Hey, Jericho. I know it's been a while but I was hoping you could swing by the station? We have some news on your sister."

Jericho didn't really care for police stations. "What news? What's up?"

"Um, I tried getting in touch with your parents first, but I was told your father had passed away. My condolences. They say your mother is not doing well either, so I thought maybe it would be better to speak with you instead of upsetting her—"

"Just spit it out, Gabe," Jericho finally snapped.

"We think we found Mercy's body, but we're going to need you to give a positive ID."

Jericho's head swam, and for a split second, he thought he was going to pass out. He ducked into the stoop of a vintage clothing store, letting the weight of the other man's statement carry him down until he sat on the pavement, his elbows braced on raised knees.

A positive ID on bones? That made no sense. She'd been gone for years. She would have been dust. "Where?" he asked, practically choking on the bitter bile rising in his throat.

"If you could just—"

The sound Jericho made was somewhere between a shout and a snarl. "Where the fuck did you find my sister, Gabe?"

"We pulled her out of the bay five hours ago."

Jericho shook his head, his brain rejecting the information. "That doesn't make any fucking sense."

"Please, we don't know any more than that. She didn't have prints in the system and DNA is going to take weeks.

Could you just help us out here?"

Help them out. Help them out… As if they were the ones whose whole world had just imploded.

He made a disgusted sound. "Yeah, Gabe. I can help you out."

THREE
ATTICUS

Atticus wasn't sure how long he'd been sitting there, staring at the door, wondering if that had actually happened or if he'd slipped into some kind of fugue state and hallucinated the entire thing. It had to be the latter. It had to be.

Atticus didn't hook up with strangers, he didn't allow men to order him around, didn't slam them up against walls so he could drop to his knees for them…no matter how sexy that man was, or how dark his eyes were, or how soft his lips, or how low and raspy his voice was when he spoke.

His lids fluttered shut. *Open up for me. Give me your tongue.* He couldn't stop the shiver that rolled over him. As much as Atticus wanted to pretend he'd imagined the whole thing, he could still taste Jericho on his tongue, his lips were still red, and his throat still sore. He'd practically begged to suck him off. Atticus shook his head. He'd been so close to getting out of the interaction without embarrassing himself.

Jericho had been leaving. He could have just let him go

40

and gone about his day, but a tightness in his chest he'd never experienced before had overwhelmed him. Not knowing if he'd see him again had stolen his breath and forced him to act on instinct. And his natural instinct had been to kneel. For him. Christ.

And now, he didn't know what to do with that. Was that fear? Had Atticus—somebody who'd never truly experienced terror—in that moment been afraid of not seeing Jericho again? Maybe he was just bored. He'd been in a dating slump since his brothers had decided to start mating for life like psychotic penguins. He'd never had much luck with the opposite sex. Any sex, really. He just found people...tedious. And he would rather focus on work, on doing things he was good at.

He pulled his phone free, pulling up Kendra's Instagram, scrolling through tone deaf posts about annoying baristas and breaking a strap on her Balenciaga handbag. One he'd bought her when they'd first started dating.

Dating Kendra had been easy. It was like dating an inflatable doll. She was all surface, just like him. He never had to worry about hurting her feelings. She didn't have any. She was vapid and shallow. Any perceived slight had been easily forgiven as soon as Atticus opened his wallet.

If he was being honest, he'd never felt anything for Kendra, but that wasn't uncommon for people with his diagnosis. He'd chalked it up to his bad genes. He was just wired wrong. She'd never asked for flowery confessions of love. She didn't care if he'd rather work until midnight. She'd only asked for material possessions. That should have

been enough for him. Why couldn't she have just been enough for him?

Now there was this fucking man, this total stranger, and Atticus had felt…bereft when he'd left him, a sensation he hadn't even thought possible. It just made no fucking sense. Was this how Adam had felt? Or August? Was this why they were so violently protective of Noah and Lucas? Why had they been so eager to embrace this feeling? It was…awful. It made him feel like he couldn't take full breaths. It made him feel like he couldn't concentrate, and he didn't have the kind of job where one could be distracted by brown-eyed men with zero boundaries.

He jumped at the knock on the door. "Come in," he barked.

Noah stuck his head around the door, pulling a face. "Is that how you talk to your employees? You sound like a dick."

"Why are you here?" Atticus asked, his sour mood worsening. He couldn't seem to wipe the scowl off his face.

"Wow, who pissed in your bran flakes this morning?" Noah asked, slipping in and closing the door behind him.

"Nobody. What do you want?"

Noah had never been to Atticus's office, yet he was giving *him* a look like Atticus was the one acting out of character. "You tell me. Thomas said you needed somebody to come pick up a bunch of documents because he needs them tonight but you didn't have time to drive up to the house."

"I meant a courier service, not you."

Noah plopped down in the chair opposite him, sprawling like it was his home and not Atticus's office. "Wow, your

hospitality skills suck, bro. Seriously, what's your damage? You're even more butt-clenched than usual."

He opened his mouth to tell him to fuck off but heard himself say, "What does fear feel like?"

Noah blinked at him. "What?"

"It's a valid question," Atticus muttered.

"You good, bro?"

Atticus was the opposite of good. "My chest feels tight, and my mouth is dry, and I can't tell if I'm experiencing fear or anxiety or having a fucking heart attack."

"Yeah, you do look kind of like a corpse. Doesn't a heart attack make you sweat and, like, make you have pain in your left arm? You're a doctor, shouldn't you know if you're having a heart attack?"

"I just don't understand what's happening to me…"

"Well, that makes two of us. Did something happen before you started to feel this way? Did somebody give you bad news? Did somebody, like, try to scare you?" Noah asked.

Well, he certainly couldn't tell Noah about Jericho. He'd tell Adam and Adam would hold a press conference about it. "I don't want to talk about it."

Noah narrowed his eyes, studying Atticus intently. "Wait…is this about a…girl?"

The hesitation before Noah said girl made his eye muscle twitch. Was he so obvious? "No."

A slow smile formed on Noah's face as he leaned forward. "Is this about a guy? Have you finally kicked open the closet door? Do you—do you have a boyfriend?"

"No!" he snapped, closing his eyes as his blatant

overreaction called him a liar. "No," he said again, quieter.

Noah rolled his eyes. "Okay, so obviously there's a person who's got you tied up in knots. Who are they?"

Atticus wanted to talk to somebody but also wanted nobody to know that he'd so easily been ensnared by a total stranger. "You can't tell anybody."

Noah's tongue darted out to wet his lower lip, and he nodded. "Okay. What did you do?"

Atticus meant to give the barest of details but, instead, word-vomited the whole story to a stunned Noah.

When he finished, Noah said, "Twice? You've seen him twice and both times you—" He made the fingers of one hand into a circle before pretending to violate it with a finger on the other hand.

"You don't have to be crude."

Noah snorted. "Save the righteous indignation, bro. I'm not the one blowing strangers in my office."

Atticus should have just kept his mouth shut. "It was just a temporary insanity thing. I think."

"But why? He sought you out. He clearly wanted to see you again. Why not just be friends with benefits? Why are you so pressed about this?"

Atticus scowled harder. "One, I'm not gay. Two, we're not friends. Three, every time I see this guy, I lose all sense of self control." *And self-respect,* he added silently.

"Have you never just wanted to get naked with somebody? Like you've never just been...like, horny for a guy you met at a bar or wherever somebody like you goes and does non-work related things?" Atticus shook his head. "Aren't you

almost forty?"

Atticus gave him a dead stare. "You're not being helpful."

Noah sighed. "Listen, it sounds like you just really have chemistry with this guy. What's the harm in seeing where it goes? It's not like he's going to get pregnant." His gaze raked over Atticus. "Or get you pregnant."

He could feel himself starting to turn red. "That's not the point."

"What is the point then? You work all the time. You are at Thomas's beck and call. You have zero vices. You're essentially an android just waiting to mirror the next stranger you meet. Maybe you aren't even into him, maybe you're just treating him the way he wants to treat you?"

Atticus gave it the consideration it deserved, but then dismissed it. Mirroring people was second-nature to him, but he had an awareness of it. He did it when it served his needs. It was useful for acquiring grant money, networking, and convincing the world that he wasn't dead inside. "That's not how that works. If I could just figure out what this feeling is, I could just move on with my life."

"I mean, how would you describe your normal mood? Like, do you feel happy or sad? I know you feel irritation and rage. I've seen it first-hand. But when you're not around other people, how do you feel?"

His brows knitted together. "I don't."

Noah's jaw dropped. "You don't?"

He shrugged. "Why would I?"

Atticus watched as Noah tried to connect the dots. "So, when you don't have somebody whose behavior you can

mirror, you just shut off? You don't have a show that makes you happy or music that makes you feel relaxed?"

Atticus frowned. "What? Why would fictional characters make me happy? And music is simply a collection of notes. It's pleasant, I guess."

Noah scrunched up his face. "Oof. Okay, we don't have to unpack all of that, but I'm going to say this. If this guy makes you feel anything at all, maybe you should just lean into it and see what happens. Worst case scenario you have really great sex…or really mediocre sex. Either way, you got off. This could be really good for you."

Atticus wanted to dismiss the idea just because it was Noah who had it, but maybe he was right. Maybe once all the tension had released in the form of physical intimacy, maybe then he could just forget about Jericho once and for all and get back to his normal life.

"I'll think about it."

Atticus did think about it. He thought about nothing else until almost nine o'clock that night. Calliope had found Jericho with little effort. Atticus had his address five minutes after he'd called. He was a mechanic. Owned his own shop in a rough neighborhood on the other side of town, a shop he apparently lived over.

Atticus had told himself he would wait a few days just to make sure this was really something he wanted to do and not him just having some kind of midlife crisis. Instead,

he paced about his too-silent apartment thinking about the weight and taste of Jericho's dick until he couldn't stand it anymore. He switched into a pair of black joggers and a gray hoodie, making sure he left his expensive watch at home. When he couldn't think of anything else to distract himself, he ordered an Uber. No way he was leaving the Volvo to get stripped down to the frame and scrapped for parts.

The ride to Jericho's was excruciating. He opened his mouth at least a dozen times to tell the driver to turn around, but he snapped it closed each time. Jericho had told him the ball was in his court. He'd said that. Sort of. But he hadn't asked him to show up at his house unannounced. But Atticus hadn't invited him to his office for oral sex, so he supposed that made them even.

Once the driver dumped him outside of the door just to the side of the office, he stood there with his finger hovering over the buzzer, trying to convince himself to turn around and go home but, instead, standing there like an idiot. When a group of rowdy teens walked by and gave him a strange look, he finally jabbed at the button on the call box.

Almost immediately, a harsh rasp came through the speaker. "Yeah?" Had he woken him? Maybe he should go. Still, he stood there, willing the words to come. "Hello?"

He had to say something. "It's me—um, Atticus." Silence stretched between them for so long that he finally just said, "I'll go."

There was the distinct sound of a lock disengaging. "It's open."

Atticus pulled the door open, taking the steps two at a

time. The staircase didn't end at a door but spilled out into an open space with a glass wall that looked down into the workshop below. There was a couch pushed against the glass and a fairly expensive television sitting on a coffee table at viewing distance. There was a small kitchen tucked away in the corner and closed doors on either side of the space. Bedrooms maybe.

Jericho was standing in the small kitchen space, shirtless, barefoot, those same jeans from earlier slung low on his hips. The colorful sleeve tattoo bled onto his shoulder and covered half of his chest. He had a beer in his hand and he looked...hot, but also rough, like he'd somehow fought a war since Atticus had seen him just hours ago. He floated closer, uncertainty growing as the distance between them narrowed until they were standing just a few feet apart.

"I didn't think I'd ever see you again," Jericho said, eyes glassy. "Definitely not this soon."

Atticus shrugged. "Me neither."

"You probably shouldn't be here right now," Jericho warned, taking another swig from his beer bottle.

Atticus's brow hooked upwards. "Why's that?"

Jericho pressed fingers against his eyes, rubbing hard. "I'm just... I'm not in a good headspace right now."

"Then why did you let me up?" Atticus asked, not offended, just genuinely curious.

When Jericho raised his head again, his expression was bleak. "Because part of me doesn't want to be alone. Part of me wants to take my bad mood out on you."

Goosebumps erupted along Atticus's skin, his nipples

hardening and cock stirring. He stepped into Jericho's space. "Okay."

His eyes widened in surprise, but his face remained stony. "Seriously, Freckles. I've had a bad day, and I kind of want to hurt someone. I have no idea what I'll do to you if you stay."

"I think I can take it," Atticus said, not at all certain that was true.

Jericho surged forward, spinning Atticus around until the counter dug into his hips, trapping his cock against a drawer with a metal pull. It hurt, but he stayed silent. He nipped at his ear. "Last fucking chance."

Atticus steeled himself for whatever came next. He'd never had penetrative sex with a man, had honestly never made it past hand jobs and rubbing off on each other. He could handle pain. He wasn't afraid of the act itself, just of how overwhelmed he felt with Jericho pressing him into the counter, his voice somewhere between a threat and a plea, like he didn't know if he wanted Atticus to stay or go.

Atticus already knew it didn't matter. "I'm not leaving."

Jericho's hands were under his hoodie, dragging it over his head and tossing it away, before Atticus even finished speaking.

"God, I love all these freckles," Jericho muttered almost to himself, licking and biting at his shoulder as if to prove it.

Atticus liked the warm press of Jericho's chest against his back, the pleasure/pain of his tongue and teeth on his skin. He pulled Atticus back against him, his hand slipping into Atticus's sweatpants, a low rumbling sound escaping when

he closed his calloused palm around his aching cock. "No underwear. And you're already hard for me."

He said it like he was pleased, like Atticus had done something well. He could quickly become addicted to this sensation. As Jericho stroked him slowly, his whole body flushed, breath hitching when the rough fingers of his other hand teased at the stiff peaks of his nipples.

Atticus took some solace in knowing Jericho was hard, too. He could feel it pressed against his ass each time he pushed back against him.

"You trying to tell me something?" Jericho teased.

Atticus shook his head. "I honestly don't know."

Suddenly, Jericho's hands disappeared. "Come with me."

Atticus blinked at the abrupt change but did as Jericho asked. The closed door led to his bedroom, which was essentially a mattress and box spring on the floor and a side table that looked like it was a hand me down. The room was sparse but clean. Even his bed was made. Before he could hope to guess what would happen next, Jericho pinned him to the wall and kissed him deep. "I'm negative, on PReP. You?"

Atticus did his best to follow another shift in the conversation. "I'm negative, but I'm not on PReP."

Jericho caught his lips in another dirty, opened-mouth kiss. "There are condoms if you want. I just really want to be inside you."

Atticus felt hot enough to blister, flushing all the way to the tips of his ears. He swallowed audibly. "Okay."

Jericho pulled back then, examining him. "I mean, I can

bottom. I prefer to top, but if that's not your thing…"

"I don't have a thing," Atticus blurted. "I've never—" He cut himself off. "Never mind. You can top. I'm good with that," he promised.

He lurched forward, capturing Jericho's mouth for only a second before a hand pressed him back against the wall once more, holding him there.

"You've never what?" Jericho asked, studying him intently.

Atticus gazed at a spot on the wall over Jericho's shoulder. "I told you, I'm not gay. I've never done…that before. It's not a big deal. I'm a doctor, I've got the mechanics down. Can we just go back to the sex part because the talking part is killing my mood." He tried to kiss him again, but Jericho held him still, continuing to study him.

When Atticus couldn't take it anymore, he said, "Do you want me to go?"

There was another pause, and then Jericho swayed into his space, fitting their lips together in a soft, barely-there kiss. "Nah, Freckles. I don't want you to go. I just think I found myself a different distraction for the night."

Jericho took his hand and led him to the bed, removing Atticus's sweatpants, letting them pool around his ankles. He awkwardly removed his shoes and socks, stepping free of them.

As soon as he was naked, Jericho shoved him back on the bed, following him down, forcing him to retreat farther up the mattress to make room for him.

Jericho didn't lie on top of him, just hovered over him, knees forcing his thighs apart, holding all his weight on

his palms as he leaned down to kiss him softly, teasing his tongue along the seam of his lips but not pushing in. "Come on," he murmured lightly. "Open up for me. You know what I want."

Atticus hated how easily he yielded, mouth opening beneath Jericho's so he could sweep his tongue inside. He hated the way his cock leaked the moment Jericho took charge. He hated how much neither of those statements were true.

It was too much—this crushing want was too much for somebody who never felt anything. It was like thinking you were pressing your tongue to a battery when it was actually an electric fence. Still, he knew he wasn't going to stop this. He was becoming addicted to the shock of adrenaline that coursed through him with the slightest touch from Jericho.

"We—We can skip the seduction part and get on with it," Atticus said, tone grumpy.

Jericho moved to lie beside him, turning on his side, one jean-clad calf hooking over Atticus's naked one. He took two fingers, gently running the rough pads over Atticus's lips. "Oh, no. We're not doing that. You had your chance to leave and you refused, so now, I'm going to spend the rest of the night taking you apart piece by piece until you're begging for my cock, until you can't think of anything else but me inside you. Got it?"

Atticus's insides shivered at his words. "I don't beg."

Jericho's chuckle was infuriating, humiliating even. He pressed his lips to Atticus's ear. "Who are you kidding, Freckles? You know you'll beg if I tell you to. You'll do

anything I ask if I want you to." As if to prove his point, he rasped, "Open your mouth."

Atticus's eyelids slid closed, but he complied, his embarrassment growing. Jericho slid those two fingers inside, rubbing them along Atticus's tongue. He tasted vaguely chemical, a little like dirt or motor oil maybe, but it only made Atticus harder.

"Suck," Jericho demanded.

Atticus closed his lips around his fingers, nursing as Jericho fucked them in and out of his mouth.

Jericho gave a pleased rumble. "See? It's okay, though. Your secret's safe with me. I won't tell. Nobody has to know how much you love this but me." He pulled his fingers free, smearing them across his lips. "I wonder what else I can make you do for me?"

Atticus fucking wondered, too. He was in over his head.

FOUR

JERICHO

Jericho couldn't have asked for a better distraction than this. Atticus, naked and willing in his bed, looking so fucking vulnerable it made Jericho want to comfort him and violate him at the same time. God, the way he sucked on his fingers, the way he did anything Jericho asked. It made it so easy to forget how he'd had his heart ripped from his chest a couple of hours ago.

He didn't want to think about that. Instead, he focused on Atticus. He bent his head and licked over one nipple before sucking it into his mouth, tugging lightly with his teeth, his cock throbbing at the way Atticus's breath hitched.

He gave his other nipple the same attention, letting his fingers skim over his belly, feeling the way the muscles dipped as he passed. He stopped just above the base of his erection but made no move to go further. Not yet.

As he played with him, alternating between kissing his pliant lips and teasing his nipples, Atticus began to squirm, his frustration obvious. Jericho just rubbed soothing circles

54

over his lower belly with his thumb, not willing to move any quicker. He was planning on making a meal out of Atticus and he wouldn't be rushed.

He rolled on top of him, settling between his knees to kiss down his chest, his fingers smoothing over his ribs, letting his mouth follow their path. By the time his lips brushed over his lower abdomen, Atticus was trembling. Still, Jericho ignored the flushed cock jutting out from a nest of red curls, instead nosing along the place where Atticus's leg and torso met, tonguing and sucking at his balls.

Atticus made a noise of disappointment when Jericho stood, walking to the side table and grabbing the lube, holding up the condom, showing it to Atticus, who stared at it for a long moment before shaking his head. Jericho knew it was stupid to just take him at his word, but he didn't want anything between them, and Atticus was plenty old enough to make his own decisions, older than Jericho even. Neither of them really had a great deal of respect for their lives or the lives of others. This was probably the least reckless thing they would do all week.

He dropped the lube on the bed, shucked his pants and underwear, then sat between Atticus's splayed legs. Jericho ran both hands over his torso before lightly dragging his fingertips along his inner thighs. It was like his whole body was blushing under Jericho's attention. A light sheen of perspiration coated his skin.

"Bend your knees. Heels on the mattress." Jericho's nostrils flared as Atticus complied without question. "Open your legs for me. Wider. That's good. That's really good. I

want to taste you."

Atticus's breath left him in a rush as he lifted his head. "What?"

Jericho dragged his gaze upwards to meet his. "I want my tongue inside you."

"Fuck," Atticus managed, sounding undone as he flopped his head back down on the pillow.

Some deep, primal part of Jericho liked being the one who unwound Atticus. Was it selfish to want to be the only one who made Atticus feel…something? Probably, but he didn't care. He didn't care about anything but hearing him fall apart. He needed to let go and Jericho needed to be the one who got him there.

He laid between Atticus's legs, running his thumbs along the inner flesh of his thighs before he tried to spread him open. His muscles clenched instinctively. "Relax for me." He nosed at the base of his cock, running his tongue along the underside before sucking the tip into his mouth.

Atticus made a lost sound, his hands clenching in Jericho's hair almost like he wasn't sure if he wanted him to stop or take more of him. It didn't matter, Jericho wasn't giving Atticus what he wanted until he begged for it. That was the deal.

He pulled off, sucking at his balls until Atticus tried to pull him back up to his cock. Jericho chuckled, ignoring his urging. This time, he pushed his legs back, leaving his hole exposed so he could put his face in the heart of him, laving his tongue over his hole, tasting him the way he wanted.

Atticus made this sort of half-bitten moan each time

Jericho's tongue probed him, twisting handfuls of his hair until he was a little worried he might tear it out. Listening to Atticus fall apart made him want to forget the plan, made him want to just thrust into him and force his body to rearrange itself to accommodate him. He didn't know why he needed Atticus to submit, but he did. He needed him to admit only Jericho could be this for him, whatever it was.

He reached for the lube, cursing as he accidentally poured too much onto his fingers, before righting the bottle, earning a soft laugh from Atticus. He looked up and grinned. Atticus smiled back, lids fluttering shut as Jericho massaged the pad of his fingertip against the tight ring of muscle. This time, when he took Atticus's cock into his mouth, he took him to the back of his throat, working a finger inside in time with each sucking pull of his lips.

Atticus clenched around him, but then seemed to force himself to relax. Jericho started slowly, trying not to think about how it would feel when it was his dick sinking into the tight heat of Atticus's body and not just his finger.

Each time Jericho grazed his prostate, Atticus whimpered, precum leaking onto his tongue. The next time he pulled back, he pressed a second finger in with the first, slowing when Atticus hissed, advancing only as he relaxed around him.

He took his time working him open, using the sounds Atticus made as a guide, enjoying listening to the way his breaths began to quicken, his noises growing impatient, feeling the way he began to squirm with impatience, just for him.

"I think I'm good," Atticus whispered, voice raw.

Jericho pulled back, standing before he reached down and dragged Atticus to the edge of the mattress. He made a show of slicking the lube over his cock before bracing his hand on the bed, leaning over him, working his length between his cheeks to tease it over his hole. He made no move to breach him, though, just put the slightest bit of pressure before retreating again.

Atticus groaned. "What are you waiting for?"

Jericho kissed him deep, loving the way Atticus sucked greedily at his tongue. "You know what I'm waiting for, Freckles. I told you I wasn't going to fuck you until you were begging for it. Until you couldn't think of anything but me inside you. Are you there yet?" he taunted against his lips.

"Yes," he said, voice bordering on a whine. "You know I am."

Jericho dragged his lips over his chin, his jaw, nosing behind his ear. "I need the words. I need to hear you beg." When he pulled back to look at Atticus, indecision played across his face, like he was battling between his pride and his need. "I told you, nobody's gonna know. Nobody but me." He pressed in just the slightest bit, loving the way Atticus gasped. "It's going to feel so fucking good when I slide inside you. I know you want it, too. Look at how hard you are just thinking about it. Just give me what I want and I'll give you what you need."

"Please…" Atticus managed, like it physically hurt him.

"Please what, Freckles?"

Atticus squeezed his eyes closed, voice strained as he

said, "Fuck me. I want you inside me. I—I want you to do the things you said. Please." When Jericho didn't move, Atticus's eyes opened once more, gaze pleading, his voice catching on a choked sound. "Please…"

Something broke in him at the sound and he sank into Atticus in one go, not stopping until he was buried. He pressed their foreheads together, trying not to come on the spot from the sucking heat of his body.

"Just move. Please. This is torture," Atticus muttered.

Jericho chuckled. "Not exactly a glowing review."

When Atticus lifted his legs to wrap them around his waist, all the humor faded away. Jericho lowered himself until he was braced on his forearms, working himself in and out with shallow thrusts, letting Atticus get used to the sensation.

When he pulled almost all the way out and slammed back in, they both moaned. It wasn't long before Atticus was rolling his hips up to meet each of Jericho's downward thrusts and he knew they were both close.

He stood, catching Atticus beneath his knees, splaying them wide as he fucked into him like he wanted. "Touch yourself for me. I want to see what I missed earlier while my cock was in your mouth."

Atticus was clearly too far gone to care about his pride because he moaned when his hand wrapped around his own leaking erection. Jericho couldn't take his eyes off of him, not sure what he liked more, the confident slide of Atticus's fist as he jerked himself or how his face looked as he did it, head back, lips parted, eyes closed.

Jericho couldn't hold out much longer. He fucked

Atticus the way he'd been thinking about fucking him since the cabin, driving into him, hard and fast, chasing the shocky pleasure that rocketed through him each time his cock slammed home. He was so close, so fucking close, but he wanted to feel his body spasm around him. "Fuck. You look so good. I just want to watch you come."

Atticus's gaze flew to him as he cried out, his release shooting across his belly and chest, a tiny bit even reaching his chin.

"Oh, fuck," Jericho managed, eyes rolling at the way Atticus pulsed around him.

Atticus's gaze was glued to where their bodies were joined, watching as Jericho drove into him for another full minute before his orgasm punched through him. He captured Atticus's lips, moaning into his mouth as he rode the waves of pleasure coursing through him.

When he could think again, he gently released Atticus's legs, but didn't stop the lazy slide of their mouths until Jericho licked the drop of cum that had landed on his chin.

"You came a lot. You clearly needed that," Jericho said, then laughed. "I needed it, too."

He flopped down beside him, his feet flat on the floor as they were still at the foot of the bed. Almost immediately, Atticus sat up. Jericho practically clotheslined him, his arm barring his exit. "You're not leaving."

"Am I a hostage now?" Atticus asked, not sounding particularly bothered by the notion. "It's just sex, right? You fuck and then leave. That's friends with benefits, no?"

Jericho furrowed his brow. "No? Friends with benefits

implies that we're friends, right?"

Atticus looked away, once more attempting to stand. "My mistake."

Jericho again barred his retreat. "My God, do I have to tie you to the bed? I'm saying if you want to be friends with benefits, you could try actually being friendly."

Atticus sort of deflated. "I've never had a friend before. I don't think I'm qualified."

Jericho understood that better than most. "Well, most of my friends are barely old enough to drink. But I've had a really shitty fucking day so can you just…just stay? For a while at least," Jericho asked, hating how desperate he sounded.

Atticus stared straight up at the ceiling. "Yeah. Okay."

"Thank you," he said, unable to keep the mild exasperation from his voice.

He wasn't used to needing other people. He didn't even like most people. His brother, the boys—they were like when people go through war together. They had bonds nothing could touch. They had family, but most of their scars were homegrown. Blood didn't mean shit to them. He cared about the people who stuck.

"So, why was your day so bad?" Atticus asked, his gaze cutting to Jericho before returning to the ceiling.

"My sister died." It was weird to say that out loud.

"I'm sorry," Atticus said, not sounding particularly sorry but trying to school his features into something that resembled regret. "How did she die? Is that okay to ask?"

Jericho shook his head, still trying to wrap his head

around the answer. "Multisystem organ failure."

Atticus nodded. "Was she sick for a long time?"

Jericho shrugged. "I don't know. She disappeared eight years ago."

There was a very long pause before Atticus asked, "And they just called you out of the blue to tell you she died? Were you listed as her next of kin?"

"It's not like that. I don't know what the fuck is happening. My mother is too sick to deal with all of this. Mercy disappeared when she was seventeen. When she went missing, they said she ran away from home to do drugs. My parents believed it because they always believed the worst about her and she did do drugs. But my brother and I didn't believe it. She wasn't that far gone on drugs, not yet. And she wouldn't have just disappeared without telling Felix and me, since she knew we'd never rat her out to our parents. Then today, out of the blue, they pulled her out of the bay, looking completely healthy on the outside—minus the…bloating—but inside, she was a disaster. They have no answers for me. They say they're investigating but what is there to investigate, really?"

Atticus nodded. "That's a lot. I can see why you don't want to be alone."

Jericho frowned. "You can?"

"I imagine that you're running every conceivable scenario in your head, trying to figure out how your sister went from teen runaway to a slab in the morgue. That's what I would be doing."

"She was only twenty-five," Jericho said, the pain hitting

him like a tidal wave, forcing him to hold his ground until it passed again.

Atticus frowned. "Multi-system organ failure in a twenty-five-year-old isn't that common."

"They said something called sepsis caused it. Complications from a kidney transplant. There was a very fresh incision."

"Your sister received a kidney?"

He shook his head. "She apparently donated a kidney and there were…complications."

Atticus sat up a bit, turning his body towards him. "Transplants are highly regulated. When a patient receives a kidney or donates a kidney, there's a paper trail for miles. You can get a baby easier than you can get a kidney. There are weeks of physicals and blood work, weeks of post op care, medications, and follow visits. There's no way they would just let a girl who just donated a kidney wander out of the hospital."

"The detective on the case is my ex, and he doesn't seem all that interested in following up on it. His bosses don't, anyway. To them, she's just a drug addict who got herself into some trouble."

"I have people. I'll look into it for you."

"You have people?" Jericho asked, a faint smile forming and then sliding away just as quickly.

"I told you, I'm a professional. I have a whole team."

Jericho sat up. "Cut the shit. You're a doctor and a murderer? Nobody becomes a dual MD-PhD and moonlights as a contract killer. What's your game?"

"You do when you're a psychopath raised by a man with an agenda. Being an upstanding member of society is what allows me to get rid of people who have forfeited their right to be on this side of the firmament. I was...raised for this."

"Being a serial killer is your birthright?" Jericho asked.

Atticus scoffed. "I don't consider myself to be a serial killer. They have signatures, rituals, fetishes. I'm just doing a job. I don't even like it. My brother, August, he fucking loves it. The twins, too. For the rest of us, it's just...work."

Jericho blinked at him. "So, you were serious in the cabin when you said you killed with your brothers. That wasn't some kind of, like, metaphorical thing? Your whole family kills people?"

Atticus shook his head. "No. My dad keeps his hands clean. He's like the foreman; he organizes the jobs. We're the grunts. My brother's fiancé is shadowing him, learning the ropes."

"Like an intern?" Jericho mused.

Atticus nodded. "We have a computer whiz, but we don't even know what she looks like. My other brother—the one who likes to kill people—his husband is psychic and a former FBI agent so we use him when we need quick intel." He stopped talking abruptly before saying, "I'm sorry. It's tacky to talk about this after you telling me you just lost your sister. My father would be very upset with my lack of manners."

Jericho knitted his brows together. "Wouldn't your father be upset that you just blabbed some huge family secret to a guy who you've known for five minutes?"

Atticus flopped back down on the bed. "I watched you

cut a guy's fingers off during a racist game of Jeopardy. I guess I thought there was a cone of silence thing happening here. Don't friends have secrets?"

Jericho grinned at that. "Yeah. They do."

"Good."

"I get it. Why you do what you do. In my neighborhood, there are a lot of people who prey on the weak, the vulnerable. People they know can't go to the cops—especially right now—for fear of being deported. So, me and my boys, we look out for them, take out the trash."

"Trash like Trevor?" Atticus asked.

"Yeah, trash just like Trevor." Jericho gave him a humorless smile. "There, now, we both have something to lose."

Atticus reached out and grabbed Jericho's hand. His palm was warm and his grip awkward, but when he squeezed, Jericho knew he was trying to comfort him. He didn't pull away. After a few minutes passed, he said, "Please, let me help you look into your sister. It won't bring her back but, if nothing else, it might give you some peace of mind."

Jericho knew he should say no. But he had no faith in the police. There was too much bad blood between him and Gabe. He didn't think Gabe would go so far as to not follow up on a lead to spite him, but he'd never been particularly thorough…with anything, really. "Yeah. If you wouldn't mind."

Once more, Atticus squeezed his hand. "I don't mind. Do you want pizza? I'm suddenly starving."

Jericho laughed at the jump in topics before shrugging. "Yeah, pizza sounds…pizza sounds good."

FIVE
ATTICUS

" **...and that's how I ended** up in a straight porn movie."

They sat naked, tangled in Jericho's sheets, a pizza box between them. They hadn't discussed anything of importance since they'd agreed on dinner.

Atticus blinked at him, chewing his pizza thoughtfully. "Fascinating. I can't figure out how much of what you say is true and how much is bullshit."

Jericho grinned at Atticus's deadpan delivery. "I'll leave you to wonder," he said, stuffing the crust into his mouth and chewing obnoxiously before swallowing the huge bite. "You could tell me something about you, then I wouldn't feel compelled to fill the silence."

Atticus snorted. "I already told you I'm a psychopathic vigilante who comes from a family of serial killers. Everything after that seems trivial, no?"

"Why *did* you tell me that?" Jericho asked. "I would think something that big would be a sort of top tier secret. One saved for deathbed confessions. Why blurt that out to

66

a complete stranger?"

Atticus thought about it for a long moment. Why had he just blurted out a huge family secret, one he'd been furious to find that Adam and August had revealed so easily? Jericho was reckless. He had a look in his eye that belied this cavalier attitude about his own safety and welfare. A look that made Atticus want to follow suit.

"It's like you said in the cabin, how often do you meet somebody you don't have to lie to?"

Jericho's grin slipped away as he studied Atticus. "You lie a lot, huh? I found a bunch of pics of you online. You at cocktail parties and award dinners. You posing with city council members. All big smiles and relaxed shoulders, nothing like you are with me."

Atticus took another bite, contemplating Jericho's statements, wondering if he was meant to explain himself, deciding he would either way. "I—My father says I'm a mimic. That I simply imitate the behavior of others without even trying. I give what I get. It's superficial, performative. My brother, Adam, can do it, too, but he's too reckless. He likes to play with people, cause problems. He's chaos. My father uses me as the public face because I'm essentially a mirror just reflecting people back at themselves with nothing behind my eyes."

"That's bullshit. Not the mirror thing, but the nothing part. That's not true." Atticus's heartbeat shot up as Jericho closed the pizza box and tossed it on the floor. He pushed Atticus back onto the pillows, following him down. He immediately opened his legs, letting Jericho settle between

them. He really hoped he didn't want to hook up again. He didn't think he could do what they'd done again after that much pizza.

"I don't want to have sex again," Atticus blurted.

"Ever?"

Atticus wished he could say yes. "Just…not right now. Pizza…"

Jericho shook his head. "You really have no concept of intimacy. It's fascinating. Me, I'm super touchy-feely. I like kissing and hugging and cuddling, even hot hookups sometimes end up as sleepovers."

Fury rocketed through him, like a shock wave at the thought of Jericho doing this…wanting this with anybody else. It made no sense. Atticus had just told him they were friends with benefits, less than that. Just benefits. But he didn't want to think about Jericho kissing or fucking anybody else, and he certainly didn't want to think about him…comforting them or cuddling them. What the fuck?

Jericho placed a soft kiss on his lips. "Come back."

"What?" Atticus asked, voice thick.

"You definitely checked out there for a minute."

"I was just thinking how absurd your last sentence was," he lied. "I understand intimacy. It's just not something I'm capable of."

Jericho searched his face, frowning, before dipping his head to fit their lips together in a kiss that lingered. When Jericho's rough knuckles trailed across his cheek, he gave a ragged shudder. Atticus flushed as Jericho tugged his chin down, slipping his tongue inside.

Part of Atticus wished he would just kiss him like they'd kissed in the cabin, raw and angry. Painful and aggressive. This softness, the slow teasing slide of Jericho's tongue over his, the way he caressed the side of his face, it made his chest tight, just like in his office earlier.

"See?" he said between kisses. "This is intimacy."

"This is just me mirroring you," Atticus said, even as he lifted his head to capture Jericho's mouth once again.

"You're a terrible liar," Jericho teased, sucking on Atticus's bottom lip. "The minute I kiss you, your whole body relaxes. You hate it—hate that I have that effect on you—but it's true. You like me taking charge."

Atticus frowned. "That's just a physical response. A reaction to yours."

Jericho threaded his other hand in Atticus's hair, running blunt nails along his scalp before tipping his head to the side to run his nose along his neck. He used his teeth to tug at his earlobe before rasping, "No, Freckles. It's psychological. Some part of you recognizes the dominant part of me. That's not mirroring. If it was, you'd be trying to control everything, trying to maintain our perceived power dynamic."

"Perceived power dynamic?" Atticus managed.

"Mm, this idea that because you're older, a little larger, make more money, that somehow you're the aggressor between us. But it's not true, is it?"

How the fuck would Atticus know? He had no gauge. Sex with Kendra was rare and often perfunctory. She preferred her toys. Was he really…submissive to Jericho? *Open your*

mouth. Give me your tongue. Open your legs. He knew the answer. He just hated it. Or hated that he didn't hate it.

Jericho was kissing him again, those deep, drugging kisses that had Atticus's cock hardening between them. "Whenever I kiss you, touch you, tell you what to do…your eyes get all hazy and you just do it. You're so…obedient. It's so goddamn sexy."

Was it? Did Jericho truly like Atticus like this? Why did he care? It had to be mirroring. Atticus didn't have feelings. Not the big ones. He could be angry and irritated and even embarrassed, but attachments, empathy? He wasn't capable. What was happening to him?

Jericho was lazily rocking against him now, his cock sliding along the groove of Atticus's hip. "You like not having to think. You like being told what to do. You're quickly becoming my favorite." *Favorite what?* Atticus thought, sure he was as red as the tomato sauce on their pizza, but Jericho was still talking. "You're not a mirror with me, Freckles… No matter how much it annoys you."

"I don't know what you're talking about," Atticus finally managed, eyes rolling behind his eyelids as sparks of pleasure rolled over him with each new rocking movement.

"Okay, Freckles. If you say so," Jericho said, his voice breathless but no less amused. "Wrap your legs around me."

Atticus complied without question, only further proving Jericho's point, but it seemed he'd found a distraction. His hands went under Atticus to wrap around his shoulders, holding him in place so he could work himself against Atticus with purpose.

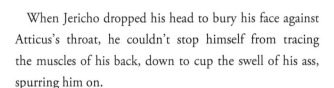

When Jericho dropped his head to bury his face against Atticus's throat, he couldn't stop himself from tracing the muscles of his back, down to cup the swell of his ass, spurring him on.

Jericho panted words into his skin as he moved. "Mm, yeah, that's it. Just like that. Fuck, you make me so hard. Fuck. Fuck."

Atticus felt Jericho come, felt the sudden wetness on his hip, but before he could even contemplate what he was supposed to do about it, Jericho sat up, swiping fingers through his release and smearing it over Atticus's cock before closing his fist around him.

Jericho gave a few slow tugs, gaze locking on Atticus. "Use my fist to get yourself off." Atticus hesitated for only a minute before giving two hesitant rolls of his hips. "You can do better than that. Show me."

Atticus threw his forearm over his eyes, not wanting to look at Jericho as he began to work up into his palm. It was a little sticky and Jericho's hand was sandpaper rough, but that didn't stop him from chasing his release. Hell, it somehow made it hotter. But it wasn't just the tight squeeze around his cock, it was his other hand skimming his lower belly, rubbing his inner thighs, trailing the pads of his fingertips over the skin just above the base of his cock until it felt like he was just one overstimulated nerve ending.

Every third stroke, Jericho would twist his hand, rubbing his thumb over his slit. "Fuck, you're leaking so much," Jericho said, like he was talking to himself. "You look so hot like this, so fucking needy. I love watching you work

for it. Come on. Look at me."

Atticus made a sound in the back of his throat at his words, forcing himself to do as he was told, gaze locking on Jericho's almost black eyes. Then a hand, those clever fucking fingers, were sliding between his cheeks to play over his hole. Just that touch was enough. He came hard for the second time that night, spilling over Jericho's fist.

Jericho gave a rough laugh as he wiped his hand on the bed before collapsing beside him. He looked far more put together than Atticus, who was the color of a naked mole rat and breathing like he'd just run a marathon.

They lay there in comfortable silence for a while. "Stay the night?"

Atticus shook his head. "I have to meet my father on the other side of town at six a.m."

It wasn't a lie. He did have to meet Thomas, but it was just for a couple of signatures. It wouldn't take more than ten minutes. But sleeping beside Jericho all night sounded… dangerous. He didn't want to lose it like his brothers had. He couldn't start thinking of Jericho as anything more than he was. A distraction. He wouldn't get all tangled up in knots like Adam and August. He had some self-control.

Jericho gave him a knowing look but just smirked. "Your loss, Freckles. I make a great pillow."

Atticus let himself gaze longingly at Jericho's hairless chest, wanting to explore his body as thoroughly as Jericho had explored his. Well, maybe not exactly how Jericho had explored his. But it didn't matter. He needed to get up and walk out before he gave in to temptation.

He stood, finding his clothes. "Put your name and number in my phone."

Jericho didn't argue, just grabbed his phone. "It's locked."

"1-9-8-2."

"You really need to be more careful with who you just give information to," Jericho teased, unlocking his phone and loading his contact information.

"Do you really think we do anything incriminating on an unsecured line?" Atticus asked.

"I suppose not."

"I'm going to have my people look into your sister... Mercy. I'll do it immediately and let you know what they find."

A shadow swept across Jericho's features, the tightness from before returning. Grief. Atticus recognized it, even if he couldn't quite understand it. He gave a stilted nod.

Once Atticus was dressed and his Uber en route, Jericho stood, shoving his legs into a pair of joggers that were lying on the floor, not bothering with a shirt. He insisted on walking him out. Down in the shop, the light was on and the sound of boys laughing and shouting could be heard, though not the words they spoke.

On the stoop, Jericho wrapped his arms over his chest as if to protect himself from the crisp fall wind. It had been so hot just the other day, but the temperature had plummeted, right on time. The leaves were already changing.

"I'll be in touch," Atticus said.

He turned away only to find himself spun back around and pushed against the brick wall, Jericho's lips millimeters

from his. "That's not how you say goodbye to me."

He gave Atticus a kiss that curled his toes and then he was gone, the door slamming behind him, leaving Atticus just standing there, the icy wind beating against his face.

Atticus made sure he was in and out of the meeting with his father but also did his best not to raise any questions. He couldn't handle a Thomas interrogation today. He needed to get to work but found he was in no real hurry to do so. He was exhausted and distracted. Each time he closed his eyes for even a minute, thoughts of last night flooded in. He ached in the best possible way, but each twinge sent him right back into his dirty memories. He needed to talk to somebody. Somebody who wasn't related to him in some way.

He called the only person he'd ever thought of as a friend.

It rang only once. "Morning, Sunshine."

"Hey, Calliope," Atticus said, trying not to sound as mopey as he felt.

"What's wrong? Why do you sound like Eeyore? Did you have a fight with your father? Your brothers? Did you not get the Padget grant?"

"No, nothing like that. I'm just having a bad day," he said, his tone implying it was very much something.

"Don't lie to me," she scolded. "Come on, tell Mama all about it. I need a distraction anyway. I'm going blind trying to run down the bugs in this code."

Atticus pushed the button on the side of his leather seat, slowly reclining it until he was out of sight of the general public, sulking as he stared up at the Volvo's pearl gray interior. "It's just…there's this person…this guy…" He trailed off, not knowing how to explain what was happening to him.

There was the sound of a chair squeaking. "Is this about *him*? Your cabin fever *Brokeback Mountain* hookup?"

Atticus gave a heavy sigh. He knew he shouldn't have told her that. But he'd needed somebody to talk to on his way home that night and Calliope was his only constant that didn't share a last name with him. She always answered when he called and she kept their conversations to herself.

He hadn't lied to Jericho about not having any friends. Calliope wasn't a friend, exactly. She was family. Sometimes, she was more like a therapist or a priest. He told her things he'd never tell the others. Maybe it was because he'd never seen her face. The anonymity made it easier for him to confess all his sins and vent his frustrations. She never judged him or questioned his feelings like the rest of the family did.

There was this notion that all psychopaths were these automatons just going through life pretending they were humans, but that just wasn't true. Psychopathy was a spectrum. Maybe he couldn't feel guilt or remorse or love the way a neurotypical person did, but he had a lot of feelings about everything else and six brothers who had no empathy and no way to process his moodiness. Atticus had empathy but only for himself.

Luckily, Calliope had enough empathy for a hundred

people—it was just wrapped in a hard shell of nosiness and sarcasm. But he needed to talk to somebody about Jericho, about what had happened between them. It wasn't like he could tell his father. He would wind up in a case study with Thomas watching his relationship from the other side of the glass. He shook his head. Not a relationship. Friendship. Hookup… Whatever. His father wouldn't understand.

Atticus didn't have any animosity towards his father. He understood why Thomas did what he did. He knew he felt called to do this. But, sometimes, it was hard knowing he'd been adopted strictly for the betterment of science.

So, he had Calliope. She kept his secrets and talked him off ledges and didn't say he was whining or petty or… disagreeable. Even though he was. He knew he was. He didn't want to be the little black storm cloud of doom and gloom everybody thought he was, but that was just who he was as a person.

Calliope didn't judge him and she didn't make fun of him like they would. "Not just the cabin. We hooked up in my office and then again at his place last night."

"Hooked up?" she prodded. "Like, heavy petting or did you guys do the horizontal tango?"

Atticus rolled his eyes but still said, "The latter."

"Oh," she said, then, "Oh! So, did you…pitch or catch?"

He could feel himself flushing again. Luckily, nobody could see him. "The second one."

"I—actually, yeah, that kind of makes sense. You're a total bottom."

"Wow," Atticus muttered. "I don't think you're allowed

to say that."

Calliope scoffed. "You gonna report me to the gay headquarters? Is PFLAG going to come take my ally card away? Why so glum? Did it not go well? Did you not like it?"

Atticus sighed dramatically. "I liked it just fine." Massive understatement of the year. "That's the problem. Have you ever met somebody who you just let...take you over?"

"You getting laid, Sunshine, or demonically possessed?" Calliope teased. "Though, if the sex is good enough, it could feel like a little bit of both."

"A demon would be easier to get rid of." Because he would actually want a demon expelled from his body. But not Jericho. And that was a big problem.

"So, who found who first?" she asked. "I can't imagine you guys exchanged contact info after your post-murder gropefest in the cabin since you needed me to look him up."

Atticus frowned. He never had learned how Jericho found him. "He found me, but I don't know how."

"He found you in the middle of the work day? Like, he wanted you so bad he showed up for a midday booty call? What did he say when he showed up?"

There was a loud crinkling like a chip bag rustling and then Calliope was quietly munching in his ear. "You're enjoying this," he said, irritated.

"Of course, I am. This is better than a telenovela. All my boys are finding their happily ever afters. I have to admit, I didn't think you'd be the next to fall, but I think it's good for you. You need to lighten up."

Atticus shook his head. "I don't lighten up around him,

I completely lose my mind around him. I lose all ability to say no."

"Did you *want* to say no?" she asked cautiously, still munching.

Of course, he didn't. That was the fucking problem. Why weren't people understanding this? "Noah said I should just hook up with him. Be 'friends with benefits,'" he air-quoted to nobody.

"You told Noah?" She sounded somewhere between shocked and hurt. "I thought you weren't out to the family."

"I'm not out because I'm not gay. I'm…experimenting."

"Okay," she said carefully. "But you experimented doing butt stuff and you've never really felt anything for the girls you've been with in the past. Maybe that's because you're hardwired to like men."

Atticus snorted. "I've never felt anything for anybody because I'm a psychopath, Calliope."

"Yet, this stranger has got you twisted up in knots. So, he makes you feel *something? Right?* Enough to get naked with him three times."

Atticus rubbed a hand over his face. "None of this matters. It's just a…phase. Eventually, I'll stop wanting him, and then I can just go back to normal. I'm just in a weird place right now."

Calliope munched another chip in his ear. "Literally or metaphorically?"

"I'm literally in a parking lot right now. But I actually called you for a reason."

"Other than to tell me you got laid?" Calliope asked.

"Yes, other than that. My...friend just found out his sister died."

"Oh, grief sex. That's intense. It's good you were there for him."

Atticus ignored her. "But she was missing for eight years before that. They said she donated a kidney just before she died and passed away from sepsis. Something's not adding up. You know how highly documented transplants are. Can you see what you can find out?"

"Sure. What's her name?"

"Mercy Navarro. I texted you her date of birth, too. Can you look up the autopsy report and also get me her case file from the police?"

"I'm on it. Give me a few hours."

"Let me know when you've got something."

SIX
JERICHO

When Jericho rolled out of bed at seven or so, he carried out his normal morning routine with a dopey half smile that just refused to go away. Atticus had been a pleasant and surprising distraction from the shit sandwich of his day. Jericho had never really thought pizza and mutual orgasms would be enough to shove aside the images he'd seen in that morgue but, somehow, focusing on Atticus had done just that.

For a time.

As soon as he opened his bedroom door, reality punched him square in the diaphragm. A sulky Felix sat curled on the couch in a pair of flowy black pants and a sheer floral robe, his eyes red and face wet with tears as he looked at Jericho's laptop.

"What are you doing, little brother?" Jericho asked, following the scent of coffee to the kitchen.

When he turned to face Felix, coffee in hand, he found his mouth was in a hard line as he glowered at him with narrowed eyes. "I've been planning our sister's funeral, unlike you, who decided to get laid...again." When Jericho didn't dignify his brother's dig with a response, he continued. "That *was* your boyfriend you walked out of here at two in the morning, wasn't it?"

Jericho took a deep breath and let it out, reminding himself that Felix was just lashing out because he was hurting. "He's not my boyfriend and yeah, that was him. What did you want me to do? Sit around wallowing about something we suspected for years? You were downstairs drinking and playing video games. Did I judge you? No. I know your default setting is judgey, but dial it down a bit. She was my sister, too."

Felix rolled his eyes, taking a delicate sip of what Jericho was certain was green tea. "Point of order. I was downstairs playing video games because your boyfriend is really loud in bed. I couldn't listen to him moaning, 'Oh, God. Oh, fuck,' anymore. You certainly couldn't be worthy of all that."

Jericho couldn't help the grin that spread across his face, which only made Felix roll his eyes as he snorted with derision. Atticus had been a little bit loud. It had been hot as fuck. He really had done anything Jericho asked, had begged for it, had given in so easily. He'd wanted Jericho to take charge—had needed it to take that pressure off him. Jericho suspected that trying to cure the sick while seeking vengeance on the living was likely exhausting for somebody like Atticus. He'd needed to be able to turn his brain off and not think.

That was fine with Jericho. He would happily let Atticus

play pillow princess if that made him happy. He found Atticus's response to him almost as hot as his touch. Besides, gay or not, Atticus had seemed to love Jericho inside him, and if he got to experience Atticus coming from inside his body, that was more than enough for him.

"Gross. You're thinking about banging him right now, aren't you? Dude, what is wrong with you?"

Jericho pulled himself from his dirty thoughts. "Shut up."

As far as comebacks went, it wasn't great, but he didn't know what else to say. He'd never let anybody occupy this much real estate in his head before. Everything about Atticus seemed to demand Jericho's full attention. He'd never been anybody's first anything. Any other day, he would've run screaming in the opposite direction. He didn't deflower virgins, even if it was only of the gay sex variety. He didn't want to be anybody's experiment.

But last night, Jericho hadn't been thinking clearly. At least, that was what he'd told himself. He took his coffee and sat beside Felix on the couch. His younger brother instantly gravitated closer.

"What are you looking at?"

Felix's voice caught on a sob. "Caskets."

Jericho's heart shredded into a million pieces. "Felix… Mercy didn't want to be buried. She wanted to be cremated, remember? We all talked about it that one really bad night. The night we took you with us to that super depressing movie and then we ate burgers and you puked in the bushes? And you were moping because you wanted to go to the water tower but we said you were too little but

you whined until we agreed?"

"I didn't whine."

"While we were up there, she said she wanted us to spread her ashes right there because it would piss off Ma and Papi? Remember?"

Jericho didn't know if that was still true. In Jericho's head, she was still seventeen years old. She still wore her jeans too low and tank tops with skulls and knives to piss off their father and dyed her gorgeous dark brown hair black to irritate Ma. But that wasn't true. She'd lived eight whole years somewhere else. Eight years she'd been in the same city but never came to see him and Felix, never called. Part of him was furious, but that anger was eclipsed by the fact that she was dead. She had died and been thrown away like trash.

"Shouldn't people have a chance to say goodbye?" Felix asked, a tear rolling down his cheek.

"What people, *didi*? It's you, me, and Ma, and she doesn't know who we are most days. The best thing we can do for her is just do what she wanted when we last knew her and put our efforts into figuring out where the fuck she's been for the last eight years. I want to know how she ended up where she did. Don't you?"

Felix deflated, tucking himself under Jericho's arm. His baby brother was all extremes. Sweet or salty, furious or exhilarated, deliriously happy or inconsolable. He was a constantly swinging pendulum knocking down anything in his way, a pent up ball of homicidal rage one moment and a big, sucking hole of neediness the next.

Jericho blamed their parents. They had put all their pressure on him as the oldest, and then Mercy, constantly reminding them not to squander the opportunities given to them by immigrating to this country. But they'd spoiled Felix. By the time he was born, they'd decided they could loosen the reins a bit.

Then everything fell apart in such rapid succession. Mercy disappeared. Their father learned he had bone cancer, and then their mother was assaulted. Attacked in broad daylight in front of her own store, her head struck violently enough to cause a bleed that left her catastrophically injured.

Jericho had already taken over his father's business by the time his mother was injured, and he'd done the best he could to raise a teen when he was barely an adult himself. He'd tried to hold onto hope that Mercy would return, that his mother's brain would somehow fix itself, even though the doctor's said there was no going back and that her level of traumatic brain injury would require constant around the clock supervision.

"How are you going to do that?" Felix asked around a sniffle.

Jericho didn't know how to tell Felix just enough to keep him from digging too deep. While he knew about Atticus being at the cabin and that he was rich, he didn't know it was a family operation. "My...friend has connections. People who might be able to help."

"Like the mob?"

Jericho gave a half smile. "No. He's just a rich dude with friends in high places, who know how to cut through red

tape."

Felix leaned back and looked at him. "Why would a rich dude want to date you? No offense."

Jericho poked him in the side. "Much offense, dick." Jericho sighed. "We're not dating. Not yet. But there's just something about him. He's under my skin."

"Sounds like an STD if you ask me," Felix said, his judgey expression nailed firmly back in place.

Jericho could handle judgmental Felix over sad Felix any day. "You just don't like anything that takes my time away from babysitting you and your friends."

Felix scoffed. "Babysitting? You and I both know you couldn't do what you do without us. You say it all the time—the trash doesn't take itself out. And there's a lot of trash in our neighborhood."

Sometimes, Jericho felt guilty about dragging his brother and the others into his mission. It wasn't intentional. After he found the men who assaulted his mother and gave them a taste of their own medicine, people in the neighborhood began to come to him. How could he say no? But he was just one person. One person playing pied piper to a bunch of angry, directionless teens with trauma. He just gave them a target to focus their rage on.

"I know. You're right. But I need to get downstairs. Customers are going to start showing up at any minute. Maybe let's just not worry about the arrangements just yet. Okay?"

Felix stared at him hard for a long moment before giving a hesitant nod. "Yeah, okay."

"Get dressed. Don't you have classes this morning?"

"I don't know why you're so insistent I go to college. I don't need to have a degree to design clothes. I have a natural talent."

Jericho snorted. "You know it was important to Ma and Papi. So, get to class, Mr. Natural Talent."

By the time Jericho got downstairs to open the shop, there were already people waiting. He pushed up the bay doors and was grateful to see Arsen was already in the office, ready to work. He had braided his blue hair down the center of his head, revealing the shaved sides, essentially giving himself a fake mohawk.

"I saw your rich man leaving this morning," Arsen said by way of greeting, his accent heavier than usual. "Felix said he is very…enthusiastic."

Jericho rolled his eyes. "Shut up."

Arsen grinned, revealing perfect white teeth. But before he could retort, a girl in a halter top rested her arms and boobs on the counter. "Hi, Arsen," she said, giving him her best *fuck me* eyes. "Can you look at my tire? I think there's a nail in it."

Arsen frowned. "Did I not look at your tires last week? Where do you drive with all of these nails and screws?"

Jericho couldn't help but smirk. Arsen was completely clueless to the girls throwing themselves at him with regularity. Like the other boys that flocked to Jericho's for shelter, he was same-sex oriented. That was how they'd all ended up there. It was a safe haven for those who had been brave enough—or stupid enough—to come out in

a neighborhood that clung to their painfully traditional "family" values.

Arsen gave Jericho a look—letting him know he thought this girl was ridiculous—before stuffing a rag in the back pocket of his coveralls and following the girl around the corner. The girls completely overlooked that Arsen was gay. They just didn't care. They were determined to win over the Russian boy with his blue hair and aqua eyes that Jericho knew had to be contact lenses.

Unlike Atticus. Those pretty blue eyes were all his. He shook the thought away, forcing himself to go about his day, unwilling to distract himself with memories of last night. He didn't last long. He spent most of the day getting caught up in not just the things they'd done last night but all the things he planned on doing to him the next time he had him all to himself.

If it happened again. God, he hoped it happened again. Now that he'd had a taste, had been buried inside him, he didn't think he could go without doing it again. Atticus had his hooks in him. It was alarming how much Jericho liked that. Maybe *he* was a masochist.

Two days. Atticus didn't contact him for two whole days. Not a text or a phone call. Jericho had spent two restless nights hoping for the buzzer at his door to go off, letting him know Atticus had finally given in and wanted more. But there was just…silence.

Jericho tried to keep himself busy with work. He really did. It wasn't like he didn't have his own life. His shop was busy from dawn until dusk. People knew Jericho was honest and wouldn't screw them over. He also let people make payment plans. That made him popular in their middle class neighborhood.

Still, Atticus was never far from his mind. At least twenty times a day, he pulled out his phone to text him. But something always stopped him. He'd lied to Atticus the other night—had lied right to his face. He'd told him he was a touchy-feely guy, that he had sleepovers with his hookups. It was all bullshit. He was affectionate with his brother, his mom, but he'd never been overly doting. It was just Atticus. He was so determined to not feel things for Jericho that it forced him to push back, to find a way to show Atticus that his stubbornness was a guise. He didn't understand it, this attraction to the other man. Maybe he really did just have a thing for gingers.

Still, if Atticus didn't contact him soon, he was going to just assume he'd gotten cold feet and had no intention of helping him solve Mercy's murder. He couldn't have that looming over him. He felt like she couldn't be at peace until he found some way to solve the mystery of her disappearance and death.

Jericho had just handed keys over to a customer when his phone vibrated in his pocket. It was a text. From Atticus. **Have news. Let's meet. Lunch time?**

Jericho's stomach dropped. Obviously, this was about Mercy. **Yeah, okay. Where?**

Jericho watched the dots dance before Atticus finally sent: **The morgue.**

What the fuck? Jericho typed out his response with shaking hands. **What?**

Atticus's response was very quick that time. **Just trust me.** Followed by: **Please.**

Please. Just that word sent a shock of awareness through him. He'd been so loath to say it the other night. Had fought until he couldn't take Jericho's teasing anymore. Was it just easier for him to say it in the light of day? Somehow, Jericho didn't think so. Some part of him wondered if Atticus had realized how easy it would be to manipulate him with just that one word, but he pushed the idea aside.

This was about his sister. This was about Mercy.

Hello?

Jericho pulled himself from his thoughts. **Sorry. Yeah. Okay. I'll be there at noon.** Atticus's only response was an address.

He was useless for the rest of the morning. When the time came to leave, he left the shop in Arsen's hands and tried not to run to his old Ford Bronco. It wasn't a long drive, but it felt like there was a lead weight on his chest, like each breath was sucked through a straw. He turned up the music, hoping the sound might drown out the voice in his head screaming that whatever he found would change his life forever.

Last time, when he arrived at the morgue, a sharp-nosed man in scrubs had ordered him to wait on a bench until Gabriel arrived. This time, a middle-aged woman behind the

desk flashed him a sympathetic smile. "Jericho Navarro?"

"Yes?" he asked, not sure why he hesitated.

"They're waiting for you right through those doors."

"They?"

"Yes. Dr. Mulvaney, Professor Blackwell, and Dr. Abbot, our Chief Medical Examiner."

"Oh," was all Jericho could manage.

When he pushed through the doors, the knot in his chest loosened when he saw Atticus, even though his expression was grim. He swallowed hard when he noted they stood at the head of an autopsy table, a body laid out before them. Mercy.

"He—" He cleared his throat and tried again. "Hey."

Atticus nodded. "Jericho, this is Dr. Abbot. He re-examined your sister's body to make sure the initial medical examiner didn't miss anything."

"Did he?"

The doctor nodded. "Yes, but I'm afraid it doesn't offer much insight. When Dr. Mulvaney informed me that your sister had a history of drug use, I decided to test a hair sample for any indications of drugs in her system."

Jericho swallowed the lump in his throat. "And…"

"It appears your sister was a heroin user." Jericho tried not to wince, but he wasn't sure he managed it. "However, it appears she'd been clean for at least five months."

"How can you tell that?" Jericho asked.

Dr. Abbot shifted his weight from one foot to the other. "When tested, each centimeter of hair reflects around one month of time. So, the farther down the hair strand we

go, the longer it was since the last time the victim ingested drugs. For your sister, it appears to be five months or so."

Jericho's face twisted in anguish. "You're telling me my sister was a drug addict for eight years, then got clean and died?"

The man looked sympathetic, more so than Atticus, who watched Jericho with an unreadable expression. The professor's face most reflected how Jericho felt—this strange mixture of sorrow and resolution. Like the outcome had been foreseeable but still heartbreaking.

Jericho once more cleared his throat, hoping he could get rid of the lump that seemed to live there now. "Is that it? Is that what you wanted me to know?"

Atticus turned to the medical examiner. "Tim, do you mind if we have a few minutes with the body?"

The man shook his head. "Take your time." When he passed Jericho, he clapped him on the shoulder. "I'm very sorry for your loss."

"Jericho, this is my brother-in-law, Lucas."

"The former FBI psychic?" Jericho asked.

"Current psychic, former FBI guy," Lucas clarified without humor.

"Okay..."

"I had my analyst search every conceivable way for your sister, but we have no information from after she went missing. We know that before she left she was suspected in some shoplifting cases and was a known associate of some low-level gang members in the area, but then she just disappeared."

Jericho felt his face flush. "Yeah, the cops figured that out years ago."

"I thought, since we've exhausted all the usual ways of learning what happened to your sister, we could try an unusual way. I think we should let Lucas try to find something."

"Psychically," Jericho said, voice devoid of expression.

"I… When I touch people or objects, I'm able to pick up on vibrations, impressions, images."

Jericho was trying not to be rude, but he didn't believe in psychics or any of that witchy-woo-woo stuff.

Lucas gave another tight smile. "I'll be happy to demonstrate if you need a bit of proof. I'm used to it in this family."

Atticus moved towards Jericho. "Do I strike you as somebody who believes in carnival sideshow psychics? He's the real deal. Let him show you if you need some proof. We just want to help you find out what happened to Mercy."

Hearing Atticus say Mercy's name broke something in Jericho. He blinked back tears as he nodded. "Yeah, okay. Show me."

Lucas beckoned him closer. "May I have your hand?" Jericho held it out. Before Lucas gripped it, he said, "It's often better if you think about whatever it is you want me to see. At least, if you don't want me roaming around in your head."

Jericho frowned but nodded. The memory that floated to the surface was the one he and Felix had recalled the other day. The three of them at the top of the water tower. Mercy's

inky black hair was caught in the wind and Jericho's legs dangled from the scaffolding. They'd made Felix sit with his back to the cistern.

"If you tell Mom we brought you up here, I'm going to bring you back up here just to toss you off," Lucas said, startling Jericho so much he almost jerked his hand away. "Shut up. I'm not a baby. You are a baby. A little tiny baby. Ma and Papi's little pet. They'd kill us both to protect you."

It was surreal hearing Mercy and Felix's conversation out of the mouth of a stranger. Jericho pulled his hand free. "I believe you. Now, what?"

Lucas gazed at him with sharp green eyes. "Now, if you want, I can touch your sister's hand and see what—if anything—I see."

Fuck. Were they really doing this? His eyes dragged to Atticus, who seemed to instinctively move closer, stopping before they were touching but standing close enough for Jericho to feel the heat of his body even through the light jacket he wore. "Let him do it. We need some kind of jumping off point and right now, we have nothing. She just…vanished."

Jericho wiped a hand over his face, covering his mouth before nodding.

Lucas stepped forward, pulling back the sheet enough to reveal one bloated, discolored hand. Jericho turned away, swallowing the bile climbing his throat. "Just do it."

SEVEN
ATTICUS

No matter how often Atticus watched Lucas do what he did, it never got any less weird or any less fascinating. It wasn't that Atticus didn't believe in Lucas's gifts. There was no refuting the evidence. Lucas most definitely knew things he couldn't know if not for some kind of psychic ability.

But unlike his brother, August, it had taken Atticus a bit more time to adjust. If Atticus had to pinpoint one thing—other than enthusiasm for murder—that showed how different Atticus and August were, it would be how they'd processed Lucas's psychometry. August, with his off the charts IQ, had not only accepted Lucas's abilities unflinchingly, he'd used them to his advantage on several occasions.

Atticus, however, had…not. He'd thought Lucas was attempting to somehow scam August or bait him into revealing their family secrets. Good thing he wasn't or they'd all be in prison because August had spilled his guts to Lucas on day one.

Kind of how he had with Jericho. That was different,

though. Jericho and he had killed together. Well, Jericho had killed Trevor, but Atticus had aided and abetted. Had one gotten caught, the other could have done some serious jail time as well. Mutually assured destruction guaranteed loyalty. At least in the Mulvaney household.

Atticus kept his eyes on Lucas, unsure what to expect, but he couldn't ignore Jericho. There was a tension in his stance, an energy that radiated off him. He was barely hanging on. Even Atticus could see it. If Atticus was to reach out and touch him, attempt even a sliver of kindness, it might send Jericho over the edge. So, instead, he did the only thing he could think to do. He stood beside him... just in case.

Lucas sucked in a breath—that telltale sign he'd made some kind of connection with whatever it was within him. He pinched his lids shut harder, tilting his head almost as if he was trying to see better. "There's a man with her, walking her somewhere. He's got a hand around her upper arm, not forcing her but...controlling her."

"What does he look like?" Atticus prompted.

"Over six feet. Brown hair, brown eyes. Sharp chin. Bad skin. He has letters or a word tattooed on his chest, but his shirt is obscuring my view. There's another on his neck. A rose with bloody thorns. And on his hand, but it's too distorted to make out. Looks homemade or like some kind of jailhouse job." He fell silent, his head tilting the other way. "Now, she's in a hotel room or basement. It reeks of weed and sour sweat. She's not alone. There are others. Half-dressed girls, guys with tattoos. Maybe a house party?

Another girl is injecting her with heroin. It doesn't feel coerced, but she has a large bruise on her face."

Jericho's shoulders straightened, his chin jutting forward, his fury palpable.

Atticus dragged his gaze back to Lucas. "Can you see anything else? Anything that might help? Anything closer to her time of death?"

"I can try. I can't really control what I see. But I'll try." He took a deep breath and let it out, squeezing his eyes shut. Then, suddenly Lucas seemed to…change. His teeth clacked together hard, shivers wracking his body. His skin turned a greenish gray color.

Jericho turned then, frowning when he looked at the change in Lucas's appearance.

Lucas's eyes were still firmly clamped shut, likely immersed in the tragic last hours of Mercy's life. "I'm sweating b-but I'm s-so cold. My stomach hurts bad. Like I swallowed a bottle of acid. I'm so thirsty. I try to say something, but my tongue feels too big for my mouth."

"Somebody's there with you?" Atticus asked.

"There's a man there. In scrubs. They're dirty. He's dirty. Greasy hair, bad teeth. He's playing a game on his phone. I can hear the music. It's annoyingly upbeat. My throat hurts. I try to talk but he just looks up and then back to his game. I hate this place. It was nothing like they said."

Atticus glanced at Jericho, who was still standing there, dumbstruck. "Like who said?"

Lucas dropped Mercy's hand, stumbling backwards. "I'm sorry. That's all I could get." He turned to the sink, quickly

washing his hands before splashing water on his face. "She was very…disoriented at the end."

"Thank you," Jericho managed, voice shredded.

Lucas gave Atticus a hard look, then a nod towards Jericho. He was clearly trying to give them some kind of signal, but it was lost on Atticus, as most things seemed to be. Lucas shook his head, giving a slight wave as he left the room.

Before Atticus could speak, Jericho was stomping to the exit as well, forcing Atticus to jog to catch up.

Jericho appeared to have zero interest whether Atticus followed or not. He tried not to take that personally. A woman in a tight black dress and a lanyard walked towards them from down the hall. When she passed, Jericho barked, "Bathroom?"

The startled employee pointed vaguely down the hall, then side-stepped Jericho and scurried away as Jericho continued to trudge down the hall like a man on a mission.

Atticus put a hand on his shoulder, but it didn't slow Jericho down. "Are you okay? I mean, I know you're not okay, but are you okay to—I don't know—drive? Function? Be alone?"

"I'm fine," Jericho muttered gruffly.

That was a lie. Jericho was most definitely not okay. When he entered the bathroom, Atticus followed, locking the door behind him. Jericho gave him an irritated look just as Atticus realized it was a single restroom with only a toilet and a sink. Did Jericho really have to use the bathroom? Honestly, Atticus didn't care. He didn't think it was a good idea to leave him alone.

Jericho's nostrils flared, but there was a resignation in his eyes. "I can't do this with you right now."

He sounded…tired.

Atticus frowned. "Do what?"

Jericho gestured between them. "This. Whatever this is. I can't…be nice right now."

Atticus's brows knitted together. "Have I ever asked you to be nice?"

Jericho slammed his fist into the ugly blue tile. "I'm serious. I feel like I'm two seconds away from snapping. I need to punch something, hit something, rip it apart. I'm so fucking angry."

Atticus caught his gaze. "You can hit me. I'd consider it a personal favor if you avoided my face. I already get enough shit from my brothers about my botched jobs. But if hitting me will make you feel better, go ahead."

Jericho stared at him for a full minute, his chest rising and falling rapidly, searching Atticus's face, like he was trying to read a foreign language. Atticus didn't see him move, didn't even register it until he hit the wall, the frigid tiles bleeding through the thin dress shirt. Jericho's hand was around his neck.

For a split second, Atticus truly expected Jericho's fist to connect with his face. But instead, he crashed their lips together, their teeth colliding before Jericho forced his tongue into Atticus's mouth. Atticus didn't fight him. He relaxed against the wall, letting Jericho take what he wanted. He would let Jericho do whatever he needed to feel better. His father would say it was the right thing to do.

Okay, maybe Thomas wouldn't have said this particular way of soothing Jericho was the right thing to do, but the sentiment was the same. But this was obviously what Jericho needed. He was frenzied—his kisses gluttonous, his hands brutal, fingers squeezing Atticus's throat as he nipped at his lips, bit his jaw, tugged on his earlobe with his teeth.

When Jericho guided Atticus's hand to his zipper, he didn't hesitate, undoing his pants one handed before plunging inside to wrap his palm around Jericho's only half-hard cock. The angle was awkward with barely any room for Atticus to touch Jericho the way he wanted, but it didn't seem to matter. Jericho suddenly buried his face against Atticus's neck, working himself into his tightened fist as a ragged sob fell from his lips.

It was Atticus who felt like he couldn't breathe. He didn't know how to make this better for Jericho. All he could do was hold him. He cupped the back of his head, focusing on his panting breaths as Jericho clung to him, desperately chasing his release, his tears hot on Atticus's skin.

There was nothing sexy about it. It was raw, and sweaty, and even a little painful. Atticus wasn't even hard. It wasn't about that. It wasn't about the sex. It was about...comfort. It was about giving Jericho some kind of pressure release before he hurt himself or somebody else.

Some part of Atticus admitted he was doing this for purely selfish reasons. If Jericho was going to lose it, if he was going to try to fuck his way into forgetting what he'd seen—what he'd learned—it was going to be with Atticus. Nobody else. He wasn't going to dissect the why of it. If

Jericho needed somebody, it was going to be him. Just him.

Jericho groaned, his release spilling over Atticus's hand. When he made no move to pull away, Atticus just held him tighter. He didn't know what else to do. Jericho was still crying. Atticus could feel his tears soaking his collar. He didn't rush him, just raked his fingers through his hair, hoping he found the motion as calming as Atticus had when he was a child. Comfort had been rare back then— something that occurred only in those brief moments where his mother was sober—but he'd liked the feeling. It had been…soothing. Jericho needed soothing.

When he finally stepped back, he wiped at his now puffy eyes with the back of his hands, clearing his throat before reaching down and fixing his clothing. "You want…" His gaze fell squarely on Atticus's crotch.

Atticus followed his eyes, then shook his head. "No. No, I'm good. For now," he added lamely.

For a second, Atticus was sure Jericho was going to just turn and leave, pretend the whole thing had never happened. Instead, he pressed his forehead to his, then kissed the tip of his nose. "Thanks, Freckles. I think I needed that."

Atticus was used to cocky Jericho, teasing Jericho. This Jericho was different but no less enticing. This Jericho had needed solace and it was Atticus who'd given it to him. Atticus, the psychopath, had made Jericho feel a little bit better after a super shitty day. That shouldn't have made him feel good but it did.

"I'm sorry if I just sprang Lucas on you. I was afraid you might hear the word psychic and run before he could show

you he was legit."

Jericho nodded, a small smile tugging at the left corner of his mouth. "Yeah, I probably would have." He looked away and then back, the tiny trace of humor replaced by a look of utter desolation. "What do I do now?"

"You didn't recognize the man Lucas described?"

Jericho shrugged. "I live in a pretty rough neighborhood. Tall guy with brown hair, brown eyes, and tattoos? Hell, he could be talking about anybody, even me."

Atticus nodded. "I'll ask Lucas to give the description to our analyst, Calliope. See if she can run it against NCIC to look for felons with those tattoos. Maybe if we have some hits, Lucas can narrow it down to our guy."

"Why are you doing this for me?" Jericho added.

"Because my father raised me to act like a decent human being even if I'm not," he lied. Jericho's face fell at Atticus's generic answer, and that heavy weight in Atticus's chest was back. He didn't want to be the reason Jericho looked like that. He couldn't be. He grabbed Jericho, pulling him back in, forcing himself to be honest. "Also, because seeing you upset makes me feel…unsettled."

"Unsettled?" Jericho asked, a heat rushing into those dark brown eyes that definitely finally had his dick taking notice.

Atticus nodded. "Yeah, I don't want you to be sad. I like when you're…you."

"And who am I?" Jericho teased, a tinge of cockiness returning to his voice.

Atticus smirked. "The guy who flirted with a psychopath next to a dead body."

"I couldn't help myself." Jericho swayed into his space, running his tongue along the seam of Atticus's lips before pulling away again. "You just don't like taking care of me. I think you want me to take care of you."

It wasn't said with any malice, but Atticus bristled just the same. "I just don't like doing things I'm not good at. I'm not good at taking care of people. And I don't need anybody to take care of me."

Jericho snaked his fingers through Atticus's belt loops, tugging him closer. "Now, that's a lie, Freckles. And lying is a sin. You just took very good care of me." Atticus hated the way he flushed at the compliment. "But you can't hide from me. Your neediness radiates off of you. Your need to be perfect. Your need to be the best." Jericho grew bolder as Atticus swallowed audibly. "I don't mind babying you, Freckles. I don't mind all those big feelings you pretend you don't have. I like taking care of you."

"You don't even know me."

Jericho snorted. "I'd wager I know you better than almost anyone." He gripped his chin. "Does anybody else know how easily you submit?" He captured Atticus's bottom lip with his teeth, tugging gently, before letting it go. "Does anybody else know how you sound when you moan my name, when you beg me to fuck you, how your eyes get all cloudy when I tell you to open up for me?"

Atticus could feel himself falling under Jericho's spell. Whatever magic his words carried pulled him under to that place where nothing mattered but him.

A shriek erupted, bouncing around the tiles of the empty

bathroom. Atticus's heartbeat skyrocketed until he realized it was his phone.

Jericho stepped away from him. Atticus pulled his phone free from his pocket, groaning when he saw it was his baby brother, Adam.

"Yeah?" he answered.

There was no small talk. "Family meeting. Devon's on 3rd. Back room. Now."

"What? Why not at Dad's?"

Adam ignored his question. "Thirty minutes."

Adam ended the call, leaving Atticus to stare at his phone. Finally, he looked up. "I have to go. Family stuff. Talk later?" Jericho nodded. Atticus swallowed hard. "Maybe you could come to my place tonight?"

Jericho grinned. "Yeah, I can do that. That way you don't keep my brother up all night screaming my name again."

Atticus glowered at him. "I did not scream your name."

"Whatever you say. See you tonight."

Then he was gone.

Devon's was one of those old school family restaurants with private rooms in the back and a stage where the owner's wife and daughter sang to the guests. They specialized in scratch cooked comfort foods, but the Mulvaneys frequented it for their soundproofed back rooms and the staff's willingness to mind their own business.

When Atticus arrived, he found the entire family waiting.

No, not the entire family—Aiden was missing as usual. But, this time, Thomas was also not in attendance. Lucas and Noah were, however.

August sat at the head of the table, Lucas on his left side and Adam on his right. Noah sat beside Adam. The twins, Asa and Avi, sat across from them with Archer, who glared at his drink as if it had called the meeting. Atticus was sure his brother wasn't used to waking before two or three in the afternoon.

"What was so important you called me away from… work?" Atticus asked, earning a smirk from Lucas, who stared pointedly at Atticus's rumpled clothing. "Are we finally having an intervention for Archer's drinking?"

Archer snorted, then downed the remainder of his drink, snagging a bottle off the shelf behind him and refilling his glass. "It's possible. Nobody's told me anything." Had he brought his own booze?

"Us either," the twins said in unison.

"What's with all the cloak and dagger shit?" Lucas asked, staring at Adam.

Noah looked to Adam, confirming it was his baby brother who had arranged this meeting. "Yeah, why are we here, babe?"

"Anybody else talk to Dad today?" Adam asked.

They each exchanged glances. Atticus took the seat opposite August, settling in for what he was sure would be a tedious meeting. "This is about Dad? Is he…missing?"

Adam shook his head. "No. He's…distraught."

"Distraught?" Atticus echoed blankly.

Adam nodded earnestly. "Yeah, genuinely distraught."

Noah frowned. "What do you mean? How do you know this? You aren't the best at context clues, babe."

Adam scoffed. "Dad was day-drinking. Fucking Blue could have picked up these clues."

"Who?" Archer asked.

Nobody answered.

"I mean, Archer is day-drinking and he hasn't been distraught a single day in his life," Lucas murmured.

Archer tipped his glass in a mock salute, but Adam was adamantly shaking his head. "You don't get it. When was the last time you saw Dad hammered? Ever?"

"He was drunk?" Atticus asked, mind reeling.

Adam nodded.

The twins looked at each other, doing that creepy twin thing where it seemed like they were having some sort of silent conversation. Finally, Avi said, "The last time Dad was drunk was the day Aiden said he was moving across the country."

"Exactly!" Adam exclaimed, as if that somehow answered anything.

"Exactly, what? Have *you* been drinking? Why did you drag us here?" Atticus asked. "Some of us have day jobs."

"I thought you were at the morgue with your boyfriend," August said, arching a brow, the slightest smile on his smug face.

Atticus's heart seized in his chest as all eyes swung in his direction. "W-What? He's not my boyfriend. He's just a friend. I can help out a friend. You're not the only one who

has friends, you know." Asa's eyes went wide as he gave his twin a 'wow' look. Atticus waved a hand. "Why is it so hard to believe I have a…friend?"

"Okay, then. I thought you were at the morgue with your 'friend,'" August said, hooking his fingers at the word friend.

"No. Don't do that. No air quotes around friend." The others snickered. "Oh, you know what? Fuck you."

"Wow, this dude has you rattled," Asa mused. He looked at Lucas. "You've seen him. What's he look like?"

"Sexy. Definitely a bad boy type. Way out of his league." Atticus could feel his jaw drop as he stared at Lucas in betrayal. "He clearly doesn't know it, though," Lucas continued quickly. "Because, even in his grief, it was clear he was into Atticus."

Un-fucking-believable. "Are we here to talk about my love life or Dad's day-drinking?" Atticus snapped.

"Love life?" Asa and Avi parroted at the same time.

Atticus shot them the finger but then sat back and crossed his arms, not caring if he looked like he was pouting or huffy. "Can we get back to why you dragged us all here?"

Adam sighed heavily. "Aiden sent papers to Dad. He's petitioning the court to dissolve his adoption."

"What? Why?" Atticus asked, rocketing forward again.

They all looked around in confusion as if one of them might secretly have all the answers.

"Why now?" Archer asked, though he didn't sound particularly bothered by the news.

"Do you think it was our talk with him the last time he

visited? Do you think we drove him to this?" Adam asked.

"That was months ago," August recalled. "It can't be that."

"What is his fucking problem with Dad?" Asa asked. "Like that man has given him everything and he's been a total fucking brat. I mean, I know he was almost an adult when he showed up but he could at least show some respect. Dad gave him everything. A home, an education, a job."

"It makes absolutely no fucking sense," Avi said, shaking his head.

Atticus was nodding when he noticed Lucas and Noah shooting meaningful glances back and forth at each other. "You two. What's with all the eye contact? What do you know?"

Noah looked seconds from breaking, but Lucas gave him a barely discernible shake of his head. August frowned at his husband, who did his best to school his expression into one of perfect innocence.

Adam cut his eyes to Noah. "Do you know something?"

August and Adam squared off against their significant others. Noah broke first. "We don't *know* anything for sure, but it seems pretty fucking obvious what's happening here."

When they all stared at him blankly, Lucas said, "Really? None of you see it?"

"Well, why don't you enlighten us?" Archer said, voice droll, as he ran a finger around the rim of his glass.

"Thomas and Aiden...you know..." Noah trailed off, nodding like that would somehow make them connect whatever dots lingered. When none of them finished his vague statement, he scoffed. "Oh, my God. They're hot for

each other."

Atticus's hand went to his chest like some scandalized maiden clutching her pearls. "That's absurd. He's our brother."

Noah snorted. "Is he, though?"

Lucas leaned forward. "It's not the scandal you guys think it is. You said Aiden was almost an adult when Thomas took him in. I don't think they've done anything, but I think maybe Aiden wanted to."

Asa tilted his head. "Why do you say that? What do you know? You've never even met Aiden. Did our father say something to you? Wait, did you *see* something…like *see* see something?" He poked at his temple in case it wasn't clear what he meant.

Lucas shook his head. "No. Nothing like that. I just… I get a feeling…"

"You get a feeling that our brother wants to fuck our dad?" Atticus said, shaking his head as if rejecting the idea subconsciously.

Noah rolled his eyes. "Aiden isn't sixteen anymore. He's older than Adam. Aiden never saw your dad as a dad because they weren't that far apart in age. Not in the grand scheme of things. I mean, it makes sense."

"How does that make sense?" Adam asked, looking bewildered.

Noah scoffed. "News flash: your dad is massively hot. Like, a full on smokeshow. You have to know that. I imagine, when Aiden was sixteen, Thomas was probably everything he ever wanted."

"Dad would never cross that line," Avi snapped. "He's not a pedophile."

Noah shook his head, raising a hand. "Nobody's saying that. Teen boys have unreciprocated crushes on older guys all the time. Hell, I totally wanted to bang my math teacher. Older men are hot. Part of me thought I'd end up with some older sugar daddy who'd pay all my bills," Noah teased.

"You were half right," Archer muttered.

Lucas shrugged. "It makes total sense when you think about it. Aiden develops a crush on Thomas, confesses his interest, Thomas spurns his advances, Aiden leaves humiliated and never comes back. Thomas wallows in his guilt."

Atticus looked around at each of his brothers. He could tell their wheels were turning as they, like him, replayed every interaction he'd ever seen between the two of them, but he couldn't remember even one significant memory that stood out to him. He really was self-absorbed. "Why now? Why would he suddenly petition the courts to dissolve his adoption decades later?"

"I don't know, but he pulled the trigger on it and Dad is inconsolable," Adam said. "Do you think Dad loves Aiden like that, too?"

"I told you, Dad's not some pervert," Asa snapped.

Adam rolled his eyes. "I'm not saying he was into Aiden back then, but maybe he is now? Maybe that's why Aiden makes him, like…sad?"

Avi looked to Asa. "It kind of makes sense. When was the last time Dad even went on a date?"

"Then isn't it better for everybody if the adoption is

dissolved?"

"Not if Aiden's cutting ties with all of us. If Thomas really is into him, then maybe he thinks he's losing his only tie?" Noah offered.

August pinched the bridge of his nose. "Dad's going to be humiliated once the press gets a hold of this."

Asa and Avi looked at Lucas. "So…do we ask Dad?" Asa asked.

Avi nodded. "Yeah, like, do we try to get him to talk to us about his feelings for Aiden?"

Lucas frowned. "Why are you all looking at me?"

"Because you're the one who thinks our brother wants to bone our dad," Adam snapped.

"*And* you're a shrink," Archer reminded him.

Lucas reacted to the news as if he'd forgotten that bit of information. "Oh, yeah. Okay, so I think we can all agree that none of you are even remotely qualified to broach this topic with your father. You will literally ruin everything and leave him worse off than you found him."

"Wow. Tell us how you really feel," Archer said, amused.

"So, what do we do?" Adam asked.

Lucas shrugged. "Keep an eye on him. Make sure he doesn't get too sloppy and humiliate himself."

"Do not talk to Aiden," Noah said. "Not about this at least. Technically, this isn't our business."

Once more, Archer scoffed. "Technically…"

"Do you have something to contribute other than snide comments?" Noah asked, giving what Atticus called his 'mom stare,' like he thought he could shame a room full

of psychopaths.

Archer rolled his eyes. "Did you want me to contribute more? Do you truly wish to hear my opinion on the matter?" When nobody chimed in, he said, "Fine. I think Aiden never should have been brought into this family. He's not like the rest of us in a number of ways, but more than that, Thomas didn't want him for the experiment. He didn't take him in because he was like us. He took him in because he was nothing like us. Why do you think he went and adopted Adam after he'd said there would only be six of us. He meant six psychopaths, not six kids."

Noah winced. "Wow. Harsh."

"What do you mean, nothing like us?"

Archer sighed. "Aiden isn't a psychopath. Surely, you must have noticed that. Whatever problems he had, it didn't come from a lack of empathy or remorse. It came from trauma."

"That can't be true," Atticus said, knowing deep down it definitely was.

"I imagine giving five children everything you have, loving them, caring for them, meeting their every need, knowing they can never love you back, probably gets pretty lonely. Maybe he thought Aiden could be the one who loved him back. Which, if that was Dad's angle, he got it, just not how he'd pictured it." Archer dumped more whiskey in his glass. "Careful what you wish for, am I right?" he asked, gazing at everybody over the rim of his glass.

"This family's a fucking nightmare," Atticus muttered.

EIGHT
JERICHO

Jericho looked out over a sea of younger faces. Not as many as he'd hoped, but more than he'd imagined given the short notice. He'd asked them to meet him after work in the back of the shop, in the space he'd created to keep them safe and out of trouble back when he was barely old enough to do the same for himself.

By the time Jericho had finally shut the bay doors and turned off the sign for the night, the usual suspects had already gathered. Levi and Arsen sat perched on the back of the large ratty couch, while Felix and Nico sat on the cushions. Cree, Lake, and Seven had also managed to make it. They sat on the pool table, perched like gargoyles.

Jericho looked at each of them. "I need your help."

"Anything, man," Nico said as the others nodded along. "What's up?"

Jericho cleared his throat, swallowing down the wave of sadness that hit him. "I got a lead on Mercy's killer or, at least, somebody who might have answers about what

112

happened to her."

"Who is it?" Felix asked, raising slightly to tuck his feet beneath him.

Jericho shook his head. "I don't know. That's why I need your help."

"What's the lead?" Lake asked.

Lake was appropriately named. He was long and lean with wavy brown hair and eyes the color of a lake and he was…very still. There was no other way to describe him. He never raised his voice, never lost his temper. He was almost the antithesis of Felix, except they were both eerily soft-looking considering how deadly they were. They just attacked their tasks in very different manners.

"Someone said they saw her being…dragged off by a guy I'd never heard of. I don't have a name yet, but I have a description. Over six feet tall. Brown hair. Brown eyes. Sharp chin. Bad skin. Has a word tattooed on his chest. Has a rose and thorns tattooed on his neck. Some kind of jailhouse tattoo on his hand, but it's too muddy to make out. Ring any bells?"

"Man, that could be half the town," Seven said.

Jericho nodded. "I know. That's why I need you guys to ask around… Discreetly."

Seven's real name was Stanley, after his father—Stan Symanski—a notorious bookie, who ran a gang of thugs who helped him with his collections business. Seven was one of ten sons born to Symanski, all named Stanley— thanks to the man's over-inflated opinion of himself—all with different mothers. To keep track of them, he called

each of them by order of their birth, which was how Seven got his moniker.

Stan was a piece of shit, definitely not worthy of burdening his sons with his name or reputation. Luckily, Seven looked like his Egyptian mother with her rich copper skin, sea glass eyes, and dark brown hair he often hid under a backwards ball cap. While Seven's mother was accepting of his same sex preferences, his father was not, which was how Seven came to be one of Jericho's boys. There was safety in numbers.

"You want all of us to start asking around about the same dude but keep it quiet?" Arsen asked, his tone implying that was impossible.

"Who was this person who tipped you off?" Felix asked, tone suspicious.

Felix was already threatened by Atticus and he and Jericho barely knew each other. He didn't think telling them that Atticus had brought his family—a psychic, no less—into this would help smooth out any future encounters.

"A friend of a friend," Jericho finally said, vaguely.

"A friend of the friend you're sleeping with?" Felix persisted, eyes narrowed.

"I didn't say that," Jericho hedged.

"You didn't not say it," Nico pointed out.

Felix's shrewd gaze burned a hole through Jericho as he pressed on. "It was him, wasn't it? The rich ginger? He has friends in this neighborhood? Friends we, somehow, don't know?"

Levi raised a brow. "That sounds sus, man. Who is this

dude? Is he a cop? How does he know this guy? Does he know Gabe?"

Jericho's mood soured at his ex-boyfriend's name. They hadn't parted on good terms, and seeing him at the morgue hovering over his dead sister, his face screwed into a mask of fake sympathy—a mask he put on a hundred times a year in his job as an investigator—had been too much. Jericho hadn't wanted him to touch her and hadn't even wanted to speak to him.

It wasn't lost on him that he hadn't had the same response to Atticus. But Atticus hadn't tried to fake a sympathy he didn't feel, hadn't tried to make himself feel better by hurling platitudes he didn't mean about better places and God's plan. When Jericho had tried to hide and isolate himself from his grief, Atticus had followed, had persisted, offering physical comfort when he couldn't offer an emotional response.

He shook the memory away. "This has nothing to do with Gabe."

"So, there's another cop on the case?"

Jericho was starting to regret teaching them to question everything. "Sort of."

"Sort of?" Lake questioned.

Jericho sighed. "Look, just trust me. His info is legit. He's a retired Fed."

Lake questioned. "Fed? Like the FBI?"

Before Jericho could even answer, Felix was leaning forward. "A retired Fed who saw some guy with our sister but then didn't say anything until your rich boyfriend

started poking around? Why did he wait?"

"I never said Atticus was the friend," Jericho pointed out.

"You don't have any other friends besides us," Levi said.

Christ. They were relentless. "Fine. Yes. Atticus has a friend and that friend gave me the information. Information he didn't have until now."

"You're hiding something," Nico assessed. "Why not just tell us the truth? You know your brother isn't going to let this go."

Felix's chin jutted forward, his gaze hardening.

Jericho shook his head. "It's nothing. The information is legit. Can we just move past this and on to finding out who this guy was?"

They all shook their heads in unison.

"You wouldn't let us get away with being this dodgy," Seven pointed out.

He wasn't wrong. But Jericho was a big fan of do as I say not as I do. He didn't want to have to explain where he got this information, but it was clear they weren't letting this go.

"No. Not until you tell us the truth. You don't lie to us. We're your family," Arsen reminded him.

They were hitting him with the big guns. They were his family. He was theirs. They knew more about each other than their blood kin. They each had enough on the other to bury them, to send them away forever if they wanted. But they never would. They would never rat each other out. They'd die first. That was what made a family in Jericho's world.

Finally, he sighed. "My friend's brother-in-law is a retired

FBI agent. But he's also—" He hesitated, knowing what was about to happen. "He's also a psychic."

The sudden silence was deafening as he stared at several shocked faces. Then chaos erupted, each of them talking over the other.

Nico scoffed. "Bullshit."

"Are you crazy?" Levi asked.

Arsen frowned, seemingly confused. "Psychic, like they see the future?"

Finally, Felix said, "You can't be serious. You fell for some psychic's lies? You would be the first person to tell us this was all bullshit."

"You didn't pay him, did you?" Lake asked.

Jericho could feel himself getting angry. "It's not bullshit, and I didn't have to pay him anything. I didn't even ask him to be there. Atticus set it up. He wanted to help."

"Of course, he did," Felix sneered.

"Psychics aren't real," Seven pointed out, looking disappointed in Jericho.

"Yes, they are."

They all turned to Cree, who'd been silent up until that point. He leaned against the wall, ankles crossed, arms folded over his chest. He was...pretty. Long chestnut hair that flowed past his shoulders and huge eyes so dark they were almost black. He was one hundred percent indigenous—part of the Nehiyawak tribe. He'd been adopted at the age of five by 'good Christian' parents, who had treated him like a second class citizen since his arrival.

"My grandfather had the gift. It's real," he said, his tone

final as if he wouldn't hear another word to the contrary.

It worked. Cree never wasted his words. He only spoke when he could think of no other way to emote his feelings. He was smart and shy and was always watching. He always picked up on the minute details the others glanced over in their excitement. The others accepted Cree's declaration at face value, turning back to Jericho.

Seven tilted his head, his gaze piercing. "So, what do we do if we find this guy? Make a citizen's arrest?"

"Nothing," Jericho said adamantly. "You do nothing. You come directly to me. Nobody else."

"It's been eight years. How do you even know this guy's still on this side of the ground?" Felix asked.

"I don't. I don't know anything, but even if he's dead, he's bound to have had other friends. Somebody will remember Mercy."

"Meeting over?" Cree asked.

"Yeah, we're done."

Arsen and Levi slid down to sit between Felix and Nico, already reaching for the controllers. Arsen looked to those still standing. "You staying?"

The three exchanged glances, then shrugged.

"Sure," Cree said, taking a seat on the ground in front of the others. Felix handed him his controller and began to section off pieces of the boy's hair, working it into an intricate braid. Cree was very protective of his hair, but, somehow, Felix was the exception to the rule.

Seven snagged the controller from Nico, shoving himself between him and Arsen. "You staying, man?" he asked,

looking at Jericho expectantly.

"No, I have a date. I probably won't be home tonight. Make sure you lock up when you leave. I'll be back before the shop opens."

Felix shot him a sullen look, but Jericho ignored him, jogging upstairs to shower and scrub the grease and dirt off before he headed over to see Atticus. He tried to ignore the shock of awareness that shot through him at the thought. There was just something about him. Part of Jericho couldn't help but wonder if he had the same effect on Atticus.

As he scrubbed himself, his mind raced. Why did he care if he had the same effect on Atticus? Could he even have those feelings for anybody? Did Jericho want to…date Atticus? Dating seemed such a weak word for something that stemmed from death and exploded in passion every time they were within two feet of each other. Jericho wanted to own Atticus. To keep him. To protect him. He wanted to be his safe place to land. Wanted Atticus to be as vulnerable out of the bedroom as he was inside it.

Jericho saw Atticus's building four blocks before he arrived. There was no missing the towering complex or the palm trees jutting from the top, which indicated there was a rooftop pool. When Jericho pulled into the valet, a kid of about twenty jogged over in a white uniform with gold accents. He gaped at the vehicle as he took the keys.

"Did you restore this yourself?" he asked.

"Yeah, took a while to run down all the parts."

The kid whistled. "This is an '88 Eddie Bauer edition, right?"

"You know your cars, kid," Jericho said, impressed.

"Yeah, my dad was big into vintage American cars. All we ever get around here is a bunch of overpriced junk. This is a classic," he said reverently. "Are you a collector?"

Jericho laughed. "Me? No. I'm a mechanic. When I found it, it was a mess. I wasn't sure it would ever see the road."

The kid frowned. "What are you doing here? Like, isn't this place a little…bougie for you?"

"I'm visiting a friend. Atticus Mulvaney."

The kid winced. "Oh, yeah. He's…intense."

Jericho barked out a laugh loud enough to attract the attention of the other valet. "You're not wrong about that." He clapped the kid on the back. "Keep her safe for me."

"Yeah, definitely."

Jericho walked past the desk attendant, who was on the phone and didn't seem overly concerned about whether he belonged in the building, though she did give his jeans and t-shirt a once over as he hit the button for the elevator.

On the way up, he couldn't help but smile at the thought of Atticus terrorizing the staff with his prickly attitude. He was just dying for somebody to put him in his place. Jericho definitely felt like he was the man for the job.

Atticus lived on the top floor. The elevator spit him out into a small room with only a single set of double doors. Did he have the entire floor to himself? Jericho wouldn't

doubt it. He was old money rich.

He rang the doorbell and then stepped back slightly. Did Atticus think of this as a date? Were they doing dinner? Were they staying at his place? Technically, he was still in the closet, swearing that this was just a phase, that he wasn't gay. Jericho had been gay for a long time, and what they were doing felt pretty fucking gay, but he wasn't going to force Atticus out of the closet if he wasn't ready.

When five or so minutes went by and Atticus didn't answer, Jericho lifted his arm to ring the doorbell once again, startled when the door swung open. Atticus stood in a towel, his dark auburn hair standing up in wet spikes, like he'd just come from the shower. Yet, he couldn't help but notice his body was completely dry.

"You're early," Atticus grumbled.

Jericho raked his gaze over Atticus, from his pink face to his flushed torso, until his eyes snagged on his obvious erection tenting the cotton fabric around his waist. Jericho smirked. "Looks like I'm right on time, Freckles."

Before Atticus could formulate some kind of argument, Jericho pressed him back against the open door, capturing his mouth in a filthy kiss as he tugged the towel from his clenched fingers.

"Need some help with this?" he murmured as he wrapped his hand around the velvety skin of Atticus's hard length. Atticus didn't say anything, just canted his hips forward into his fist with a moan.

"Were you jerking off thinking about me?" he teased, sweeping his tongue between Atticus's lips. As always, he

was pliant, letting Jericho take control, take whatever he wanted without question. It was so fucking hot.

He ran his other hand over Atticus's bare hip, his fingers slipping into the furrow of his ass, his own cock throbbing when he found his hole was slick. He looked up into Atticus's now crimson face. "You're wet. Were you fingering yourself, Freckles? Were you getting yourself ready for me?"

Atticus was breathing hard but he still didn't say anything. Jericho knew he should close the door. Anybody could step off that elevator and find them right there in the doorway, but knowing that only made it hotter. He released his cock and spun him around, trapping him against the door. He yanked his shirt off and tossed it away, hastily pushing his underwear and jeans down to his thighs. He teased the head of his cock between Atticus's cheeks until it caught on his rim. "Are you already wet for me? Could I just push right in? No prep? Could I fuck you right here against the door? Is that what you want? Is that what you were thinking about when you were fingering yourself open for me?"

Atticus pressed himself back against Jericho's cock. He squeezed his eyes shut, biting down on Atticus's shoulder hard enough to leave an impression as the tight heat of his body closed around him. He made no move to go deeper. He wasn't done playing with him yet. Instead, he let his hands roam his torso, tug at his nipples, tease around his cock, mouth at his neck, his shoulder, anywhere he could reach.

When Atticus tried, once more, to push back on Jericho's cock, he made a tsking noise. "Uh-uh. You don't get what

you need until I get what I want. Understand?"

Atticus gave a whine of frustration, his voice raw when he said, "What do you want?"

Jericho chuckled, tugging at Atticus's earlobe before saying, "You know what I want, Freckles. I want to hear you ask for it. I want you to tell me how badly you want my dick in your greedy little hole."

"I hate you," Atticus muttered, but there was no malice behind it.

Jericho buried his smile against Atticus's shoulder as he slipped free, once more teasing the head of his cock against him, before dragging his teeth along his shoulder. "Come on, let me hear it. Say, 'fuck me, Jericho.'"

Atticus's back rose and fell against Jericho's chest for a good thirty seconds before he muttered, "Fuck me, Jericho."

Jericho didn't know why he enjoyed torturing him so much. "Say it like you mean it, Freckles." He wrapped a hand around his cock, giving it a few tugs. "I can feel how hard you are, how ready you are. It's going to feel so fucking good when I'm buried inside you... Just tell me what I want to hear, make me believe it, and I'll fuck you so hard your neighbors will call the cops."

Atticus pressed his cheek to the door, squeezing his eyes shut. "Fuck me, please. Please..."

"Please, what?" Jericho prompted, pressing in just enough to make them both groan.

"Please, Jericho."

Jericho was leaking at the raw desperation in his voice. He kissed his shoulder, then his cheek, whispering in his

ear, "See, that wasn't so hard, was it?" before burying himself in one hard motion.

Atticus's mouth fell open in a silent cry, and Jericho had to bite down hard on his shoulder just to keep from coming right there on the spot. There was just something about this man. Jericho was addicted.

"Fuck, you're so fucking tight," Jericho muttered, his speed increasing as he chased the sparks of pleasure that spiked through him with each hard thrust. "I've been thinking about being inside you for hours. Do you know how hard it is to concentrate on my job when I can't stop thinking about you?"

Atticus still remained silent, but he reached back, gripping Jericho's ass, as if trying to pull him closer, get him deeper.

"You want more?" Jericho teased through gritted teeth.

"You know I do," Atticus panted, arching his back.

Jericho gripped his hair, twisting his head back to give him a kiss, increasing his speed and intensity until the door was slamming hard against the wall and every fucking thrust was making them both moan into each other's mouths.

Jericho finally reached around to grip Atticus's cock, working him in time with his brutal thrusts, concentrating on the head until Atticus finally reached that point where he was no longer worried about being embarrassed and was just whining and gasping, "Oh, God. Oh, fuck."

Jericho would usually try to prolong their pleasure, but the truth was, he couldn't stop. The tight grip of Atticus around him felt too good, and the way he was moaning and

muttering beneath his breath was just too much. He didn't want to come before Atticus. "Come on. I wanna feel you come on my cock before I breed this tight little hole."

Atticus sucked in a sharp breath, a strangled sound escaping before his hole pulsed around him, his release spilling over Jericho's hand.

Jericho's eyes rolled, his hips falling off rhythm as he gave two more hard thrusts, then emptied himself inside. He kept his arms around him, didn't pull free of his body, just dropped his forehead to his shoulder, drawing in much-needed oxygen. As he softened, he slipped free, but they still continued to just linger for another few minutes before he finally stepped back and turned Atticus around, pressing a kiss to his flushed cheek.

"Damn, Freckles. You really know how to make a guy feel welcome." He fixed his pants but didn't bother retrieving his shirt. "What's for dinner?"

NINE
ATTICUS

When Atticus went into his room to find clothes, Jericho followed, looking this way and that, as if he was trying to take it all in. He had no idea what could be so interesting about the large, bright space. It was very…minimalist. The decorator had called it Scandinavian decor. While he appreciated the clean lines, the Scandinavians clearly overestimated Atticus's need for blankets. They were draped over couches and folded neatly in woven baskets. Hell, there was one draped over a ladder that led to nowhere.

He'd had no interest or input in the design of his own apartment. When he'd found the place, Kendra had instantly made herself at home, referring to the place as theirs. Atticus hadn't cared enough to correct her. He'd figured it was going that way, anyway.

Kendra had hired a decorator—with his money, of course—but had turned into such a nightmare that three designers had quit within the first six months. They'd split up before the fourth one could complete the job. Atticus

had considered just giving her the place and moving elsewhere but the family had freaked out. August had even threatened to put a bullet in her head if Atticus gave her a million dollar apartment as a consolation prize.

Atticus hadn't really liked Kendra, but he hadn't wanted her dead, so he kept the apartment and paid the decorator double to just do whatever she wanted and not bother him about it. On any given day, he barely even noticed where he was, anyway. He worked most nights until dark and then came home and went to bed, except on the nights when he was working for his father, and then it didn't really matter where he bedded down for the night as long as protocols were followed.

Atticus slipped on a pair of athletic shorts, stiffening when Jericho's arms came around him from behind. "What are you doing?"

Jericho chuckled. "Hugging you."

"Why?"

Jericho kissed his shoulder, lips lingering as his hands splayed over his belly. "Because I like touching you. You smell good, and you're warm."

Atticus did his best to relax. "Oh."

"You really don't get touched very often, huh?" Jericho mused.

"I was raised in a family of psychopaths. We aren't real big on cuddles."

"Not even your father?" Jericho questioned.

"My father did his best with us. He was always very aware of our bodily autonomy. If we didn't want to be hugged or

kissed, he kept his distance."

Jericho inched back. "Does it bother you?"

Atticus snatched Jericho's hands before they could slip from around him, pulling them back into place and holding them there in case he tried to leave again. He leaned back, liking the feel of their skin touching. "No. I just... I don't know how to process affection."

Once more, that infuriating chuckle. "You don't have to process it, Freckles. You just have to feel it."

Atticus shook his head. "I don't feel things. At least, not the things you *want* me to feel."

Jericho pressed a kiss behind his ear, then at his hairline. "I don't want you to feel any kind of way. I just want you to accept that you like my touch. You're a doctor. You have to know people require touch. That it's therapeutic."

"I'm not most people."

Atticus felt himself start to protest further when Jericho stepped away, but then he was taking his hand. "Come here."

Atticus let Jericho pull him towards the bed. He watched as he slipped off his shoes and then laid down, patting the spot beside him. Atticus followed him down hesitantly. When he went to lie on his back beside him, Jericho made a noise. "Uh-uh. Head on my chest. Just wrap yourself right around me, Freckles."

Atticus stiffly did as he asked and intended to stay just as he was. Jericho needed to know he wasn't capable of this sort of intimacy. Jericho's heartbeat thudded beneath his ear, his fingers absently playing at the nape of his neck before petting through his hair.

Jericho's chin brushed the top of Atticus's head as he said, "Tell me about your day. What was your family drama?"

Atticus had no intention of doing that. But when he opened his mouth to say as much, what came out was, "My brother's in love with my dad."

Jericho's fingers paused at his hairline for a count of ten before he started to stroke him again. "Wow. That's..."

"Yeah," Atticus confirmed.

His lids grew heavy as Jericho said, "But your brother's adopted like you, right?"

Atticus nodded. "Aiden wasn't like the rest of us. He was way older when Thomas took him in. He was supposed to be the last. There were going to be six of us. But then, suddenly, he brought Aiden home and he was already sixteen, almost seventeen. Adopting him never made any sense to the rest of us, especially when my dad went out and adopted Adam. Then there were seven of us."

"Does Aiden live around here? Is he the one who told you that?"

"Nobody told us. Not officially. Aiden sent my father papers to dissolve his adoption. It sent him into a tailspin. Lucas and Noah said it's because Aiden is in love with my dad."

Jericho's fingers dug deeper, blunt nails dragging over Atticus's scalp, leaving an almost sedative-like calm in their wake. "Do you think they're lying?"

Atticus felt his hand come to rest on Jericho's belly. "No. I think we just didn't see it. It makes sense in hindsight. He's constantly saying that Thomas isn't his dad, just ours."

"Do you think they've..." Jericho trailed off.

Atticus trailed his finger from Jericho's belly button to his waistband, liking the way the skin beneath jumped. "No. No way. My father has this strict moral code he lives by. He'd never cross that line. Aiden left for college and never came back. At least, not for long. Sometimes, he comes home for jobs, but he avoids Thomas. He always avoids Thomas."

Atticus dipped his fingers below Jericho's waistband just a bit, making Jericho's breath hitch as he said, "How do you feel about this information?"

Atticus paused, trying to process if he felt any particular way about it. "I feel stupid for not having realized this was happening. I feel stressed because I know this is going to make my life harder, especially when the paper gets a hold of the dissolution."

"Why would they care?"

"Because my father is a celebrity. He's created this carefully crafted lie that we're all one big, happy family. Every public event we attend is choreographed, an operation he plans right down to the minute."

"You don't feel bad for him?"

Atticus frowned, his fingers sweeping upwards. "No. I feel concerned that Thomas might fall off the deep end if he's hurt and compromise all of us."

"You don't care about your father at all?" Jericho prompted.

"I don't want him hurt. I am grateful to him for all he's given us. I would...mourn the loss of him. He's...my father. I don't know how that translates into feelings of love or affection."

Jericho's hand moved lower, his fingertips sweeping along Atticus's spine. "Why did you follow me into the bathroom this afternoon?"

Atticus blinked at the sudden shift in topic, finding it hard not to focus on his touch. "What?"

"Why did you follow me?"

Atticus frowned. "Because I knew you were upset."

"And?" Jericho prompted.

"And I wanted to make sure you were okay."

Jericho's lips brushed the top of his head. "Why?"

Atticus didn't know where Jericho was going with this. "Because I don't like when you're upset."

"Why?" Jericho asked, softer this time.

"Because I don't like the way I feel when you're upset."

Jericho made a sound that rumbled against Atticus's ear. "That sounds like an emotion to me."

Atticus sighed. "I have emotions, just not the kind you're looking for."

"I think you've just convinced yourself that's the case."

"You saw me back at the cabin. Did I seem particularly emotional while you were cutting Trevor into bite-size pieces?" Atticus asked.

"Did I?" Jericho countered.

"Maybe you're a psychopath, too."

"Nah, Freckles. I just learned not to waste my feelings on people who don't deserve them."

"And who makes that determination?" Atticus asked.

Jericho's chest rose and fell beneath his cheek. "In my neighborhood, I do."

Atticus shifted, resting more of his weight on Jericho. "So, you named yourself judge, jury, and executioner?"

"No, I was…nominated for the position."

"So, not a judge, but a King?" Atticus mused.

"I didn't want the job, but somebody had to do it. After my mom was attacked, I was so fucking pissed, and the cops didn't have enough evidence to do anything, so I took care of them myself. When word got out, I realized there were a lot of people being taken advantage of out there, people who couldn't do what I did."

Atticus ran a hand along Jericho's side. "Kill without remorse?"

"Yes."

"But you don't kill alone."

"No. My crew doesn't weep over dead bodies either. You don't have to be a psychopath to kill people. You just have to have the conviction that the world is a better place without them."

"So, you feel nothing when you kill?" Atticus asked, craning his head to look up at Jericho.

"No. Not nothing. When I tortured and killed the men who attacked my mother, I felt…exhilarated. I liked their pain, their suffering. It was what they deserved."

Atticus shivered, but not out of fear or revulsion. It was…excitement. "You don't lose sleep over all the blood on your hands?"

"Hell, Freckles. Most nights, I go to sleep with a big ol'

smile on my face. Does that bother you?"

Atticus scoffed. "No. Honestly, I'm a little jealous."

Jericho frowned, looking down to study his face. "Jealous? Why?"

"I wish I enjoyed killing the way my siblings do. I don't feel guilty or morally conflicted about it. I know it needs to be done. But I just...don't like it."

"Why not?"

Atticus stiffened. "If I tell you, you'll just make fun of me like my brothers."

Jericho flipped Atticus onto his back to hover over him. "I like to tease you because I think you're sexy as fuck when you're all riled up. I tease you because it makes you blush all the way to the tips of your ears. I tease you because it gets my dick hard when you get all prickly. I tease you, Freckles, because I cannot get enough of you."

Atticus heard himself swallow. "I'm not...prickly."

Jericho snickered. "Freckles, a cactus is tame in comparison. Tell me why you don't like killing."

Atticus blew out a frustrated breath. "Fine. It's dirty, unsanitary. There's blood and body fluids and toxic chemicals. I've ruined a dozen pairs of shoes. The way people scream and whine when they know they're about to die is...tedious. Most of the places are hot and cramped and, sometimes, I'm stuck waiting for my target for hours— hours that could be spent in the lab or working on grants for my research. Killing is hard."

Jericho laid on top of Atticus, resting his weight on his forearms. "I could kill for you. I don't mind."

Atticus frowned. "Like, you'd just go instead? Don't you have your own kill list to take care of?"

"I don't seek out targets, they come to me. Most days, I'm just a mechanic and babysitter. I wouldn't mind killing for you, Freckles."

Atticus could feel himself pouting, but he couldn't stop himself. "You act like I'm some damsel in distress."

"No. I act like you're the delicate flower you are. It's not a bad thing. You like mom cars and bow-ties and submitting in bed. I'm here for it. Honestly, I like the idea of being the one who handles your needs." He rolled his hips against his suggestively. "All your needs."

Atticus didn't know whether to be flattered, turned on, or offended. He was basically calling Atticus soft, saying he needed somebody to take care of him. He wanted so badly to protest but the truth was…Atticus did want somebody to take the reins. Did it make him a bad person that he didn't want to pay bills or change a tire or slit the throat of some Columbian drug lord? What was wrong with Atticus wanting to be taken care of as long as he provided something in return?

"And what about you? What about your needs?"

Jericho captured his mouth in a kiss that lingered. "I just need you."

"Surely, you need more than that."

"I'm a simple guy. I need good company. A hot meal. Hot sex. Somebody who lets me lead."

"I'm not great company."

"I don't know. I find you pretty fucking entertaining.

Who else would know off the top of his head that Asia has forty-eight countries?"

"I don't think my knowledge of geographical trivia is enough to keep you entertained."

"When we run out of things to talk about..." Jericho trailed off to kiss him softly. "I'll just strip you naked..." The second kiss lasted longer, was a little dirtier. "...and slide into this tight little body until you're screaming my name."

Atticus could feel himself growing hard again. He pulled Jericho down until his mouth lingered just over his. "You're obsessed with me screaming your name. I've never, ever screamed your name."

Jericho chuckled. "Oh, but you do beg for it. 'Fuck me, Jericho...please,'" he mimicked, but there was no malice behind it. If anything, he was turning himself on.

"So, no dinner?" Atticus teased.

"Oh, I plan on eating. I got something you can put in your mouth as well."

Atticus snorted with laughter. "Wow."

Jericho grinned and then laughed. "Too much? It was too much."

"A little, yeah."

"Fine. Let's figure out dinner. We can watch a movie or something."

"I don't own a television."

Jericho blinked at him for a full minute. "You're killing me, Freckles. Tell me you at least have a laptop."

Atticus nodded.

"Perfect. We can watch something on there."

"Like what?" Atticus asked.

Jericho kissed his nose. "Whatever you like."

Atticus shook his head. "I don't really like anything."

Jericho got a mischievous look in his eye that made Atticus inexplicably nervous when he said, "Then I'll introduce you to my favorite movie."

"Okay," Atticus agreed hesitantly. "Wait, what's your favorite movie?"

"I feel like, if I tell you that, you'll preemptively judge it."

Atticus gazed up into dark eyes. Objectively speaking, Jericho was beautiful in a rough and tumble kind of way. He was younger than Atticus, maybe by a good decade, but he had tiny crinkles in the corners of his eyes, and when he frowned, little lines formed on his forehead. It made Atticus itch to touch them. "I'm going to judge you, anyway. Might as well get it out of the way."

"Fine. *Labyrinth.*"

Atticus barked out a surprised laugh. "You're lying."

"I'm not. My mom used to watch it with my brother and me. David Bowie in tight pants was my sexual awakening. That bulge…"

Atticus felt himself smiling. "So, it's your favorite movie because you think David Bowie is hot?"

Jericho's smile faded, his gaze dropping to Atticus's lips. "No, Freckles. It's my favorite movie because when he said, *'fear me, love me, and I will be your slave,'* I realized that I had a very specific kink."

Atticus felt goosebumps rise along his arms. "David Bowie?"

"No, somebody willing to submit to me anytime I wanted. I realized I would do just about anything for somebody willing to be good just for me."

Atticus couldn't even bring himself to get offended. "Is that what you think you're getting from me?"

Jericho dipped his head, pressing his lips to Atticus's ear. "I know that's what I'm getting."

"So, I just give you all the power. Let you make my decisions for me?"

"You want so badly to be upset about it," Jericho said, running his tongue along the shell of his ear. "But I can feel how hard you are just thinking about it. You don't want to make decisions. You don't want to do the hard things. You want to play mad scientist in your lab while somebody else takes care of you. I'm offering to be that somebody."

Atticus felt a strange pang in his chest at the idea of leaving the hard stuff to Jericho. Did it make him a bad person? Shouldn't he be rising to the occasion, doing his best to grow as a person? What was he talking about? He was a psychopath who murdered people. Who cared if it was the right thing? Who cared if letting Jericho baby him made him a bad person? He'd never thought of himself as same sex oriented, but there was no denying he was Jericho-sexual. He just did it for him in every way.

"Don't get quiet on me now," Jericho rasped, still nibbling on his ear in a way he found pleasantly distracting.

"I'm thinking," Atticus managed.

Jericho laughed softly before biting down hard enough to make Atticus hiss. "Think all you want, Freckles. But we

both know you're already mine."

Atticus fought to find a way to make this feel like his decision and not just some foregone conclusion. "We could... I could try...on like a temporary basis. Just to see if I'm even capable of being with someone like you. It could be like a...business arrangement."

"What kind of business are we talking about here?" Jericho teased.

"It has to bother you that we barely know each other," Atticus said.

Jericho shook his head. "We live very dangerous lives. If we don't jump on the things we want when we want them, we might never get to." Jericho had a valid point. He could feel himself wavering. "I'm not letting you go, Freckles. I'm just not. You can call it a business arrangement, an affair, a kidnapping, some kind of midlife crisis. But whatever you call it, you're mine. And I protect what's mine."

Atticus flushed. "I can protect myself."

"Yeah, but we both know you don't want to."

Atticus hated that Jericho was right, hated that he saw through him so easily. "Let's just figure out who hurt your sister and then we'll...and then we'll see."

"Whatever you say."

Jericho hopped off the bed before grabbing Atticus, pulling him up, too. "Grab your laptop. I'm going to order dinner."

Atticus frowned. "You don't know what I want."

Jericho grinned. "What do you want?" Atticus's brain ground to a halt, indecision stopping him in his tracks.

"Yeah, that's what I thought. I'll pick. Anything you don't like?"

"No mushrooms," Atticus said, tone sullen, even to his own ears.

"On it. I'll meet you back in bed in ten."

Was this normal? Was any of this normal? He really wanted to talk to Noah or even Lucas. Atticus froze. He identified with Noah and Lucas. He identified with the two of them more than he did his own brothers.

What the fuck did that mean?

TEN

JERICHO

Atticus insisted on paying for dinner, rolling his eyes when Jericho protested. He'd assured him he had more money than he could ever spend in five lifetimes. It wasn't said with any sort of ego, just a statement of fact. He had a valid point. Jericho gave in. He wasn't poor, but he wasn't stupid enough to compare their financial situations.

After they ate, Atticus made popcorn—something he seemed genuinely surprised to find in his own kitchen—and Jericho convinced him to watch a movie in the bedroom. He propped himself up on a few of Atticus's overstuffed, but insanely soft, pillows, then patted the space between his open legs. Atticus hesitated for a minute before sitting where Jericho wanted him. He hooked his chin over Atticus's shoulders to watch the laptop propped on his thighs but found he liked the smell of Atticus's shampoo and the subtle scent of his cologne far more than watching the movie. Cologne he'd clearly put on for Jericho after his shower.

If Jericho had expected Atticus to take the movie seriously,

he was mistaken. He kept a running commentary as they watched, none of it particularly kind. Maybe it should have annoyed Jericho that Atticus wasn't enjoying the movie, except he was enjoying it in his own way. Mocking it clearly made him happy, and Atticus happy was such a singularly bizarre experience that Jericho watched him more than the screen.

"This is not even remotely possible, medically speaking. No wonder children are so stupid," Atticus said around a mouthful of popcorn, eyes wide as he watched a group of muppets volley their heads back and forth. "This is a kid's movie?"

"The eighties were wild. But you should know that, right?" Jericho teased. "You're the elder millennial."

Atticus frowned. "You act like I'm ready for the retirement home. I'm not that much older than you. What? Ten years, maybe? I get enough of that from my brothers."

Jericho laughed. "Well, you are the eldest, right? Comes with the territory."

"Yes, well, sort of," Atticus hedged.

Jericho prompted. "Sort of?"

"I'm the oldest and Adam is the youngest, barely, but the rest don't really refer to themselves by birth order. We go by order of adoption, not by age."

Jericho chewed on that for a minute before asking, "Why?"

Atticus sighed. "Thomas taught us to be human. He showed us we could exist in society. He pulled most of us from horrific situations and gave us everything we could ever

want. We only became a family when Thomas picked us, so that's what we focus on. Most of us don't even know our real ages, and half of us don't remember our original names."

That stopped Jericho short. His life hadn't been easy, but he'd had parents who loved him, even if they were a little strict. He'd never wanted for anything. Up until Mercy went missing, his life was pretty idyllic. To hear Atticus talk so casually about how he and his brothers had so little identity before they were adopted was crazy. It was sad. But not to Atticus, apparently, who was already fully focused on the movie once more.

"I think Sarah's being a bit of a drama queen. Like, Jareth is laying out a pretty solid offer. I mean, she's the one who sacrificed her own brother during a temper tantrum. How's he the bad guy?" Atticus asked, taking a piece of popcorn from the bowl and absently feeding it to Jericho over his shoulder.

Jericho's heart squeezed at the casually affectionate gesture before he rolled his eyes at himself. It was just a piece of popcorn. "You don't have to convince me. That masquerade ball alone would be enough to make me say yes. Do you know the kind of planning and commitment that takes? Granted, it was just a dream, but I imagine with him being king, he could make it happen if he wanted to."

Atticus shrugged. "Maybe, but it doesn't seem like those goblins have a very good work ethic. He'd have to find contractors outside the castle and it seems pretty rural. It's hard to find good help these days."

Jericho chuckled. "In their defense, they are theoretically

all babies he turned into goblins so I imagine that limits their capabilities."

Atticus made a thoughtful sound. "Child labor laws are very strict. Plus, they likely lack the basic understanding on the intricacies of planning a ball?"

Jericho snorted. "But not you? Plan a lot of balls, do you?"

Atticus bristled, tone pouty. "I'm just saying, that as somebody who's had to put together more than one fundraiser, I can't imagine a toddler pulling it off. Just obtaining a liquor license alone would pose an insurmountable problem and, believe me, you cannot host a party without liquor. It's impossible. The guests will revolt, including your own family. And, sometimes, people get thrown in the pool. I speak from experience."

Jericho snickered and Atticus cut his glance to the side, relaxing when he saw the other man wasn't making fun of him. Who knew psychopaths were so delicate?

Atticus examined his face for a long minute before smacking a kiss onto his lips and returning to the movie in front of him.

Jericho licked his lips, tasting salt and butter, feeling like he'd been sucker punched. Atticus hadn't initiated contact between the two of them since that night in the cabin and he certainly hadn't given any type of affection unprompted before. Yet, he seemed perfectly relaxed in Jericho's arms, cozy even.

Jericho kissed his temple, then his cheek.

Atticus didn't openly acknowledge the casual affection

but Jericho got to watch the flush run from his neck all the way to the tips of his ears before he took a handful of popcorn and stuffed it in his mouth, pointedly refusing to make eye contact again. When he brought his hands around to run across Atticus's stomach, he shivered. Atticus was definitely in shape, not an ounce of fat on him, but sitting as he was, he had a belly, and Jericho found he really liked it.

"I swear, if you try to have sex with me right now…" Atticus muttered, a trace of humor in his voice.

"You'll what?" Jericho prompted. "What are you going to do if I slip my hand into your shorts and wrap my hand around your cock and jerk you off?" He heard Atticus audibly swallow, his exhaled breath shaky. "I'll tell you what you'll do. You'll sit here and you'll let me. You'll let me do anything I want to you, and we both know it." Jericho pressed a kiss to Atticus's throat, feeling the rapid pulse beneath his lips. "Kiss me."

Atticus turned his head, pressing their lips together, but waited for Jericho to deepen the kiss, to slip his tongue inside to find his.

God, why was that so fucking hot? What did it say about Jericho that being with Atticus, taking care of him, controlling him—being the only one who could—made his dick harder than anything ever had before? There was something so…potent…about being the only person in the world who got to see somebody like Atticus at their most vulnerable. Jericho was grateful it was him and not somebody who might twist Atticus into something dark and ugly.

"You taste like salt," Atticus murmured against his lips.

"I like it." Jericho's hand was just sliding into Atticus's shorts when his phone rang. They both looked at each other. "Answer it," Atticus urged. "They wouldn't call this late if it wasn't important, right?"

Jericho picked up the phone, putting it on speaker. "Yeah?"

"I may have a hit," Seven said.

It took Jericho a long moment to process Seven's words. "You found him?"

There was a hesitation before he said, "Um, maybe. I found somebody who knows somebody who says that the guy you're looking for sounds like a dude who used to run with the 4Loco crew a while ago."

"What's 'a while ago'?"

Seven sucked his teeth. "Man, I don't know. A while ago. They say he was homies with a dude named Bryan Alvarez, street name Magic. Says your boy goes by Scar."

Jericho scoffed. "Scar? Like from the Lion King?"

Seven snickered. "Scar, like he has a burn scar on his left cheek from where he took a blow torch to somebody and it malfunctioned."

What kind of idiot melted his own face with a blow torch? The same kind who hung out with people who had street names.

"Do we know his name? Like, anything other than Scar? Do we know where he likes to hang?" Jericho asked, his hand still casually stroking Atticus's belly.

There was a sound like Seven shifting and the sounds of the crowded city streets filtering through the bedroom

before he said, "They say he took over running the crew when this Magic dude went away upstate for statutory rape and trafficking of a minor. But they paroled him for good behavior and now the guy has gone underground or something since Magic came back to reclaim his throne."

Gang policy was always so goddamn dramatic. A bunch of barely legal, low-level thugs, fighting for territory, fighting for clout, killing for street cred, so desperate to prove that they were the baddest, the toughest, abusing and butchering anybody who stood in their way. Kings of shit. A modern day tragedy.

Still, something caught Jericho's attention and held it, the popcorn in his stomach threatening to revolt. "Trafficking?"

Seven hesitated. "Yeah, man. He's 4Loco. They run girls out of that crack den on 5th and Compton. You know the one."

Jericho wracked his brain. Had he known that? "It's not our territory. I have a hard enough time dealing with the shit in our own backyard. Where do I find this Bryan Alvarez?" Jericho asked. "Did they give you a heads-up as to where he might be?"

"Nah, man. Sounds like this shit happened a while ago. I'll keep asking. I'll update the guys, see if they can find out any more."

Atticus stretched to grab his own phone off the table and scrolled until he found what he was looking for.

Jericho sighed, voice tense. "Yeah, okay. Keep me posted."

Jericho disconnected just as a chipper voice said, "Hey,

Sunshine."

Jericho's brows shot up. It had to be almost midnight. Who was that fucking awake at this time of night? Atticus ignored the sunny greeting. "I need you to track down a Bryan Alvarez for me. Not sure of the spelling, but he did time for statutory rape and human trafficking. Runs with the 4Loco crew. Goes by Magic."

This was the illustrious Calliope. It had to be. She was clearly used to dealing with Atticus and his lack of niceties. Jericho listened to rapid-fire typing.

"Got him. Bryan Alvarez. Thirty-six years old. Son of Darren and Dinita Alvarez. Did two years for possession with the intent to distribute, six months for domestic battery, six years for statutory rape and trafficking of a minor. What else do you want to know?"

Holy shit. Did this chick work for the FBI? It would take Jericho six months to run down the information it took her to do in less than five minutes. No wonder Atticus was so cocky about the woman. If Jericho had this kind of information at his fingertips, he'd be cocky, too.

"Well, for starters, is there a list of known associates attached to his record, and do any of them go by the street name Scar?"

There were another few taps on the keyboard. "He's in a gang, sweetie. He's got about a hundred known associates. I don't see anybody who's specifically listed as going by Scar. Though, there are more than ten that should."

"Fuck. We'll have to do this the hard way. Can you take the mugshots of his known associates—focus on ones with

facial scars—shoot it over to Lucas, and see if any of them are the man he saw in his vision?"

"Sure thing, sweet cheeks."

"Do you have the last known address of Bryan Alvarez?" Jericho asked, directing the question to Calliope.

There was a long pause. "Um, let me check," the woman said hesitantly. "Got it. I'll text you the address."

"Calliope, right?" Jericho asked.

"Yeah. Jericho, right?" she countered, humor evident.

His brows shot up and he watched Atticus once more flush to the tips of his ears.

"Yeah. That's me. Thanks for the info, Calliope."

"Anytime, Jericho," she said.

"Just send the info," Atticus snapped.

"Already sent. Bye, Sunshine. Text me if you need me."

Atticus disconnected without another word. Jericho fisted his hand in Atticus's hair, tilting his head so he could murmur against his ear, "You been talking about me, Freckles?"

Atticus scoffed. "Yeah, I told her all about the pain in the ass who kept showing up without an invite." Even as he said it, he turned himself to give Jericho better access to his ear.

Jericho chuckled softly, watching goosebumps erupt along Atticus's skin. "You came to me, Freckles. Remember?"

Atticus turned his head to let Jericho plunder his mouth before pulling away to say, "You came to my office first."

"You came to my house," Jericho teased. "You said you weren't leaving, no matter what I did. You begged me to fuck you, remember?"

"I remember," Atticus managed, seeking Jericho's lips

once more.

After that, there was no talking, just kissing and touching and the occasional breathy sigh or moan. It didn't go anywhere. Atticus had made it clear he wasn't in the mood for more than that, which was fine with Jericho, even if he was hard enough to pound a nail through a two by four.

By the time they slowed, the movie was over. Atticus put his laptop on the side table. Jericho rolled them so Atticus was the little spoon. He could feel him gearing up to tell Jericho that he had to leave. "Don't even try to tell me I can't sleep over, Freckles. You're sleeping in my arms tonight. Deal with it."

Atticus harrumphed like the spoiled brat he was. "Fine. I'm too tired to argue."

"Such a gracious host," Jericho murmured, letting his lips trail over whatever skin they could reach.

After a few minutes, Atticus asked, "What are you planning on doing with our friend Bryan?"

Jericho didn't stop his lazy exploration. He touched his tongue to Atticus's shoulder before scraping his teeth along the spot.

Atticus shifted slightly when Jericho's fingers began to trail along his chest and belly. Atticus was so into being touched. He loved it. He gravitated towards it without thought. It was so hot.

Finally, he said, "Fine, but I'm just going to keep you company. I told you, I don't like the killing part."

Jericho shook his head, dropping a kiss to the nape of his neck. "I just want your company, Freckles. I'll do the

wet work."

That seemed to settle him. "Just don't tell my brothers. I'll never hear the end of it."

"Already thinking of introducing me to the family?" Jericho teased.

Atticus shrugged. "I'm sure you'll meet them eventually. Too many of them know about you now. If I don't bring you to them, they're going to come find you. They're probably already watching you."

Jericho supposed that should have concerned him, but what were they going to learn? That he was in the same business they were? "So, you did tell them about me."

Atticus heaved a heavy sigh. "Not exactly. It just... happened. It's complicated."

Jericho curved his hand over Atticus's hip. "Does it bother you that your family thinks you're gay?"

Atticus shrugged. "My family doesn't care about sexuality. Most of them are gay. Seems statistically impossible, but I'm the only one who's ever seriously dated a woman."

Jericho's stomach soured, his lip curling in disgust. "Kendra."

"Did I tell you her name?" Atticus asked.

Jericho's grip tightened. "I do my homework, too, Freckles. I saw all the articles about the two of you. She looks like a real bitch, if I'm being honest."

Atticus gave another soft laugh. "She was a real bitch. I'm pretty sure she was a psychopath, too. My brother, August, was sure she was just a narcissist. Whatever she was, she had an agenda and woe betide the creature who got in her way."

"What did you see in her?" Jericho asked, hating the way his stomach clenched.

"Do you want me to be honest?" Atticus asked.

No. "Yeah."

"Nothing. She was just relentless in her pursuit of me and I was too busy working to keep fighting her. I'm sure she assumed that, as the eldest, I'd inherit my father's money because there were plenty of other, hotter Mulvaneys she could have tried for, but she went for me with the same single-mindedness she attacked everything."

"Why didn't you just get rid of her?"

"Like, kill her?" Atticus asked.

"No, like just tell her to fuck off?"

"She was pretty and knew which fork to use and she kept out of my way as long as she had access to my black card."

"She sounds lovely," Jericho grumbled.

Atticus went still. "Are you... Are you jealous of Kendra?"

Jericho could have lied, but they didn't have any lies between them. He didn't want to start now. "Yeah. Very. I don't like the idea of her sinking her claws into you."

Atticus rolled in his arms until they were face to face. "Yeah, well, she's long gone. We didn't part on friendly terms. I'm pretty sure the last thing she said to me was that I was shitty in bed. My designer didn't seem surprised by Kendra's assessment of my skills in the bedroom."

Jericho kissed Atticus's nose, his cheeks, his eyes. "Her loss, Freckles, 'cause I don't share."

Atticus flushed, seemingly trying and failing to keep his voice casual as he asked, "What about you?"

Jericho liked being all tangled up in Atticus, their calves brushing together, their chests touching, hips together. He let his hand slide around to cup the swell of Atticus's perfect ass. "What about me?"

Atticus was close enough for Jericho to feel his breath on his lips as he asked, "Have you been in a long term relationship? What about that cop? Gabriel?"

Jericho sighed. Fucking Gabe. "We knew each other from around the neighborhood. We hooked up a few times after he was given my sister's case, dated off and on. I thought he was my boyfriend."

Creases formed across Atticus's forehead. "But then you broke up?"

"Yeah."

"Did it upset you?"

Jericho shrugged. "I dated him for the same reason you dated Kendra. He was there. But neither of us were ever really invested enough to take it past casual. Good thing, too. Turned out he had a boyfriend the whole time we were together. Still does, I think."

Atticus studied his face, like he was trying to figure out if he was serious or not. "I don't share either," he finally said, his lips brushing against Jericho's. "Just so we're clear. You don't get to fuck anybody else either."

Jericho surged forward, fucking his tongue into Atticus's mouth until they were both breathing a little heavy. "Do you think I want anybody else? Nobody compares to you, Freckles. You are this weirdly perfect combination of impenetrable and vulnerable and I can't fucking get

enough of it."

Atticus swallowed hard. "You're the only one."

Jericho kissed him again. "Good. 'Cause I have no problems killing to protect what's mine. I'm sure you know that by now."

Atticus slipped his thigh between Jericho's, snuggling closer to tuck his head against his chest. "I know. I don't like killing, but I'd kill for you, too."

Jericho's stomach fluttered. "I know, Freckles. I know."

ELEVEN
ATTICUS

The first text came through at 8:15, moments after he'd sat down at his desk: Jericho asking if he'd made it to work okay. Atticus had assured him he had and donned his white coat, intent on spending the day in the lab even though his job lately was mostly fundraising.

At mid-morning, another text arrived: Jericho standing in front of a mirror, shirtless, his coveralls hanging from his waist and a look on his face that could melt solid steel. That man had been inside him last night. Twice. Well, once last night and once again this morning, but still. Fuck.

Jericho was hot, and not just to Atticus. Like, he was hot enough to sell the picture in his phone to a magazine, hot enough that, sometimes, Atticus couldn't believe this man not only tolerated him but seemed to venerate him, and acted like he was worth fighting over. Not even his brothers thought that.

Atticus didn't respond but saved the photo and made it his wallpaper. Who would ever know? He always kept his phone locked.

He was just about to quit for lunch when his phone vibrated where it sat on the counter beside the microscope. He didn't stop what he was doing but glanced over at the text bubble that popped up across his lock screen.

Do you know how hard it is to work when I keep picturing bending you over my work bench, fingering you open and fucking my load into you?

A rush of heat shot through Atticus, his face flushing and his pants growing uncomfortably tight. He almost fumbled the slide in his hand, earning a strange look from one of the techs working across from him. They hated when he was in the lab. They preferred him in his office. He knew how much they hated him.

He slipped a glove off to type back: **That doesn't sound very sanitary.**

Almost immediately, those three dots began to jump, indicating Jericho was typing a response. Why did that make Atticus's stomach flutter?

Fuck sanitary, Freckles. I want to get you dirty. Really, really dirty. I want to stuff you so full of my cum that you feel it dripping out of you all day while you're in your office trying to cure cancer and shit.

Atticus was almost positive he was bright red. He moved closer to the table to hide his obvious erection. **Don't you have cars to fix?**

I'm on lunch. Besides, I'm an excellent multitasker.

Atticus snorted, earning another startled glance from the tech, whose eyes quickly darted back to their work. **Yes, well,**

my job requires a steady hand and my complete attention.

Are you saying I'm distracting you, Freckles?

Atticus rolled his eyes but answered honestly. **Yes. You definitely are. I could be handling toxic chemicals, juggling bottles of acid. How would you feel if I died?**

Four crying emojis appeared followed by, **Fine. I'll keep my thoughts to myself but only if you promise to send me a dirty pic at lunchtime.**

Atticus flushed bright red, once more sneaking glances at his techs, grateful they were uninterested in him or his work.

How dirty? Atticus countered.

I guess that depends on how badly you want me to leave you alone? If you want me to let you work all day, you're going to have to send me something pretty scandalous.

Atticus sighed. **You know I hate guessing. Tell me what you want me to do.**

Those three dots bounced, and then another text appeared. **Okay, Freckles. I want you to lock that office door, take a seat at that big old desk of yours, open your pants, and show me how hard I get you.**

Fine. Ten minutes.

He had intended to take a quick pic and be done with it, but once he'd sat at his desk, his imagination sort of ran away with him. He opened his pants, taking his semi-hard cock in hand, Jericho's words etched in his mind. He was thinking about bending him over, pushing his fingers inside him, fucking him... Atticus tried not to imagine the edge of the counter digging into his hips, the burn of Jericho's

fingers invading his body, the sparks of pleasure that would fire along his skin as Jericho's cock slammed home.

Before he could change his mind, he clicked the button for video and began to record himself. He closed his eyes, keeping his camera trained on his hand as he let himself imagine how that scenario played out. It didn't take him long to finish, spilling onto his hand, grateful his pants were out of the way. Not that he planned on returning to the lab after this. He had paperwork to attend to.

He cleaned up, staring at the file on his phone for ten more minutes before Jericho sent a gif of Judge Judy tapping her watch. He sighed, loaded the video and hit send. After that, there was only silence. Atticus tried not to let his imagination go crazy. There was really no such thing as too far with Jericho, not emotionally, not sexually, and certainly not morally. Still, he stared at his phone with a singular intensity until another text appeared.

This time, it was just two emojis. The drool emoji and the water droplets emoji. He frowned. What the fuck did the water droplets mean? He fired off a text to Noah, who sent back a dozen laugh cry emojis before informing him it simply meant wet in a sexual context. Atticus had flushed even though he was all alone in his office. He refused to ask for further context from either Noah or Jericho. Luckily, he didn't have to.

Fifteen minutes later, he received a video in return. Jericho was in his bathroom, coveralls clinging to his thighs, his cock in hand. "Fuck, that was hot, Freckles. I had to come upstairs and take care of this. See what you

fucking do to me?"

If Atticus could have gotten hard again, he would have. Watching Jericho fist his own cock while he kept a running commentary of all the things he wanted to do to Atticus made him contemplate taking a cold shower in his office bathroom.

"Fuck. When I get you all to myself tonight, I'm going to spread you open, slide my tongue into your tight hole while I jerk you off. Then I'm going to fuck you nice and slow until you're begging to come, begging for me to fill you up." When Jericho came, he was breathing hard, his voice gravel as he said, "Oh, God. Fuck. Fuck."

Atticus jumped when Jericho turned the camera towards his face so he could see his blown pupils and sly grin. "See you tonight, Freckles. Have a good day at work."

Oh, you too, Atticus thought snarkily.

Strangely enough, he did have a good day at work. He managed to get his paperwork done, finished the journal article he'd written for JAMA, and even managed to return a few emails before his phone buzzed. He blinked, rubbing his hands over his face before he realized the sun was already setting outside his window. He grabbed his phone from the desk, realizing quickly it wasn't his regular phone but his burner phone.

He heaved a sigh. He had no interest in dealing with family shit tonight or any night, really. Ever since their realization that Aiden might have less than familial feelings for Thomas, he'd dreaded going home. Apparently, Thomas had gone from drinking his feelings to isolating, leaving

Noah and Lucas to pick up any slack.

Despite all of that, he snatched the phone up, frowning when he realized it wasn't his brothers but Jericho. He'd given him the number that morning for coordinating their...date with Brian/Bryan. But he hadn't expected him to use it quite so quickly.

There were two texts. An address and another that just said: **Meet me at the cabin. I've secured our friend.**

Jericho clearly wasted no time. He was always so decisive. He saw what he wanted and he took it. Including Atticus. He was trying really hard to be mad about it, but he couldn't muster up the energy to convince himself that he didn't want Jericho's undivided attention.

Atticus grabbed his keys and his wallet, grateful there was always a bag ready to go in his trunk, but grimacing about being back in that thick swampy muck. Fuck it, he was going to stop at one of the stash houses and grab a truck that wouldn't be traced. He wasn't bringing his baby back into the swamp. Even after three washings, the interior still smelled faintly of brackish water and rotting vegetation.

He tapped out his reply as soon as his engine turned over.
On my way.

Atticus made it to the cabin in good time. It was a lot easier to navigate the barely-there trail in a 4x4, especially when you didn't have to worry about branches scratching the paint or getting stuck in the mud. He parked the truck next

to Jericho's vintage Bronco. He loved a fixer upper. Atticus stopped short. Was that how Jericho saw him? A fixer-upper? A project? He supposed the idea should bother him more than it did. Jericho wasn't the first one to look at him and think that way. Even Thomas thought of him that way.

There was a single light on in the window but it lit the place enough for Atticus to see Jericho moving about the space. He texted Jericho to let him know he was there, even though he was certain he heard his engine. It didn't pay to spook murderers. He opened the door and Jericho's gaze raked over him, a small smile hitching his lips upwards. "Hey, Freckles. You made good time."

"I brought the truck."

Atticus noted the faint blood trail that led from the chair to the door. A chair that once had held Trevor. Something big had helped itself to Trevor's corpse, dragging it back to its den. It had been kind enough to leave the chair for the brown-haired man who was screaming behind his gag. Atticus could only assume that was Bryan.

He wasn't screaming in terror. No, Bryan was fucking pissed, enraged even. His sweaty face was bright red, and a vein in his forehead throbbed in time with his pulse as he gave them a piece of his mind, none of which he understood. He wore baggy jeans and a flannel shirt over a wifebeater, like some gangbanger straight out of central casting.

"Has he been doing that since you got here?" Atticus asked, dropping his duffle bag on the same table he'd sat on the last time he'd watched Jericho torture a man to death.

"Only since he woke up," Jericho said, unbothered.

Atticus's stomach chose that moment to announce that he hadn't had time to eat before he got there. Jericho snickered. "I brought some of those granola bars you like. They're in my pack."

"You did?"

"Yeah, Freckles. I know eating isn't a big priority for you. Can't have you wasting away." He slapped Atticus's ass as if to make a point and, once more, Bryan began to freak out behind his gag.

Atticus found the granola bars and hopped onto the table before lying back with his head on his bag, unwrapping his treat. Jericho lined his instruments of torture along the bench seat just below him so he didn't have to strain to hand anything over. Jericho really did think of everything.

"You ready?" Jericho asked.

"Sure," Atticus said around a mouthful of granola.

Jericho ripped the bandana out of the guy's mouth. "Do you fucking bitches know who I am? Do you know what you just did? My boys are gonna fucking gut you, they'll shove a blow torch so far up your ass you'll—"

Jericho stuffed the gag back in his mouth with a sigh before dragging a chair in front of Bryan, spinning it around so he could straddle the back. "Bryan, you need to take a minute and think about this. Note that we're not wearing masks. That means we're not worried about getting caught." Jericho pulled a knife from the holster strapped to his thigh. "Do you know why we're not concerned about getting caught?" he asked, opening the man's skin from the corner of his eye to the corner of his mouth while he

screamed. "It's because you're not walking out of here."

Atticus took another bite of his granola bar as the seven stages of grief overcame young Bryan. His eyes widened as he shook his head. Atticus sighed. Denial. Behind the gag, Bryan began to shout again. Anger. Soon bargaining would come. Atticus hated bargaining.

"This is going to go one of two ways. Easy or hard." Jericho shook his head as Bryan tried to somehow yank himself free of his restraints, still talking the whole time. "Shh," Jericho chided. "You don't want to miss my offer."

The man glowered at him but fell quiet.

"My offer is this. You answer my questions and you die quickly. You don't and you die slowly...screaming."

The man's gaze shot to the front door, then back to Jericho. This time when Jericho pulled the gag down, the man remained silent.

"You going to cooperate?"

"Man, fuck you, fa—"

Jericho slipped the blade between the man's lips. "I highly recommend you don't finish that sentence."

When he pulled the blade out, blood followed. The wound was superficial but tongues always bled like a bitch.

"Fucking do what you want, man. I ain't tellin' you shit. You think I'm afraid of you fucking—" He cut himself off. "You think you can do something worse to me than what the crew will do to my family if I talk?"

"This isn't about your gang, Bryan. This is about your friend. The one who goes by the name, Scar."

Atticus had thought that mentioning Scar would have

put the man at ease but, instead, his shoulders went back and his eyes darted around like this was some kind of test. "I don't know anybody by that name."

"Problem is, Bryan...you do know who he is. We know you do. That's not in question. We want to know who he is. Is he one of your gang friends? Is that why you're so scared?"

The man scoffed, the blood spraying from his lips narrowly avoiding Jericho's face. "Fuck you, man."

"You're wasting your time trying to be nice," Atticus said, reaching down to pick up the cordless drill. "Use this to pop one of his kneecaps off and he'll either die or tell you what you need to know."

Jericho rose from where he sat, taking the drill from Atticus, pushing the button down and watching it roar to life. "I've never used one of these on a knee before."

"Feel for the softest part on the sides of the kneecap. Then you want to go in at a fifteen to forty-five degree angle, ensuring it will tear through the meniscus, the popliteal tendon, and the cruciate ligament. In addition to hobbling him, it's going to make him wish you'd just hacked his leg off above the knee."

Jericho leaned over and gave him a chaste kiss. "Thanks, Freckles." He turned back to Bryan. "What do you say? If you're not going to talk anyway, let's play a little game of operation. Think I can avoid hitting any bones or major arteries?"

"If you go too slowly, he might go into cardiac arrest from the pain," Atticus warned, bored.

"Huh," Jericho mused. "Hear that, Bryan? Think you'll

be lucky to just have a heart attack and die before I lose interest in torturing you to death?"

Jericho got within a quarter inch of Bryan's kneecap before he screamed, "Wait. Wait. Wait!" Jericho took his hand off the trigger, gazing up at Bryan expectantly. The man looked miserable. "What the fuck do you want from me, man? If I tell you anything, they will murder my family."

"They?"

Bryan jutted his jaw forward, furious and terrified. "What the fuck, man."

Atticus sat up, swinging his legs over the side of the table. "I can keep your family safe, but I'm going to need more than just your friend's name and location for that."

"Man, Scar is the least of your problems. It's who he works for you should be worried about."

Atticus flicked his gaze to Jericho and then back to Bryan. "Well, let's start with Scar's real name."

When Bryan hesitated, Jericho pressed the trigger on the drill again, moving it back into position.

Once more, Bryan began to scream, "Wait. Wait. Wait."

"Last chance, Bryan," Atticus warned. "Name. Now."

"Carlos."

"Carlos what?" Jericho prompted, voice cold.

He hesitated only a second, eyes fixated on the drill. "Perez. Carlos Perez."

"See? Was that so hard?" Jericho asked.

"Where can we find this Carlos guy?" Atticus asked.

Bryan snorted. "You don't. He finds you, and you best hope he don't. You two have no fucking idea who or what

you're messing with."

"Well, then why don't you enlighten us, Bryan?" Atticus asked.

Jericho once again took a seat straddling the back of the chair. "You're dead either way, kid. Might as well go out not screaming in pain."

"Look, Scar...Carlos...used to hang with us. He took over running my crew when I got popped for pimping some whores out of The Orchid. But by the time I got out, he was running with some much scarier fucking dudes."

"Like a rival gang?" Atticus asked.

"Nah, man. No rival gang. You think my boys don't know how to handle our fucking people? This wasn't a fucking turf war. These people are fucking...sinister, man. They got money. They got connections. And they been operating in our territory for a decade and nobody even knows they're there. They're fucking ghosts."

Jericho exchanged a look with Atticus as they both processed Bryan's information. "What do you mean?" Atticus asked. "Ghosts, how?"

Bryan shook his head, staring over Jericho's shoulder out the window. "They pretend they're going to help, ya know? They're the ones you don't expect. The white knights, the ones who carry crosses and say they can fix everything."

"You sound like you're talking about a klan rally. Just tell us where we can find Carlos."

"Man, that's what I'm telling you. You don't. His boss will never let you get close enough to question him. He's just their enforcer. Their recruiter. Carlos will cut his own

tongue out before he ever talks."

Jericho looked back at Atticus, appearing equally confused. He pulled his wallet free and shoved a picture in front of Bryan. "Do you know this girl?"

Bryan shrugged, confused by the abrupt change in subject. "Maybe?"

"Maybe?" Jericho echoed, fury edging into his voice.

"Man, all these bitches look the same. Maybe. Why?"

"Because she was last seen with Carlos, eight years ago."

Bryan shook his head. "Then I hope she wasn't nobody important 'cause you ain't never gonna see her again."

"She was my fucking sister, dick."

"Man, look. I don't know what you want me to tell you. Carlos works for bad fucking people. People with money. People with power. People who don't give a fuck about people like your sister."

"There has to be somebody at the top of the food chain," Atticus said.

"I'm sure there is, bro, but you're never going to find a name. I don't fuckin' know it and the people who are unfortunate enough to know it aren't in any shape to talk anymore."

"Somebody will always talk," Jericho insisted. "Given the right motivation."

He looked down at the drill, but Bryan was shaking his head. "Man, use the drill, fucking pull my teeth out. I'm not saying shit about shit. The person you're looking for is a goddamn myth, some fucking childhood monster who sneaks in the window and steals your fucking children.

He's fucking Keyser Soze, man. He'll ruin your whole goddamn life and make sure every single person you love dies screaming, even the family dog. Even if you know him…you don't fucking know him. Your sister's dead. Just fucking kill me already."

Jericho looked at Atticus, who shook his head. They weren't going to get anything more out of Bryan. He picked up the gun and screwed the silencer on the Ruger from the bench, handing it to Jericho to put Bryan out of his misery.

They got what they came for. A name. A generic name, but it was at least a place to start. Jericho put a bullet between the man's eyes before he knocked the chair backwards and began violently stomping on Bryan.

Atticus let him go until he stumbled back, then gripped Jericho from behind, pulling him away from the corpse.

He didn't let go even when Jericho tried to wrench free. "I'm fine. I'm fine," he snapped.

Atticus held firm. "You're not fine. Who would be? Just breathe."

"What the fuck is going on? What did they do to my sister? Where was she for the last eight fucking years?"

Atticus pressed his lips to the back of Jericho's head. "I don't know. But we're going to find out, and when we do, we'll take them out, whoever they are, however many there are, all at once or one at a time. Either way, I promise you, they'll be the ones who die screaming." Jericho didn't answer but collapsed back against him. "Let's just go home."

At first, Atticus wasn't sure Jericho heard him, but eventually, he just nodded. "Yeah, okay, Freckles. Let's go home."

TWELVE
JERICHO

Jericho couldn't stop thinking about Bryan's words. Was he just full of shit? He couldn't be. Dying people didn't lie, especially not to a guy with a drill in his hand. But that didn't mean that Bryan hadn't fallen victim to whatever story these people circulated to keep them off the cops' radar. Keeping people too afraid to talk was just good business.

Jericho knew, deep down, that the most obvious explanation was that Carlos had trafficked Mercy, that he'd turned her into a junkie so she was more susceptible to his seduction, easier to manipulate, easier to lure away from her family. It wasn't a unique story in their neighborhood. It wasn't a unique story anywhere.

People had this idea that human trafficking was something that took place in third world countries. They thought of women and children packed into shipping containers, like something out of a crime show. They imagined the bad guys being far removed from their perfectly curated lives.

But the truth was, most often, the girls being trafficked

didn't even know it. They thought their pimps were their boyfriends, they thought they loved them because that was what they were told. *If you loved me, you'd sleep with this guy. It's just one time. We need the money. Don't be selfish.*

Jericho had seen it hundreds of times. Parents coming to him, distraught, because their daughters had been groomed by some much older gangbanger to believe they were Bonnie and Clyde. His stomach churned at the thought of his baby sister falling prey to some slick talking predator. But it was the most likely scenario.

Pimps could sell one girl or child thirty times a day for years without ever having to worry about restocking inventory. What enterprising criminal would turn that down? Even the simplest of gangbangers understood supply and demand. And that was all any girl ever was to them. Product.

He slammed his hand down on the steering wheel, hoping the impact would drag his thoughts away from falling down a rabbit hole of what could have happened to lead to his sister winding up in the river, missing a kidney.

His phone vibrated on the seat beside him, snagging his attention. Atticus.

He glanced in the rearview mirror to the truck tailing him. Atticus was only a vague outline on the darkened two-lane highway. "Yeah?"

There was a slight pause before Atticus hesitantly asked, "You good?"

Jericho sighed. No, of course, he wasn't. But that wasn't Atticus's fault. "I just keep running over what Bryan said.

None of this shit makes any sense."

"It sounds like a story to me. Some kind of urban legend. It's a good idea. Make up some big, bad boogeyman to keep people from looking too deep into shit, to keep them from talking to the cops. Mafia, maybe?"

The mob certainly had the pull to intimidate the neighborhood. The Italians didn't run out of his neighborhood, but that didn't mean they didn't poach girls from there. Jericho had no idea where Mercy had ended up before being dumped. The Irish and the Russians had a pretty good grip on the gambling and the guns around town but left running girls and dope to the street gangs.

The mob just didn't make sense. "Bryan said nobody suspected them. He said they pretended they were there to help. Nobody mistakes the mob for the good guys."

Atticus grunted. "He also said they were ghosts. I don't even know what that means. Ghosts. Helpers. Crosses. It's like a jigsaw puzzle with no picture on the box."

That was what was so frustrating. Jericho needed a bad guy. He needed somebody he could punish for whatever happened to his sister. But first, he needed to find out what the fuck happened to her.

Fuck, this was frustrating.

"We need to find Carlos Perez," Jericho said through gritted teeth.

"I already have Calliope on it, but it sounds like it's going to take a lot more work than it did with Bryan."

"I don't know what else to do. This Carlos guy is our only lead," Jericho said, white knuckling the steering wheel.

"I think I should talk to my father—" Atticus stopped abruptly to clear his throat. "I think *we* should talk to my father."

"You want me to meet your dad?" Jericho asked. Usually, he'd tease Atticus about this but he couldn't muster up anything close to humor.

"I don't *want* to bring you home to meet anybody."

His words were a kick to the balls. Still, he gave a humorless laugh. "Wow. Don't worry about my feelings or anything. Afraid I won't know which fork to use?"

Atticus snorted. "What? No. I am not worried about your behavior. I'm worried about theirs. They don't know how to behave around strangers. They're like...wolves."

"So, it's not about your family finding out you're less straight than you've implied?" Jericho asked, not sure why it suddenly mattered so much.

Atticus gave a frustrated sigh. "No. Look, I'm not gay, but I'm...gay for you? I don't need to clarify it or justify it to my asshole brothers. Besides, this isn't about them. It's about helping you find out what happened to your sister. That's more important."

Atticus's flustered declaration made Jericho feel warm all over. "And you think your family can do that?"

"I'm not an investigator. And, as far as I know, neither are you. I just kill people and I'm not even very good at that. My dad, Noah, Lucas, Calliope, they're like our... investigative team. That's what they do. They vet our kills, get evidence even the police can't access. There's no system Calliope can't crack, no connection my father can't exploit,

no object Lucas can't read, and no place Noah won't ferret his way into…whether we want him to or not. If I ask them to help you, they will."

Jericho's heart clenched behind his ribs. He knew better than anyone how much it would pain Atticus to ask his family for help, to bring Jericho into the lion's den. But he was willing to do it for him if it meant helping him find out what happened to Mercy. There was something telling about that. Something Jericho wasn't sure he should look too closely at. Atticus seemed to think of himself as a hopeless screw-up, but as far as Jericho could tell, he was pretty fucking close to perfect. Even if his family didn't see it.

What would Felix think of Atticus? What would the others think? Did Jericho care? Maybe a little. They were his family. The people who always stepped up when he needed help, and he always needed their help.

He couldn't do what he did on his own. There were too many people who needed help. Too many people that criminals and the government took advantage of because they weren't in the country legally, because they knew there was no way for them to fight back, and if they did, nobody would care when it went badly.

It didn't matter, though. If Felix and the others couldn't accept Atticus, they were just going to have to get over it. He didn't need their approval and he certainly wasn't giving up Atticus. Not anytime soon, anyway.

"When?" Jericho asked. "When do you want to go to your dad?"

"We'll go tomorrow. I just need to make sure my dad's…"

"Available?" Jericho supplied.

"Sober," Atticus muttered.

"Is this about the adoption thing?" Jericho asked. "Did it hit the paper or something?"

"Not yet. But it will eventually."

Jericho kept his eyes on the road as he contemplated the situation. What man drank himself into a drunken stupor over a potential scandal? Jericho didn't know Thomas Mulvaney, but he imagined any man who willingly raised a gaggle of psychopathic children wasn't prone to histrionics. It just didn't gel.

"Are you sure this isn't more about feelings?"

Atticus scoffed. "Of course, it's about feelings. My father loves Aiden. He loves us all."

Jericho's lips twitched at Atticus's indignation. "Yeah, I get that, but does he love you guys the same way he loves Aiden? Sounds like he's grieving the loss of more than a family member he barely sees. He sounds…heartbroken."

"Well, he needs to get the fuck over it because they can't just…be together. Right? Like, that would be a huge fucking scandal. My father hates unplanned scandals."

"More than he loves your brother?"

That seemed to bring Atticus up short, leaving Jericho to listen to him breathe heavily on the other end of the line for a solid minute before he finally muttered, "Fuck if I know. I never thought we'd be a family whose family tree doesn't fork."

Jericho snorted, a smile crawling across his lips. "You're being a little dramatic, Freckles. None of you are blood

related. It's definitely not ideal, but I don't think you can help who you fall for. It's not like your brother's a child, right?"

"My brother and I are almost the same age. He was the sixth adopted but the second oldest."

"So, everybody's a consenting adult. He didn't raise your brother. You said they've barely seen each other over the years. If it's been over a decade and there's still something there that is making your brother want to run and your dad want to drink...I don't think outside opinions should matter."

"Okay, yeah, but most families aren't hiding a literal graveyard worth of bodies behind their facade of one big, normal family."

Jericho chuckled. "Normal? You're all living out the musical Annie, a bunch of overachieving orphans raised by a billionaire. That's only normal for you."

Atticus made a noise of frustration. "Stop making so much sense."

A smile spread across Jericho's face, but it quickly died as the reason for their road trip punched him in the gut once more. "What do you think my odds are of ever knowing what happened to my sister, Freckles?"

Silence stretched between them for a long moment before he said, "On your own? Thirty-five percent, at most. With my family and maybe yours...I'd say your odds double."

Jericho's stomach churned. "That's still only seventy percent."

"But it's not thirty-five."

He couldn't argue with that. He honestly didn't want to.

He'd take his seventy percent and be grateful. He knew, in real life, there were thousands of people desperate for answers about loved ones, answers they'd waited on for years. Answers that would never come. It wasn't hard to believe he might end up being one of those people.

Atticus's voice disrupted his downward spiral. "Are you coming back to my place?"

Jericho's gaze flicked to the rearview mirror reflexively. "Do you want me to?"

Once more, there was a pause, and Jericho knew it wasn't because Atticus wasn't sure but because it pained him to say it. Finally, he said, "Yeah, but I need to make a stop. I have to drop off the truck at the garage and grab the Volvo."

"Get in front of me, and I'll follow you there."

"You don't have to. You can just wait for me back at my place. I can give you the codes to the door."

Jericho rolled his eyes. Atticus was the world's most self-sacrificing psychopath. "I'm going with you, Freckles. Not up for negotiation."

"Okay, fine," Atticus grumbled, but beneath his words was just the slightest tinge of relief.

If Jericho was being honest, he was relieved, too. He didn't want to be alone right now. He didn't want to be away from Atticus right now. Or ever, really.

Jericho jerked awake, his heart racing, gaze darting around the shadows as he tried to remember where he was. His

shoulders sagged when he saw Atticus starfished naked on his belly, snoring softly, back rising and falling rhythmically.

He'd been dreaming. He didn't remember the specifics, but it had definitely been about Mercy. She haunted his thoughts. He pressed the heels of his palms against his eyes, trying to rub away the remnants of uneasiness still remaining.

They hadn't made it home until well after midnight, showering and then collapsing in bed without eating. In their exhaustion, they'd left the bathroom light on and its faint white glow cut directly across Atticus's waist, highlighting the deep dip just before the generous swell of his backside. Jericho couldn't drag his gaze away. He laid back down, rolling onto his side before allowing himself to reach out and trace the steep curve of his ass, continuing his caress upwards along the knobs of his spine, then back down again.

Jericho smirked as Atticus made a happy noise in his sleep. He loved being touched, craved it even. He'd never fucking admit it, but he couldn't hide the way his body responded when Jericho so much as brushed up against him, always wanting more, even if he refused to admit it.

In sleep, he couldn't deny it. His brain wasn't reminding him of all the reasons he shouldn't want Jericho's touch; it only reacted. Once more, Jericho traced the lines of Atticus's body, letting his fingers traverse the dark furrow between his cheeks, fingertips teasing against his hole before dipping lower to graze his balls. Atticus sighed, parting his legs.

Jericho carefully scooted closer, letting his lips graze one freckled shoulder as his fingers played over his entrance once

more, testing his theory. Atticus made another appreciative noise, arching his back slightly.

Fuck. That was so hot.

Jericho's cock throbbed. He rolled, grabbing the lube that still sat on the nightstand, coating his fingers. He let his mouth explore whatever skin he came in contact with as he reached down to massage his hole. When Atticus didn't protest, Jericho pushed a finger inside, squeezing his eyes shut as his body accepted his finger in that tight heat, sucking him deeper without resistance.

He kissed his way along Atticus's throat, his ear, his cheek, pumping his finger in and out. Atticus was totally at his mercy. Totally his. He slid free of his body before pushing in with two fingers, moaning when Atticus offered no resistance. He found his prostate, rubbing over it until Atticus made a helpless sound that went all the way to Jericho's aching dick.

He couldn't stop himself, didn't want to. He pulled his fingers free, kneeling between Atticus's splayed legs. Jericho lubed his cock, blanketing himself over Atticus to run the slick crown between his cheeks until it caught on his rim.

He didn't push in, no matter how much he wanted to. Instead, he nuzzled behind Atticus's ear. "You awake, Freckles?"

"I am now," Atticus grumbled sleepily.

"Me too," Jericho said, letting Atticus feel his length pressing against his hole. "Can I?"

"Yeah."

Jericho slid inside in one smooth motion, biting down

on Atticus's shoulder to stifle a groan as the tight heat of his body enveloped him. He slid his arms beneath Atticus, holding him tight as he lazily fucked into him. He just wanted to feel Atticus beneath him, to be inside him, connected to him. He needed to feel something other than the panic he'd felt upon waking.

Atticus's breaths increased as Jericho rolled his hips against him, pressed his lips against his ear to murmur. "You're so fucking hot inside, so tight. I can feel you milking my cock."

Atticus shivered, goosebumps erupting along his shoulders. Jericho's lips followed in their wake.

"I've been thinking about this—about you—all day. Thinking about stripping you down, spreading you open, burying my tongue inside your tight fucking hole, watching you flush and stammer and grumble the whole time until you gave me what I wanted, until you were so desperate and needy you'd beg for my cock, beg for me to fuck you, use you, claim you…breed you."

Atticus turned his head so that Jericho's lips were pressed against his ear. It was so obvious that he loved Jericho's praise, his approval, his words. That he needed to please him. It spurred him closer to orgasm. Still, he couldn't stop talking, pressing the words into Atticus's skin. "When you're sleeping, you don't hide how bad you want it. Your body knows you belong to me. When I slid my fingers inside you, you arched your back, moaning like a whore for me. I swear I almost came on the spot."

Atticus shivered beneath him. Jericho released him to

run his hands along his arms, tangling their fingers together as he picked up speed.

"You like being a whore for me, don't you?" he rasped.

"Yes," Atticus said, his voice a barely-there whisper.

Jericho couldn't help the almost feral sound that fell from his lips. "Just for me. My perfect fucking whore."

"Yes," Atticus hissed.

"Say it. Say it's just for me."

Atticus's skin grew hot. "It's just for you. Just you."

Warmth pooled in Jericho's belly. He used his knees to force Atticus's thighs farther apart, rising just enough to snap his hips into Atticus in long, sure strokes that made them both moan. Atticus's fingers tightened around his, his back arching. Jericho picked up his pace, driving into him harder, chasing his pleasure. He couldn't stop staring down between them where their bodies were joined.

Atticus had never let anybody else inside his body before, had never been vulnerable like this for anybody else. Just Jericho. Only he got to claim him. Only he got to breed him, mark him.

"Fuck. Fuck. Fuck…" His orgasm hit him hard, driving his brain offline for a full minute. He didn't pull out right away, just laid there breathing heavily, mouthing at the spot beneath Atticus's hairline, their fingers still entwined, his cock growing soft inside him. He needed to take care of Atticus, but his brain was mush.

"You good?" Atticus asked with enough concern to make Jericho's chest tight.

Jericho dropped a kiss to the back of his head, finally

managing to say, "Yeah, I'm great."

"You're lying," Atticus countered.

Jericho sighed. "I just had a...bad dream."

"About Mercy," Atticus asked, hesitant.

"Yeah."

"Do you feel better now?" Atticus asked.

"Yeah, I do."

Atticus dragged their intertwined hands towards him and kissed the back of his hand in an unprompted display of affection that made Jericho's stomach swoop like he was on a rollercoaster. "Good."

Jericho slipped free of his body, sitting back on his knees. "Roll over for me, Freckles."

Atticus did as he was told, not seeming in any particular hurry. Jericho immediately honed in on his flushed and leaking erection jutting from the nest of red curls. Jericho made an appreciative sound from between his thighs. "Bend your knees for me, plant your heels. That's good. Open up for me. A little more. Mm, perfect."

With Atticus nice on display for him, he laid on his belly and swallowed his cock down, head bobbing until he found a rhythm that had Atticus's toes curling and his hands fisting in Jericho's hair as he fucked up into his mouth.

Jericho snaked his fingers between his cheeks, pushing two fingers into his cum-soaked hole, groaning at the wetness. Atticus gave a hoarse shout when Jericho massaged over his prostate with intention. "Oh, fuck. That's..."

Jericho pulled off, watching as Atticus squirmed, riding his fingers. "I love fingering this hole, love feeling my cum

inside you. You like it, too. I can tell you're close. I wanna feel you cum from the inside. I wanna feel your greedy hole tighten around my fingers."

He closed his mouth back over Atticus's cock, sucking him with an intensity that had him trying to work himself into his mouth and back on his fingers at the same time. "Oh, fuck. I'm so close."

That's the point.

Jericho didn't say that, just kept stroking him from the inside, opening his throat so Atticus could go as deep as he wanted. It only took another minute or two and then he went rigid beneath him, the bitter taste of him flooding his tongue. He swallowed it all, sucking until Atticus pushed him away.

Jericho rolled off the bed and into the bathroom, washing his hands and grabbing a washcloth, running it under the water before returning to the bed and helping Atticus clean up.

When they were both relatively clean, Jericho chucked the washcloth onto the side table before gathering Atticus into his arms, the dopamine numbing him to any feelings about his sister.

"You have the dirtiest mouth I've ever heard," Atticus said conversationally.

"Just with you, Freckles. Just with you. I know you like it."

Atticus snorted. "And if I didn't?"

Jericho shrugged. "I guess we'll never know."

Atticus shook his head. "Can you sleep now? We're meeting my family tomorrow. You'll want to be as...awake

as possible for that."

"Does the thought of me meeting your family make you nervous?"

"My family makes me nervous," Atticus intoned dryly.

He said it like a joke but Jericho could tell it wasn't. "Why's that?"

After a minute, Atticus said, "I don't think they like me very much."

Anger flashed through Jericho's system, but he tamped it down quickly. "Does that bother you?"

Atticus shrugged. "It irritates me that they don't take my concerns seriously, that they think I just sit around looking for reasons things won't work instead of seeing it as me being cautious about getting caught. But I don't sit around crying about it or anything."

Jericho dropped a kiss on the top of Atticus's head, feeling the way his fingers spasmed where they lay across his stomach. Atticus always reacted so intensely to any random sign of affection. It made Jericho sad. Was Atticus really a psychopath, or had nobody taken the time to try to love him?

"Good night, Freckles."

Atticus dropped a kiss to the skin just beneath where his head lay. Jericho was relieved when he made no move to head back to his own side of the bed. He needed the weight of Atticus to keep his brain in the off position.

Atticus tightened his grip on his torso as if he could read his mind. "Night."

THIRTEEN
ATTICUS

Jericho whistled low as they parked in front of Atticus's father's sprawling mansion. "This is your dad's house…like where he lives…every day? Like, where he wanders around in his underwear and watches television?"

Atticus couldn't help but snort at Jericho's assessment of what 'home' meant to him. It made sense, though. Jericho was fond of nudity. And television. When they were at Atticus's place, Jericho never bothered with clothes unless food was coming and, even then, only long enough to slap the money into the delivery driver's hand. It worried Atticus how much he liked that about Jericho.

Atticus stared through the Volvo's window at the resort-sized home where he'd grown up. He felt velcroed to the spot. Bringing Jericho in there changed everything, whether he admitted it or not. Once he met the family, it was real. They would know that Atticus had been lying to himself and to them forever. They would know there was somebody who seemingly cared for him—about him. He

was weirdly protective of it. He didn't want his brothers to ruin it for him…and they would. Because he'd spent years ruining things for them, whether he meant to or not.

"We don't have to do this," Jericho reminded him. "We can just go back to my place and I can use my guys. Arsen is no Calliope, but he's pretty good at finding the information we need."

"Of course, you have a guy named Arson on your crew."

Jericho snickered. "Arsen, as in Arseny. Not Arson, as in the intentional setting of fires."

A reluctant laugh left Atticus, but the sound died quickly. "No. Let's just do this. They were bound to meet you anyway eventually."

Jericho followed Atticus from the vehicle, catching his hand in his. "You could make it sound less like a root canal, Freckles."

"Once you've met my family, you'll understand."

Jericho laughed. "Understand what?"

Atticus threw open one of the double doors that made up the front entrance before looking at Jericho. "That root canals are less painful."

Jericho blinked in surprise. Atticus tried to hurry through the place to their war room—or, as Noah referred to it, the Batcave—but it was like trying to drag a child through a toy store, with Jericho digging in his heels to look at everything as they passed. "How does nobody get lost in this place?"

Atticus glanced around, distracted. "We used to get lost in this place a lot. The house belonged to Thomas's family. They've owned it for generations and it's a really weird

place. It even has hidden passages."

"No shit?" Jericho asked, sounding a little awed. "Like the movie *Clue*?"

Atticus frowned. "What?"

Jericho snorted. "*Clue*? The movie? Tim Curry?" At Atticus's deepening frown, Jericho rolled his eyes. "I swear you were created in a lab, Freckles."

Atticus rolled his eyes in return. "Lab created for what purpose? It's not killing people. I suck at that."

Jericho dragged him into a small alcove and pushed him up against the wall, gripping his chin, forcing him to meet Jericho's unwavering gaze. "Lab created for me, Freckles." He licked over the seam of his lips. "Just me."

Atticus sucked in a shaky breath, his mouth opening to Jericho's prodding as easily as his legs parted when he pressed a knee between them, his thigh applying pressure that had Atticus fighting not to grind against it.

"Oh. My. God."

Atticus stiffened at the familiar voice of his soon to be brother-in-law.

As feared, Adam piped up next, dramatically intoning, "I need bleach. In my eyeballs. Immediately."

Atticus sighed, turning to glower at Noah and Adam. Noah gaped at them without shame. Whereas Adam looked horrified, like he'd just watched a man get mauled by a bear.

Jericho released him, turning to face the two. "I'm Jericho."

"Wow, you're pretty," Noah said, breathless enough

to earn a growl from Adam. "What? I didn't say he was prettier than you, you big baby. But I have eyes."

"If you'd like to keep those eyes, I'd focus them back where they belong," Adam said, gaze locked on Jericho.

Noah snorted, hopping on Adam's back and biting his neck hard. "You're so full of shit. Quit posturing. You look like an idiot."

Adam huffed, catching Noah's legs around his waist and hauling him towards the Batcave.

"I'm Noah, by the way," Noah tossed over his shoulder. "This mannerless dick is Adam."

Jericho smirked. "Nice to meet you."

Adam dropped Noah to his feet just outside the door. He looked at Jericho, all traces of humor gone. "You know what you're getting into, right?" he asked. "With the Mulvaneys, I mean? You're literally about to enter the snake pit."

Jericho's smile turned rueful, giving Atticus a look that made him wish his pants were looser. "That's alright. Turns out I'm a snake charmer."

"Christ," Adam muttered, typing in the code for the room, then quickly pushing the door open.

Atticus couldn't help but take inventory. The twins were there, side by side, both sitting forward when Jericho entered. August and Lucas were there. Lucas smiled and gave a friendly wave to Jericho, who returned it, earning a scowl from August. Archer sat in his usual seat, booted feet kicked up on the conference table, a glass in his hand.

There was only one person missing. "Where's Dad?"

Everybody shrugged, looking around at each other, as if one of them might have the answer. When none were forthcoming, Atticus sighed. "This is Jericho. He needs our help."

Asa cocked a brow, making a show of checking him out. "I can think of a number of things I'd like to help him out with."

Avi snickered, eyes squinting like he was trying to do a calculus problem. He pointed a finger back and forth between Atticus and Jericho. "Wait. Are you two—" He poked his finger through a hole he'd made with his other fist, his look salacious. Atticus could feel himself turning crimson.

Jericho's hand encircled his wrist, his thumb stroking the delicate inner skin there in a way that was strangely soothing. "Does it matter?" Jericho asked Avi, the edge in his words and his expression telling his brother to tread carefully.

"Oh, this one's protective," Avi said. "Look at him. He's pissed. Atticus finally got himself a guard dog."

"Hope he's better on assignment than Atticus is. We don't have the manpower needed to clean up after two idiots," Adam said, staring a hole through Jericho.

"You got something you wanna say, pretty boy?" Jericho asked, inclining his head in a way Atticus found both sexy and alarming.

"I just did," Adam replied, affect flat. "We can't afford anybody around here who doesn't know how to take care of themselves, and your new boyfriend tends to screw things up...a lot."

Atticus shook his head. If Adam brought up that fucking

meat clever incident one more time, Atticus was going to use it dissect Adam's head from his body. But before he could say a word, Jericho was talking.

"I can handle myself just fine. And the way I hear it, maybe you should worry about yourself. Didn't you meet your man by fucking up a job and letting him get the jump on you? That was you, right? Seems to me you've done some fucking up of your own, so I'd be real careful who you go calling a fucking idiot, 'cause from where I'm standing, you certainly don't look like no fucking MENSA candidate."

"I am."

Asa and Avi both started laughing as Jericho's gaze cut to August. "What?"

August gave an almost reptilian smile. "I'm a member of MENSA. Have been since I was four. But you're right. Adam is an idiot. And he's going to apologize or sit there and keep his mouth shut." He threw a sharp look at their brother, who took to pouting as usual. The big baby. August gestured to the two empty seats. "Please, sit down. Ignore them."

Atticus had never been so…relieved that Lucas had somehow sanded down August's rough edges. Marriage had been good for him, good for both of them. They were settled, had a routine, a life together. Hell, they were even talking about having kids.

The idea had always seemed claustrophobic to Atticus. Not marriage in general but the intimacy between them. Kendra had seemed safe because Atticus had known he'd never truly have to worry about her wanting to share

space…emotionally. Something he'd never be capable of.

But Lucas and August, they were so in tune with each other, they were sometimes one consciousness. Literally. That had always seemed like such an invasive and stifling thing until Jericho. He fit into Atticus's life so easily. Jericho made Atticus look forward to things. A text. Dinner. A movie. Sex. Until Jericho, Atticus had mostly just been an observer. Permanently benched. But now, after just a few days, they were so immersed in each other's lives. What would that look like in a month? A year? How intertwined could their lives get before they no longer knew where one ended and the other began?

The door opened and shut with an almost imperceptible click. Atticus's eyes went wide at the sight of his father. In all the years Atticus had been a Mulvaney, he'd never seen Thomas look anything but his best. Even when his father had gotten pneumonia ten years ago, he'd still looked polished, put together.

The man dragging himself into the room was not the man he knew. He wore sweatpants and a t-shirt. Atticus hadn't even known the man owned sweatpants. He wouldn't have been surprised to find out Thomas went to the gym in business casual.

They all stared as he walked directly to the bar and poured himself a drink before plunking down at the end of the table and taking a big sip. He gave each one of them a hard look—the same look August had given Adam only moments before. Nobody said anything, just stared. Even Archer seemed taken aback. But that could have just been

 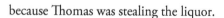

because Thomas was stealing the liquor.

Thomas slapped at the button on the speakerphone in the center of the room, barking, "You there, Calliope?"

There was the distinct sound of somebody tsking. "Yes, but I won't be for long if you're going to snap at me like that. I'm not one of the kids, bucko."

Heads all swiveled from the speaker to Thomas, waiting for him to explode. Instead, he sighed. "My apologies, Callie. I have a migraine."

Calliope snorted, tone unforgiving. "I would, too, if I'd spent the last two days marinating in booze like you're Archer."

Archer tipped his glass towards the speaker as if Calliope could see him. "They don't call it getting pickled for nothing." He looked to his father. "The key is to never get sober. You have to make your organs afraid. Make them work with the booze, not against it."

"Can we save the lecture for when my head isn't pounding?" Thomas asked, tone pleading.

Calliope was the only person who ever seemed to get through to Thomas, the only one who could get away with questioning him.

Atticus pinched the bridge of his nose with the hand Jericho wasn't holding hostage. "Can we get to why we came?"

Avi snickered. "What's our latest Scooby Gang mystery?"

"May I, Jericho?" Calliope asked.

Jericho looked at Atticus in surprise. He'd spent the first half of their long drive home explaining what he could to

Calliope in the hopes that she would be able to help piece together whatever was going on. They'd been too tired to talk when they got home, and later, when they'd woken up, they'd gotten…distracted.

Jericho cleared his throat. "Uh, yeah. Go ahead."

His hand went from stroking Atticus's wrist to clenching it as a picture of his sister appeared. She was pretty in a hard sort of way. She had the look of somebody who had wrapped herself in barbed wire and then dared somebody to scale it. She'd been hurt before somehow. Had Atticus known what she looked like aside from the horrors of the morgue? He didn't think so.

"This is Jericho's sister, Mercy. She disappeared a little over eight years ago and was not seen again until a few days ago when her body washed ashore septic and missing a kidney."

"Missing a kidney?" Avi asked, no longer amused. "Like a ritual? Like Jack the Ripper?"

"No. Like she'd donated a kidney," Atticus provided. "Though I suppose if a serial killer had anatomical knowledge, he could have excised a kidney, but the pathologist seemed pretty sure this was a donation gone wrong."

"It wasn't any legally sanctioned kidney donation," Calliope said. "I cross referenced your sister's profile with UNOS—the United Network for Organ Sharing. They keep a database of every donor, every transplant, every recipient. Your sister didn't donate a kidney, not legally anyway."

"Black market?" Archer asked. "A kidney on the black market goes for a hundred and sixty thousand, easy."

"It would explain my vision. The guy watching over your sister was in scrubs, but he did not look like your typical hospital employee. Hygiene was not a big priority with this guy," Lucas said.

"You think my sister figured out a way to sell her kidney for six figures and they dumped her when she got sick?" Jericho asked, still squeezing Atticus's wrist hard enough to leave marks.

Archer shrugged. "It's a possibility."

"It still doesn't explain where she's been for the last eight years," Atticus said.

"I'm not trying to be insensitive," Lucas said, "but she was a drug addict. How do you know she didn't just stay away of her own volition? She wouldn't be the first addict to just disappear."

"Didn't you say you saw a man dragging her down the street?" Atticus asked.

"Yeah, but that doesn't mean she was being kidnapped," Lucas said, voice dripping with sincerity. "You know as well as I do that addicts don't make great choices when it comes to their partners."

"Right, the guy!" Calliope said, excitedly. A man's face appeared on the screen. He had greasy brown hair slicked back in a ponytail, a burn scar on his face, and a meanness in his eyes that Atticus knew well. He'd taken out dozens of men and women just like him, people who were so dead inside, so morally bankrupt, that they no longer had the capacity to see people as humans, just product.

"You found him," Lucas said. "That's the guy from my

vision."

"Technically, Jericho and Atticus found him. Or, at least, his name. Carlos Perez, aka Scar. This guy's a bit of a mystery. Up until around eight years ago, Carlos was just another low level street thug. His biggest claim to fame was being the number two to this slightly bigger shitbag." A picture of Bryan popped up on the screen.

Noah popped a piece of gum in his mouth, chewing thoughtfully. "Can't we find shitbag one and two and torture them until they talk?"

"Shitbag one is in the wind. We talked to shitbag two last night. The only person he'll be talking to going forward is God," Jericho said.

"Did you learn anything useful?" Asa prompted.

"I guess that depends on your definition of useful," Atticus muttered. "Shitbag two got really sketchy when we brought up Carlos. In some kind of weird reversal of fortune, it seems Carlos now outranks Bryan. He's an enforcer for some kind of…something."

"Some kind of something?" Archer managed. "That's helpful."

Jericho sighed, clearly frustrated. "Bryan said when he got out of prison, Carlos had hooked up with some 'scary dudes' and they were nothing like your average street gang. He said they had money. They had connections."

"Like the mob or the cartels?" August asked.

Jericho shook his head. "Nah, man. Carlos said these dudes were ghosts. Said they'd been operating in our territory for over a decade and nobody knows they're there.

He used the word sinister."

"Can't we just find this Carlos guy? Did Bryan give you a hint where to look for him?" Adam asked.

"He said we won't find him unless he wants us to and that we don't want him to come looking for us. He called Carlos their enforcer," Jericho said, gaze glued to the picture on the screen.

"He called him something else," Atticus recalled suddenly. "Their recruiter."

"High-level escort service?" Archer asked. "It would explain where she's been. They keep their girls on the move. Big money. Big clients. Lotta drugs. Lotta Stockholm Syndrome."

Jericho's mouth was a hard line as he seemed to contemplate Archer's theory. "Maybe. But he was talking about crosses. He said they were helpers. That nobody suspected them. I mean, I guess they could be Epsteining. Rich dudes trading girls, but it still doesn't explain how Mercy went from escort to dead in a river."

Calliope's voice broke in. "She's not the only one."

That brought the whole room up short. Atticus sat forward. "What?"

"When my search for Carlos turned up nothing and my search of UNOS turned up more nothing, I decided to search the archives for any bodies that washed up in the river minus their body parts," Calliope explained.

"And you found more people missing organs?" Jericho asked.

There was the sound like a chair creaking, and then

Calliope said, "No. Well, yes and no."

"Which is it, Calliope?" Atticus snapped.

Atticus sighed as the silence stretched. After a minute, Calliope said, "Since it seems none of you can remember your manners today, I'll address Jericho. And only Jericho."

"What did you find, Calliope?" Jericho questioned gently.

Calliope gave a delicate sniff. "I found a fifteen-year-old John Doe they'd fished out of the water missing a lobe of his liver, but they couldn't give a definitive cause of death because there was something...peculiar about the kid's blood. They'd posited that perhaps he'd gotten a hold of an unknown synthetic drug."

"Was that the only other one?"

"No. There was a nineteen-year-old runaway from Texas who they also diagnosed as a drug overdose, but again, they couldn't identify the strange drug in her blood."

Jericho frowned. "I get the liver kid correlating to my sister's death, but how does the overdose case? She had all her parts, no?"

"Because she also had that same unknown compound in her blood. The expanded toxicology report came back this morning."

"This makes no fucking sense," Asa said.

Archer shrugged. "Maybe it's something coming in from over the border. New synthetics are popping up all the time. If all three victims were drug addicts, maybe that's how they convinced two of them to donate a body part. Maybe number three OD'd before she had the chance?"

 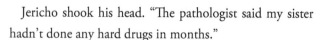

Jericho shook his head. "The pathologist said my sister hadn't done any hard drugs in months."

"The standard toxicology report only looks for amphetamines, barbiturates, opioids, marijuana, and alcohol. The only reason we know more is because Thomas asked the pathologist to run a full toxicology panel...as a friend," Calliope said.

Jericho's gaze shot to where Thomas was sitting, his elbow on the table, head propped up on his fist. He didn't acknowledge any of them but Atticus knew he heard every word. Thomas saw everything, heard everything, knew... everything. And nothing.

"Thanks for doing that," Jericho finally said to the top of Thomas's head.

"Anything for a friend of my son," Thomas said, exhaustion evident in his voice.

"Where do we go from here?" Atticus asked.

"We go old school," Adam said. "We head out to the neighborhood and we question people about what they know. If shitbag number two knew enough to call them ghosts, then there are bound to be others. We just convince them to talk."

Jericho scoffed. "Yeah, right. No offense, Abercrombie, but nobody's gonna say shit to you. No matter how much you try to look like one of us, they'll smell the money on you."

"You think we've never had to question someone before?" Adam countered.

"Ever questioned somebody without a weapon in your

hand, pretty boy? Because the people in my neighborhood aren't going to talk to somebody whose backup watch is worth sixty k." He gave Atticus a contrite look. "No offense, Freckles."

Atticus literally felt the blood drain from his face as the endearment left Jericho's lips. He closed his eyes, mentally preparing himself for the onslaught that was about to ensue.

"What—What did he just call you?" Asa asked.

"Nothing," Atticus muttered.

"Oh, no. That was definitely something," Avi said. "Freckles, was it? Well, now that's just fucking adorable."

"It's a little obvious, if you ask me," Asa said. "There were so many to choose from. Red. Ginger. Fire crotch."

Atticus could feel Jericho tensing beside him, could feel his anger. He twisted his wrist free under the table, then threaded their fingers together, squeezing his hand, silently asking him not to engage.

"Careful, I think you're pissing off his guard dog," Adam said, his tone menacing.

"I don't think he likes you picking on our big brother," Archer noted, seeming in no hurry to join them in taunting Atticus.

"Well, if he beats up everybody who talks shit about Atticus, he's gonna get real tired," Avi teased.

He wasn't wrong, but that didn't stop Jericho's hand from squeezing the life from Atticus's fingers.

Asa snickered. "Better get your man, Freckles. He looks pretty tough but I don't think he could take us—"

Glass exploded against the wall, causing all eyes to go to

 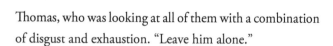

Thomas, who was looking at all of them with a combination of disgust and exhaustion. "Leave him alone."

"Dad—" Asa started.

"Not one more fucking word." Thomas jabbed a finger in Asa's direction, his tone leaving no room for argument.

"It's fine," Atticus muttered.

Thomas shot to his feet. "No. No, it's not. I taught you better than this. I taught *all* of you better than this. Didn't I? You're all grown adults with jobs, yet you bicker like children. You taunt each other like fucking children. We're here to do a job. I think Adam's right—"

"That's a first," Archer muttered, eyes dropping to his glass when Thomas cut his gaze to him.

Thomas closed his eyes for a long moment, like he was praying for guidance or peace or maybe just duct tape to wrap around his children's mouths. "If high tech isn't yielding results, then we go old school. If there's some kind of synthetic drug on the market or some kind of black market organ donation program operating out of this city, we need to find those responsible and punish them."

"I agree, sir," Jericho said, earning a snort from Adam. Once more, Thomas shot a look at Adam, who withered beneath his hard stare. "I have my own guys for that. Guys that the neighborhood knows and trusts."

"You've got guys? What does that mean?" August asked with his usual calculating curiosity.

It was Jericho who addressed him. "It means you guys aren't the only ones out there trying to keep people safe. I can handle the questioning and I can take care of whoever hurt my sister."

"You're not doing this alone," Atticus said. "If this is a network, you're going to need more than a bunch of kids."

"Those kids have more kills under their belts than most soldiers," Jericho reminded.

"I'm not saying they don't. But you're going to need more than them. Let us help you."

"You guys can't even help yourselves."

"Our familial bickering aside, we're actually pretty adept at large scale sieges," August murmured. "Use your guys to get the information, but let us help with the clean-up."

"Please," Lucas asked, Noah nodding earnestly beside him.

Jericho looked to Atticus, who nodded as well. Once more, he sighed. "Yeah. Yeah, okay."

FOURTEEN

JERICHO

Jericho was silent most of the way back to his place. He didn't even ask Atticus if he wanted to be dropped off. Hell, he hadn't even asked if he'd wanted to drive his own car. He'd just plucked the keys from Atticus's hand, held the passenger door open for him, and walked around to the driver's side. And Atticus had let him, hadn't uttered a single protest, just watched him, studying Jericho in that way he did when he was trying to gauge how to behave around him.

There was something soothing in the way Atticus just let Jericho lead, let him do what he wanted. Jericho needed it. Needed to feel like he had some control in an uncontrollable situation.

Once they were on the road, his hand gravitated to Atticus's thigh, squeezing slightly, needing Atticus's touch to ground him. After a few blocks, he felt a hand settle over his. He didn't acknowledge it. He didn't want to do anything that might cause Atticus to startle.

Affection seemed to embarrass Atticus. Well, not

affection so much as pointing out that the action could be seen as affectionate. Atticus wanted to be touched, needed it even, but he was embarrassed to ask for it and embarrassed to admit it. Atticus was so much more accepting of violence and vengeance. He didn't flinch when Jericho was hacking a person to pieces, but if Atticus was to acknowledge that he had initiated any type of affection, Jericho was certain Atticus would hurl himself from the car rather than look at him.

Now that he'd met Atticus's brothers, he got it. It clicked. Being raised as a psychopath in a house full of psychopaths must have been hell for somebody as touch-starved as Atticus. Jericho thought back to when Atticus had said he was a mirror. Was Atticus a psychopath or just reflecting the psychopaths surrounding him? Atticus was the oldest, but it was clear the others made a habit out of mocking him, teasing him.

Jericho was well versed in how boys treated each other. He was raising a household of heathens. But there was something especially vicious in the way the others treated Atticus. Jericho imagined that Atticus, with his delicate sensibilities and his constant need to be perfect, was probably annoying to his younger siblings.

It didn't mean Jericho had to like the way they treated Atticus. And it certainly didn't mean he'd tolerate it in his presence. Was Atticus an annoyingly finicky perfectionist? Yes. But he was Jericho's annoyingly finicky perfectionist and he would protect what was his, even if it meant hacking off his future in-laws' appendages until they got the point.

 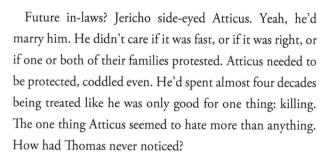
Future in-laws? Jericho side-eyed Atticus. Yeah, he'd marry him. He didn't care if it was fast, or if it was right, or if one or both of their families protested. Atticus needed to be protected, coddled even. He'd spent almost four decades being treated like he was only good for one thing: killing. The one thing Atticus seemed to hate more than anything. How had Thomas never noticed?

Thomas. The family patriarch. Jericho didn't know how he felt about Thomas. He imagined the man wasn't always the mess he'd been today. The articles about him painted him as a billionaire philanthropist, running a huge charity where he donated money almost as fast as he made it. But that wasn't the man he'd seen.

His sons had looked shocked, and shocking a psychopath couldn't be easy. Still, how often had Thomas ignored the others' treatment of Atticus? Did he not see that Atticus was nothing like them? Did Thomas also feel some kind of disdain for him as they seemed to? Atticus sure seemed to think so. But when push came to shove, Thomas had put a stop to their teasing.

"Are you really going to let my family help you deal with this?" Atticus asked suddenly, yanking Jericho from his thoughts.

He glanced at Atticus, then back at the road. "I don't know. We don't even know if this is a one-person job. These people... They could have nothing to do with my sister's death."

"Instinctively, though. You know we're onto something. Your gut has to be telling you there's something bigger at

play here, no?"

Atticus wasn't wrong. Jericho wanted to believe there was another explanation for his sister's death. Some naive part of him wanted to think his sister had run away, that she'd just needed to be free of their parents' restrictions and had lived a whole exciting and satisfying life before she'd ended up in the river. But he knew that wasn't true. He knew Mercy wouldn't have stayed away for that long by choice.

"I get that. I do. But what are we even talking about here? My sister was trafficked and then her organs were sold on the black market? Is that what we're talking about?" he choked out, suddenly feeling like he couldn't breathe.

Atticus squeezed the hand on his thigh. "I don't know. It seems hard to believe that something like that could be happening under our noses and neither of our…families had known about it." Atticus shook his head. "But people tend to mind their business, especially when not doing so could end up with them being tortured and killed, as Bryan implied."

Jericho nodded absently, his stomach churning, as he contemplated the amount of suffering his sister had endured. He was so involved in his own thoughts he almost missed his turn for the alley behind the shop. Once he parked, he noted Atticus had a death grip on his hand. "What's the matter, Freckles?"

"I could stay here while you talk to them if you want."

"Why?" Jericho asked. "I promise they're a lot more respectful than your brothers."

Well, most of them. Felix wasn't going to like having

Atticus back in their space, but he was going to have to get over it because Atticus wasn't going anywhere.

Atticus gazed out the window, notably not making eye contact. "I just didn't know if you wanted me there…"

Jericho frowned at him. "If I didn't want you here, I would have dropped you at home first."

Atticus gave a stilted nod but made no move to leave the passenger seat until Jericho walked around and opened the door for him. When he slipped from the car, Jericho stepped in close, pressing him back against the now closed car door. Atticus's whole body reacted, the tension melting from him as he waited for Jericho to take whatever he wanted. How could Jericho not want to keep him?

Jericho cupped his face, leaning in to drag his lips across his in a barely-there kiss. His lips were soft, his mouth relaxed, and when Jericho dipped his head for another taste, Atticus opened for him instantly. Jericho took his time, let himself explore Atticus's mouth, his hands slipping around his waist to cup his ass and give it a squeeze.

When he stepped back, Atticus blinked in surprise. "Thanks, Freckles. I needed that. Come on."

Jericho took his hand and led him into the garage. The shop was still open, so Arsen and Levi were both working, Levi behind the counter and Arsen under an old Jeep Wrangler. Felix, Lake, and Seven sat on the couch in the back, two of them deeply entrenched in a video game per usual. Seven was the first to notice Jericho and Atticus. He wasn't playing the game. "Hey, boss."

Felix immediately whipped around, his shrewd gaze

landing on Atticus before dropping sharply to their joined hands. The fury on his face was obvious and instantaneous. Still, he said nothing, choosing to seethe quietly.

"Where are the others?" Jericho asked.

"Cree's at the movies. Nico's with his mom," Seven said.

Cree worked at a run-down movie theater that showed old black and white movies. He didn't make any real money from it, but he loved it and the old man who owned it so he worked for pennies. Nico's mom was a raging alcoholic and mean as a snake, but Nico still went home every single day to take care of her. A thankless job if ever there was one.

"We're it for now," Lake said.

Jericho popped himself up on the pool table, pulling Atticus back between his splayed thighs, earning curious looks from the others. He'd never brought anybody home to them before. Arsen and Levi floated over, Arsen wiping his hands on a dirty rag he then stuffed in his back pocket.

"What's up?" Lake asked.

"I need you guys to go question some people," Jericho said, looking at each of them in turn, his gaze holding when he reached his brother, whose jaw jutted forward defiantly.

"Who exactly are we questioning and why?" Felix asked, tugging their mother's threadbare cardigan around himself dramatically like some girl in a movie gazing moodily at the ocean.

Jericho sighed internally. "Mercy wasn't the only body to turn up missing organs."

"That's not exactly surprising in this neighborhood, is it?" Lake asked. "The crews around here drop bodies on the

regular. That's why we're still in business."

"Yeah, but how many of those bodies are missing internal organs?" Atticus asked.

Lake shrugged. "Not many, I guess. So, you want us to ask about the people with no organs? Who were they?"

"There was no ID on the bodies," Atticus supplied.

Jericho nodded. "Yeah, what he said. We don't have any names to go on but one, and it's probably best if you keep that name out of the conversation if you want anybody to talk to you." Jericho didn't supply them with Carlos's name. He didn't want them inadvertently tipping this guy off and getting hurt. "I want you to head down to 6th and Broadway—"

"Skid row?" Felix asked, surprised.

"Yeah. These people we're looking for probably won't watch the tent cities as closely as they would the working girls and the addicts," Jericho said. "Be discreet. Offer money if you have to. But just be…cautious."

"What exactly are we asking about? If they overheard anybody talking about harvesting organs?" Felix asked, his annoyance obvious.

Atticus spoke up then. "We're looking for people who disguise themselves as helpers. Bryan mentioned crosses."

"Crosses? Helpers? Man, the church has a million different people out there every weekend trying to buy their way into heaven by pretending they give a shit about the homeless. They're every church's pet project," Seven muttered.

It was true. Without fail, each Saturday a group of people from one church or another would be out there passing out

sandwiches or blankets or socks. It wouldn't seem so fake if they weren't stopping to take selfies of each one of their good deeds and posting them with captions like #blessed. It was so disingenuous. But that brought up a good point.

"These people won't be your average Sunday morning repenters. Look for the people who are always out there. People who are a little too involved," Atticus said.

Felix flicked his gaze to Atticus like a cat flicking its tail in irritation. "Do we take orders from him now?"

"You take orders from me and he's an extension of me. This isn't about him, it's about our sister. Mercy. Remember her?"

"Yeah, I remember her. I was planning her funeral while you were banging your new boyfriend," Felix snarked, wrapping his arms tighter around himself as he sulked.

Jericho ignored Felix's tantrum. "Check the shelters, the methadone clinics. But again…discreetly. We're not looking to get anybody hurt. If you find somebody who's willing to talk, you come find me. I want to question them myself."

"Should we tell the others?" Lake questioned.

"Yeah, I want as many people on this as possible. But I cannot stress this enough, be subtle. According to our recently deceased friend, Bryan, whoever these people are, they have no problem eliminating anybody who could point a finger in their direction. We're not looking to get anybody hurt. We just need to find out who's out there in these people's ears."

"What are you going to be doing?" Felix asked.

"Excuse me?" Jericho countered.

"While we're out there risking our lives in tent city, what exactly is it you'll be doing? Is there a ball? Some gala? Some super pressing dinner party you just simply must attend?" Felix sneered.

Jericho could have told him the truth, but it didn't matter what he'd be doing. Felix knew better than to question him, especially in front of the others. This only worked as long as he had their trust. "You got a problem with the way I run things, little brother? If you got something to say, just say it."

The fury and hurt in Felix's eyes was obvious, but Jericho wasn't going to let him talk to him like that.

Lake set a hand on Felix's shoulder. "Let's just go and do our jobs."

Felix continued to give Jericho a hard stare for another thirty seconds before finally tearing his gaze away. "Whatever. Let's just get this over with."

When Arsen and Levi were back up front and the others had gone, Atticus turned to face Jericho. "Yeah, your brother hates me as much as my brothers do."

"That's not true. Felix... He just doesn't do well with change. I'm all he has left, and whenever he feels threatened, he reacts...sometimes violently. He's afraid you'll take me away from him."

"I-I wouldn't do that," Atticus said. "Family is important. Even families like mine. As much as my brothers dislike me, they need me." Atticus shrugged. "And I need them," he admitted.

"What are we going to be doing while they're

questioning people on the streets?" Atticus asked, as Jericho led him upstairs.

Jericho grimaced. "We're going to go talk to somebody who might be able to shed some light on whatever it is we're dealing with."

Atticus arched a brow. "Why does it look like you'd rather be having a root canal?"

Jericho sighed. "Because a root canal is less painful than asking my ex-boyfriend for help."

"You're going to go talk to *him*?"

The way Atticus said *him* spoke volumes, and it shot sparks along Jericho's nerve endings. Atticus was jealous. "Relax, Freckles. You know there's nobody else for me but you."

Atticus stiffened. "I wasn't even thinking of that."

Liar. "No? Then what were you thinking about?" Jericho teased.

Atticus captured Jericho's mouth, walking him backwards until his back hit the glass windows that overlooked the shop below. Oh, yeah. He was definitely jealous. That probably shouldn't turn Jericho on, but it definitely did. He needed him desperate and loved him when he was needy. He was already half-hard when Atticus went to his knees in front of him.

Jericho glanced over his shoulder, relieved to see those down below weren't paying them any mind. Atticus mouthed at the outline of his cock through his jeans. Jericho groaned. "You always look so good on your knees for me, Freckles. I can't get enough."

Atticus made a noise in his throat that could have meant

anything or nothing at all. Jericho opened his jeans, pushing them out of the way and thrusting his hips away from the glass, his hand catching in Atticus's hair as he forced his head back to his crotch. This time, the sound Atticus made was most definitely a moan. He loved to be manhandled.

"What do you want, Freckles? You want my cock in your mouth? Wanna suck me off right here where anybody can see us?" Atticus continued to mouth at his erection through his underwear until Jericho jerked his head back. "I asked you a question. You wanna blow me?"

"Yes," Atticus rasped. "You know I do."

Jericho grinned down at him, fisting his hand in his hair once more. "I just like hearing you say it. Say please."

Atticus didn't hesitate. "Please."

"Please, Jericho."

Atticus let out a shuddering breath. "Please, Jericho."

"Fuck, I love when you say my name, Freckles. It's so fucking hot." Jericho freed himself from his underwear, smirking at the thought of the view they might get from downstairs and grateful his brother was long gone. "Open up for me."

Atticus did as he was told. Jericho slipped his cock into the wet heat of his mouth, working himself in and out a couple of times.

"Fuck, your tongue is amazing. Suck me. Make me come."

Jericho's eyes rolled in pleasure, muscles tensing as Atticus's lips closed around him, enveloping him in that tight suction of his mouth.

"Christ."

Jericho watched Atticus as his head bobbed. He really was sexy as fuck. There was just something so obscene about his uptight little doctor on his knees, his hands gripping Jericho's ass as if he couldn't get him deep enough to sate him.

Jericho knotted his fingers in those auburn tresses, holding him in place so he could fuck into his mouth deep enough for him to gag, his eyes watering, but still, he didn't release Jericho. Atticus wanted this—for Jericho to take what he wanted.

That was fine with him. "You love this, don't you? Love choking on my cock. You can't get enough, huh? Fuck. You're so good for me. That's it, relax and let me do the work. Good." Atticus fumbled slightly, and Jericho realized it was him trying to shove his hand into his pants to get himself off. Jericho stifled a groan, his whole body flushing hot. "Oh, shit. Oh, yeah. Touch yourself for me."

Atticus moaned obscenely as his hand closed around his flushed cock. The sensation sent shivers along Jericho's spine.

"Fuck, yeah. Do that again. Moan for me."

Atticus flicked his gaze upwards, tears leaking from the corners of his pretty blue eyes as he did as Jericho asked.

"That's it, Freckles. Keep looking at me just like that. I'm so close. I want to watch you swallow my load."

Once more, Atticus groaned, and Jericho realized he was coming over his fist. Holy shit. That was all it took. Jericho's orgasm hit him with enough force to have him

almost double over, giving a hoarse shout as he flooded Atticus's mouth. He swallowed it all, sucking him like he didn't want to miss even a drop.

Jericho pulled him off when his body couldn't handle anymore, dragging him back up to his feet to kiss him deep, sucking the taste of himself off his tongue, before dropping kisses on his cheeks, his nose, his forehead. Anywhere he could reach. "Shit, Freckles. I should make you jealous more often."

"I wasn't jealous," Atticus muttered, tone sulky.

"Whatever you say," Jericho soothed. "Come on. Let's get cleaned up and go find Gabriel."

Atticus made a sound that was suspiciously growl-like.

"You sure you're not jealous, Freckles?"

"Maybe I just don't like law enforcement."

Jericho snickered, righting his clothes. He glanced down at the shop once more to see Arsen gazing up at him with a smirk on his face. Jericho stepped to the side, blocking him from Atticus's view. The last thing he needed was for Atticus to get self-conscious. Hopefully, Arsen kept his mouth shut, but that was the least of his worries.

Introducing Atticus to Gabe was a risky move but necessary. Atticus wasn't going to let him go alone, and Jericho really didn't want to, anyway. Some part of him wanted Gabriel to see Atticus as much as he wanted Atticus to hate Gabriel. Maybe that made him an asshole, but he didn't care. He needed to know that Atticus was as territorial as he was, as fucked up over him as he was over Atticus. That he'd kill for him. Die for him. That this

obsessive compulsion was a two-way street. That there was some kind of unspoken agreement that the only way out of this relationship—no matter how fucked up—was if one of them stopped breathing.

FIFTEEN

Atticus tracked Gabriel Vélez as he exited the police station and began his long walk across the parking lot. He looked like a cop. There was no other way to put it. He wasn't dressed in any type of uniform, but his square jaw, bulging muscles, and high and tight haircut just screamed law enforcement. How the hell was this Jericho's type? He looked like he lived on protein shakes and steroids. Atticus side-eyed Jericho. Was that what Jericho was into? Gym rats?

Atticus took in Vélez's faded jeans, freakishly white sneakers, and a black sweater so tight he must have bought it from the children's section. He caught a glimpse of his own reflection in the glass of the Bronco's side mirror, his hand floating to his flat stomach as he checked out his boring black dress pants and white button down. He fought the urge to roll up his sleeves or…something. Anything to make him look less like a—what had Jericho called him that first night?—an insurance salesman.

To his credit, Jericho looked less than enthused about

seeing his ex-boyfriend. He leaned against his truck, hands stuffed in his pockets. As Vélez approached, Atticus felt himself move closer to Jericho until their bodies touched from shoulder to hip. Jericho smirked, turning his head to run his nose up his neck until his lips rested against his ear. "Staking your claim, Freckles?" he murmured.

Atticus huffed out a breath through his nose as his dick twitched in his pants. "I hate you so much."

"That would explain why the sex is so hot," Jericho teased. "But I don't think you hate me. Do you?" He pressed a kiss behind Atticus's ear in full view of his ex. "You gonna break my heart, Freckles?"

"Can we focus on questioning Mr. Universe over there?" Atticus muttered through gritted teeth.

Jericho gave a low chuckle just as Vélez reached them. His gaze darted to Atticus, his mouth forming a hard line he tried to cover almost immediately by smiling with too many teeth. "Who's this? You didn't say you were bringing...somebody."

Something loosened in Atticus as Jericho nudged him with his shoulder. "He's not just somebody, and why would I tell you I wasn't coming alone? Like I said on the phone, I just need some information."

"Yeah, but I just thought..." Vélez started before frowning, like he was trying to solve a complex math problem, which, for him, was probably anything over simple addition. He cleared his throat, his shoulders going back as he looked Atticus over. "So, who are you?"

"His boyfriend. Who are you?"

His irritation was obvious. "A…friend, I guess."

Jericho snorted. "Speaking of friends. How's your boyfriend?" Jericho asked, expression blank. "Still living together?"

Vélez flushed, shifting his weight from one foot to the other. "Uh, yeah. He's good. What information do you need?" he asked.

Jericho smirked, like he'd expected the rapid change in subject. "Have you ever heard of a guy who goes by the name of Scar? Used to head the 4Loco crew back when their leader was doing time?"

Vélez blinked, his gaze darting over Jericho's shoulder, the muscle in his jaw popping as he seemed to clench his jaw. This all happened in less than a second—a blink and you miss it micro-expression, but Atticus caught it immediately. Had Jericho?

Vélez overcompensated, shoving his hands in his pockets to mimic Jericho's stance. "No. I came after your sister's investigation started, remember?"

Atticus frowned. How did he even know this was in regards to Mercy if he didn't know this man?

"How do you know this is about his sister?" Atticus asked.

The fury in the other man's eyes was there and gone in an instant. He was used to his lies going unquestioned. "I just assumed this was about Mercy. Is it not?"

"Mm," Atticus said, tone implying he was full of shit.

Atticus didn't see Jericho move so much as a muscle, but his weight shifted, pressing against him in a way that would

have caused him to list to the side had he not had a slightly sturdier frame than Jericho. He was trying to tell Atticus to back off. Or, at least, slow down. Some part of Atticus unclenched as he realized that Jericho had seen the other man's tells, too.

Nothing Vélez said was overtly suspicious, but he was definitely behaving like somebody who'd tripped up and said too much. Had the mention of Perez rattled him? If so, why? Was this guy such a threat that even the cops were afraid of him? Or were the cops in the pocket of his bosses?

"Did you know my sister was last seen in the company of this guy, Scar? His real name is Carlos Perez," Jericho said.

It was risky bringing up this man's name if he had the police in his pocket. Bryan had acted like the guy was Bloody Mary or Beetlejuice. Like if the name was said three times, he would appear to wreak havoc. Maybe that was Jericho's plan. It would be a great way to draw him out, have him focus his attention on them and not on Jericho's boys.

Vélez frowned, crossing his too-muscular arms over his broad chest until his sweater was clinging for dear life. "Last seen by who?" he asked, suspicious.

"Does it matter?" Jericho countered. It wasn't like he could tell a cop that their lead had come from his boyfriend's psychic brother-in-law.

Atticus could feel Vélez's trepidation grow. "Did somebody come forward? Because we've interviewed everybody who was a known associate of your sister."

"Known associate?" Atticus echoed. "That doesn't sound

 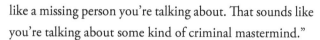

like a missing person you're talking about. That sounds like you're talking about some kind of criminal mastermind."

Vélez's eyes widened. "What?"

Jericho stiffened. "Is that how you see her, Gabe? As a criminal? Another dead junkie?" Jericho asked.

Vélez scanned the parking lot, like he was afraid of being overheard or thought, maybe, somebody watched. "Of course not. That's not what I meant."

"So, what did you mean?" Jericho snapped.

Vélez shook his head, once more scanning the parking lot before lowering his voice. "She was hanging around with some really shady people, Jericho. The people we interviewed…friends, acquaintances…they all said the same thing. She liked to party. She liked hooking up with random guys. I know she was your sister and you loved her, but she was no angel."

Jericho launched himself off the truck. "What the fuck did you just say?"

Atticus shot an arm out to block him from assaulting a police officer in the parking lot of the station before saying, "Wait for me in the car."

Jericho's eyes bulged as he looked at Atticus like he'd never seen him before. "What?"

"Wait for me in the car." When he hesitated, Atticus gave him a gentle shove. "Go."

Jericho stared at him hard for a solid minute while Atticus prayed he just did as he said without question. Finally, Jericho gave Vélez one more disgusted look, then turned on his heel, punching the hood of the Bronco before

he slid into the driver's seat, seething.

"Wow. You've really got him whipped," Vélez said, glowering at Jericho.

Atticus didn't pay any attention to Jericho, making Vélez his sole focus. He mirrored his body language, widening his stance and crossing his arms. "Listen, we both know how…emotional he gets over her. Family is never rational. And I get what you're saying, but can I please ask you a few questions?"

"I don't even know you. I could lose my job talking about this to you."

"Would it help at all if I said my father—Thomas Mulvaney—is really good friends with the city commissioner, and I'd be happy to have him relay how helpful and professional you were. Alternatively…" He let the threat hang in the air.

"Thomas Mulvaney is your father?" he asked, like he wasn't sure if Atticus was full of shit or not.

"Yeah. I'm his eldest son. Look, we both know that this guy is a dead end. Girls like Mercy… They get themselves into trouble all the time. They meet the wrong people, fall for the wrong people, and they end up dead for their trouble. It's a cold case and it's going to stay that way, but chasing down these leads makes him feel better."

Vélez's shoulders fell, the tension leaving his system. He really thought Atticus was on his side. "I don't know what he thinks he's going to find. She ran away eight years ago and somehow wound up OD'ing on some new designer drug. Somebody dumped her in the river. There's no case here."

"I know, but it would help me out if you could just give me something?"

"There's no case here," he said again, almost to himself. "He needs to understand that."

Atticus nodded along. "I'll get him to understand, but it would just go a long way towards helping him clear some things up if you'd just let me ask you some questions?" Atticus said, matching Vélez's tone.

Vélez took a deep breath and let it out, throwing up his hands. "Yeah, man. Ask your questions," he said begrudgingly.

"You weren't the first detective on the case, right?"

Vélez shook his head. "I was still a UC for narcotics back then. I got transferred later. They threw the case at me because I was a newbie and they always throw us the cold ones."

"How long after the case opened was that? A few years?" Atticus asked.

Vélez shook his head. "Like six to eight months maybe?"

Something pricked at the back of Atticus's brain but he couldn't say just what it was that rang false about the statement. "What happened to the first detective? Is there any way we can talk to him?"

Vélez snorted. "Not unless you've got a ouija board. He's dead."

Huh. That was interesting. "Oh, shit. When did that happen?"

Vélez shrugged. "Right before my transfer. That's why the spot opened up in major crimes."

"Why'd you leave narcotics? Seems like it would be a lot more exciting than major crimes, no? Got tired of being undercover?" Atticus asked, keeping his tone as casual as possible. He needed Vélez to think they were just talking, just making conversation, killing time to make Jericho think he was getting information.

Vélez's eyes shifted to the left, then back. Atticus could practically hear him attempting to carefully craft his answer. Finally, he said, "It was just time for a change. My mom was worried I was getting in too deep."

It wasn't totally a lie, but it wasn't the whole truth.

Atticus nodded as if that made perfect sense. "And you've never heard of this Carlos dude? Not even in your UC narcotics days?"

Vélez shook his head, gaze floating away from Atticus once more. "This wasn't my jurisdiction. I was working West End back then." He looked over to where Jericho was sitting in the truck. "Look, I like Jericho. We were friends once…I think. But we've run down every lead, did our due diligence."

Atticus frowned. "Was there anybody in particular who stood out? Like maybe somebody you just couldn't put your finger on?"

Vélez's eyes went wide, but he recovered quickly. "Nah, man. Just the same junkies and burnouts you always see." Atticus was prepared to take that as face value, especially since he didn't believe a word the other man said, but Vélez wasn't done. "Some cases just never get solved. His sister got involved with the wrong people and, somehow, ended

up tossed in the river. It sucks but she's not the first. Hell, she's not even the first this month. She's what we call a high risk target."

"High risk? She wasn't a sex worker or homeless. Jericho said his sister wasn't into hard drugs."

He leaned in like he was sharing a secret, his voice a conspiratorial whisper as he said, "The track marks all over her arms tell an entirely different story." He looked back over his shoulder at the building. "I gotta get back to work. If you or *your father* have any more questions, you can take it up with my boss." He gave another fleeting glance at Jericho. "Tell him I'm sorry. Truly."

He didn't give Atticus a chance to ask another question, just turned and jogged away.

Atticus slid into the passenger seat, fully prepared to have to defend what he'd done. But as soon as the door closed, Jericho said, "What'd you get?"

"You knew—"

Jericho snorted, cutting him off. "That you didn't just suddenly decide you wanted to be the dominant one in this relationship? Yeah, I don't need to be a psychic to figure that out. It was interesting watching you do what you do."

"Do what I do?" Atticus said, frowning.

"Yeah, this is the first time I've seen your mirror bit in action. It's impressive. So, what did you get?"

Atticus wouldn't exactly call it a bit. It wasn't something he practiced, just something he innately knew how to do. "Your ex is hiding something. He definitely knows who Perez is. Also, did you know the original detective on your

sister's case died?"

"Yeah. Car accident. Drove his car into one of those guardrails on the highway. Practically split his car in half. Gruesome."

"That doesn't strike you as weird?" Atticus questioned.

Jericho frowned. "Why would it? People die in car accidents every day."

"Let's just think about this logically. Bryan said they were ghosts. That they had reach. What if the cops are in their pocket? It wouldn't hurt to have a man on the inside."

"But why? The original detective hadn't gotten anywhere on Mercy's case," Jericho said.

"How do you know?"

"Gabe told…" Jericho faltered. "Gabe told me when he first picked up the case."

"Exactly. Vélez said they gave him the case because they always shove the cold cases onto the new guys, but a case isn't considered 'cold' until a year has passed, so that was a lie. How long after he took over your sister's case before you two started dating?"

Jericho's frown became a full blown scowl. "We hooked up about four weeks after he took over the case. Began our brief on-again, off-again thing until I learned he had a boyfriend. After that, we only talked about the case, then we didn't talk at all."

"You've had no contact in all the years?" Atticus asked.

"I froze him out after I learned he had a boyfriend. He talked to my parents a few times after that to update them about Mercy, but even that stopped after a few months

when they stopped asking questions."

"Why did they stop?" Atticus asked, certain he already knew the answer.

"My dad died, my mom got assaulted, and Gabe became a low priority while I was trying to raise Felix. Our neighborhood is small. When I saw him around, I went in the other direction. We weren't enemies, exactly. Most of the time, I didn't think of him at all. I had no interest in being friends."

"You said you knew him from around the neighborhood. So, he lived in this neighborhood? Your neighborhood?"

Jericho nodded. "Yeah."

"Yeah, he's full of shit. Vélez told me he didn't know Carlos because he was working West End, which is bullshit in and of itself because, if you're a UC in narcotics, you're going to know the hierarchy of shitbags for the 4Loco crew. They're the biggest gang in this area. Besides, UCs have informants everywhere. He lived in your neighborhood. He was a narc. I find it hard to believe he's never heard the name Carlos Perez, even if it was only as a guy who ran 4Loco years ago."

Jericho looked at the doors of the station. "You think Gabe played me?"

Atticus caught Jericho's attention. "I think it's a possibility. We need to at least look into him a bit more. Is that alright?"

Jericho nodded. "Yeah, we need to know. But for the record, if he had something to do with Mercy's disappearance, I'm going to kill him. Slowly."

Atticus shrugged. "I'll drive. I'll show you some of my favorite places to torture where you can kill somebody undisturbed."

Jericho's gaze grew intense. "I'm serious. I don't care if he's a cop. He's going to die."

Atticus shrugged, pulling his phone free to check his work emails. "You think I give a shit if he's a cop? We've dropped pretty much every kind of body by now from priests to politicians. We just can't leave him in the woods for the animals to scavenge like the last couple of times. We'll need to be more strategic, maybe dismembering. I know a place for that."

Jericho arched a brow. "You could act less excited about the prospect of murdering my ex."

Atticus scoffed. "If it was Kendra? If you had proof that Kendra was somehow involved with murdering innocent girls you wouldn't happily eviscerate her?"

Jericho sighed dramatically. "That's fair. But we're only killing him if he's somehow involved in what happened to my sister."

"I can't guarantee that," Atticus said. "If my father finds out he's involved in something shady—even if it has nothing to do with Mercy—there's a very good chance he could end up on the wrong side of one of my brothers."

Jericho thudded his head against the back of his seat. "His mom used to go to the same church as my parents."

Atticus gave him a flat stare. "It doesn't make him a better person. We both know he's involved in something shady. He was too evasive. Best case scenario, he's a dirty cop

looking the other way for a gang that traffics humans and drugs. Worst case scenario, he was put into the department just to clean up any messes when whatever they're doing doesn't go according to plan, which means this is a way bigger...something."

After a minute, Jericho said, "Admit it, part of you just wants him dead."

Atticus could feel his lip curling. "Where does a guy even find sweaters that tight? Is that what you're into? All muscles and no brains?"

Jericho chuckled. "You really are jealous, Freckles."

Atticus stared out the windshield at the sea of cars. "Shut up."

Atticus jumped as Jericho's hand landed on his thigh, sliding dangerously higher. "I like it. It's hot seeing you get all flustered and possessive. Especially when it leads to you on your knees for me. You look so fucking good on your knees for me."

Atticus flushed to the tips of his ears, hating the way his knees fell open, giving Jericho more access, disappointed when his hand retreated.

But when Jericho placed that same hand, palm up, on the seat between them, Atticus didn't hesitate to place his own on top, threading their fingers together.

After a while, he said, "I'll call Calliope as soon as we're home."

Home. Their home? His home? He didn't even know anymore. For once in his life, he didn't want to overthink it, didn't want anybody studying it or examining it for

flaws or potential pitfalls. He and Jericho—whatever they were—was theirs, just theirs, and nobody was going to intrude on that.

Nobody.

Except maybe Felix.

Fuck.

SIXTEEN
JERICHO

Atticus held Jericho's hand the whole ride back to his fancy apartment, even though he stayed mostly silent. It was a comfortable silence, with Atticus absently drawing circles onto the back of Jericho's hand with his thumb.

Silence didn't bother Jericho. If anything, raising and running a crew of teens—some of which had come to him as young as twelve—had taught Jericho to value the quiet. Still, to amuse himself, he turned on the radio and sang along, singing all the dirty parts directly to Atticus, which made him all flustered and flushed, Jericho's two favorite looks on him.

When Jericho reached the valet, the kid with the car obsession—who he'd learned was named Diego—jogged over and opened the driver's side for Jericho. "Hey, J. What's good?"

Jericho grinned. "Everything, D. Everything."

"Did you catch the game the other night?" Diego asked. They'd briefly bonded over a love of soccer. "Nah, man.

Work has me super busy lately. I've got it recorded, though. Don't tell me anything," Jericho said as he walked around the truck.

He opened Atticus's car door for him just as Diego slid into the front seat, both of them stepping out of the way before he sped off in the direction of the valet parking lot. As they walked into the building, Atticus asked, "What was that all about?"

Jericho frowned. "What was what all about?"

"You and him. Do you even know him?" Atticus asked, tone sour.

That shouldn't have made Jericho smile, but he couldn't help it. He loved jealous Atticus, and seeing that side of him twice in one day was almost too much. "I know him as the kid who likes my Bronco and who I talk to whenever I'm here to visit you. It's called being friendly, Freckles."

Atticus stiffened when Jericho placed a hand on his lower back, stepping away from him. "Well, I don't like it."

Jericho chuckled. So prickly.

Before he could formulate any kind of response to soothe Atticus, the elevator in the lobby dinged and the doors opened. He walked to the back of the empty car, turning to lean against the wall, facing the mirrored doors. Atticus stood just in front of Jericho, his back to him, a good two feet between them. Yeah, he was definitely mad. Why did Jericho love that so much?

As the doors began to close, he fished two fingers into Atticus's belt loops, dragging him back so his ass was nice and snug up against Jericho's now half-hard cock. When

the doors were less than an inch from each other a tiny, withered hand shot between them, triggering them to open once more.

They both watched as a little old lady stepped inside with a tiny white dog stuffed into her Balenciaga bag. Atticus tried to pull away, but Jericho held tight, hooking his chin over his shoulder to whisper, "I wouldn't do that if I were you, Freckles. We don't want to scar Nana for life with the hard-on I'm sporting right now."

Jericho watched Atticus startle in the reflection before relaxing against him. Fuck, Jericho wanted to do dirty things to him. "You look sexy as fuck when you pout, Freckles. It makes me want to do very bad things to you," he rasped.

Atticus shifted, his hands not so subtly trying to hide his own erection. The woman made no eye contact. She turned up her nose, staring straight ahead, refusing to acknowledge them at all. At the third floor, she floated off the elevator, never looking back.

Once the car began moving again, Jericho let his mouth explore Atticus's neck, up to his ear, his hands sliding around his hip to palm over his cock.

"There are cameras in here, you know," Atticus said, voice raw.

"Good. We'd look so hot on film together," Jericho teased. "I bet you'd love watching me fuck you. Maybe we should put a mirror over your bed." Atticus snorted but still pushed his ass back against Jericho, head dropping to the side to give his lips better access to the spot where his neck

and shoulder met. "Yeah, you'd definitely like that."

Jericho settled a hand around his throat as he ran his tongue along the shell of Atticus's ear, continuing to fondle his now rock hard cock. "Maybe I'll just fuck you bent over the bathroom counter so you can watch me driving into you, so you can see the way your eyes get all cloudy and your mouth goes slack. So you can watch how you make these breathy little 'uh uh' sounds each time I thrust into you, letting me know just how deep I am inside you. What do you think, Freckles?"

Jericho felt Atticus's Adam's apple bob beneath his hand as he swallowed audibly. The elevator slowed, dinging before the doors slid open. Atticus was off like a shot, practically speed-walking the short distance to his door, fumbling as he seemed to momentarily forget his key code.

Jericho caught up just as Atticus gave a surprised grunt, pitching forward, almost tripping over an enormous cardboard box. Jericho caught his arm, righting him once again, staring in confusion at the minefield of boxes waiting just inside the door. "What's all this?"

Atticus flushed, mumbling, "A television."

Jericho's heart tripped in his chest, his mouth going dry. "You bought me a television, Freckles?"

Atticus looked anywhere but at Jericho. "I bought *me* a television. But you can use it when you're here."

Usually, Jericho would tease him but this didn't seem like a ha-ha moment. This meant something. It had to. Like a way for Atticus to let Jericho know he wanted him to feel comfortable in his space. "I thought you didn't like TV?"

Atticus shrugged stiffly. "I don't. But you do. It's not a big deal."

Jericho turned Atticus towards him, cupping his face. "It's a big deal to me."

Atticus went from pink to bright red, mumbling, "I'm glad you like it."

"Oh, I love it." Jericho slanted his mouth across his, using his thumb to pull Atticus's chin down so he could slip his tongue inside. "I want to fuck you," Jericho said against his lips. "Now."

Atticus shivered. "Okay."

Jericho took his hand and led him back to the bedroom. In-between kisses, he stripped them of their clothes. When they were both naked, Jericho pushed him back on the bed, following him down to blanket his weight on top of him before capturing his mouth once more.

He took his time, relaxing Atticus with deep, drugging kisses that seemed to melt all the worry from him until he forgot to overthink everything, until there was nothing else in the world but Jericho. Was that greedy? He didn't care. He needed to be his sole focus. The one person who knew the key to unlocking the real Atticus, equal parts brilliant killer and eager submissive.

But only for Jericho.

When he tore his lips away, Atticus lifted his head, trying to follow Jericho's mouth, but he had other ideas. He slid off of Atticus, nudging him. "Roll onto your side for me."

Atticus frowned, but then did as Jericho asked, rolling away from him. Jericho grabbed the lube that sat knocked

over and forgotten on the side table, coating his fingers before settling in behind him. He dragged his teeth across Atticus's shoulder, his hand dipping to the furrow between his cheeks. Atticus's breath hitched at his touch. Jericho didn't push his fingers, just teased around his entrance, until Atticus was pushing back on him, grunting in frustration.

Jericho chuckled low. "Want something?"

There was a moment's hesitation before Atticus said, "You."

Jericho brushed his lips against Atticus's cheek. "Oh, I'm all yours, Freckles, no doubt about it."

Atticus's breathing became ragged at Jericho's statement. "I'm… I'm yours, too."

Jericho sank two fingers into the tight heat of Atticus's body. "Yeah, you are. All mine. Just mine."

Atticus made a helpless sound, trying to fuck himself on Jericho's fingers.

"You always feel so goddamn good. I can never get enough of you."

Atticus bent his top leg, letting it fall forward, clearly wanting more. Jericho ignored it for the moment, relishing the sucking heat of him, cock leaking at the knowledge that this was just for him. Nobody else would ever get this side of Atticus, only Jericho. He let his mouth explore whatever skin he found. The spot behind his ear, his shoulder, his cheek, his lips.

After a few minutes, Atticus whispered, "What are you waiting for?"

Jericho chuckled. "So impatient. What? You don't like

 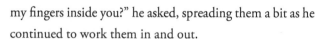

my fingers inside you?" he asked, spreading them a bit as he continued to work them in and out.

"You know I do," he said, reaching around and grabbing Jericho's dick rather aggressively, snugging it up against his entrance. "I just want this more."

"You're being very take charge tonight. I like it," Jericho teased, batting his hand away to slick his cock. "But don't forget who's really in charge."

Jericho thrust into him in one fluid motion, both of them groaning when he bottomed out. Jericho curled himself around Atticus, his lips trailing along the skin behind his ear. "This more to your liking?" he asked, lazily rolling his hips.

"Yeah," Atticus said, voice raw. "But you could go faster."

Jericho nipped at Atticus's ear lobe. "I'll move when I'm ready. I haven't been inside you in almost twenty-four hours. Don't want it to be over too quickly. Now, kiss me."

Atticus craned his head enough for Jericho to capture his lips in a long, slow kiss that had him fucking his tongue into his mouth in time with his thrusts. "I swear you put some kind of spell on me," Jericho murmured. "I've never in my life wanted anybody the way I do you. I'm not just saying that. I know you won't believe me, but it's true. I'm completely addicted to everything about you."

Atticus shivered, goosebumps erupting along his skin, his breath quickening, but he didn't say anything, just reached back and ran his hand along Jericho's hip like he wanted him closer.

Closer was fine with Jericho. He'd wanted to take it

slow, wanted to somehow convey with his body the shit he knew Atticus wasn't ready to hear out loud. But it was near impossible, especially with Atticus spurring him on, pushing back on him with each thrust like he just couldn't get him deep enough.

"Alright, Freckles. You win."

He pulled out and pushed Atticus onto his back, slipping between his legs and catching him beneath the knees, practically bending him in half as he drove back into him.

This time, he set a brutal pace, hips slinging in and out hard and fast, as Atticus's eyes fluttered closed, his mouth going slack, those breathy little grunts letting Jericho know he was doing something right.

He leaned down to kiss him before saying, "Touch yourself. I love to watch you jerk yourself off for me."

Atticus wrapped a hand around his flushed, leaking cock, and Jericho couldn't tear his eyes away from the sight as heat pooled in his belly, electricity arcing along his spine, letting him know he was dangerously close. "Fuck, yeah. God, that's so hot. You're so fucking hot. I want to watch you come for me, Freckles. Let me feel it."

Atticus gave three more hard strokes, and then was spilling over his belly and chest. Jericho groaned, hips falling off-rhythm as Atticus spasmed around him, milking his orgasm from him with an intensity that had his vision going black at the edges as he emptied himself inside before collapsing on Atticus, boneless.

They were both sweaty and sticky, but Jericho couldn't bring himself to move, or even pull free from him. He just

lay there, feeling Atticus breathing just as hard beneath him. Jericho was surprised to feel Atticus wrap his arms around him, and even more surprised when he started to scratch his back, his blunt nails following the lines of Jericho's shoulders, down his back, almost to his ass and then back up again.

This time, it was Jericho who had goosebumps, his lids heavy. He worked his arms beneath Atticus, holding him tight as he drifted to sleep.

"When did you have time to do all this?" Jericho asked.

They were both freshly showered and wrapped in towels, staring down at Jericho's non-present.

Atticus looked at the sea of boxes. "I bought it on my phone and paid a courier to drop it off. When they arrived, my doorman placed the packages inside."

Packages. More than one. Jericho had noticed earlier but was far too preoccupied to question it. "Why is it in so many boxes?"

Atticus looked like he'd swallowed a cactus. "It's a sound system and some other things."

Jericho's heart squeezed. "Some other things?"

Atticus wouldn't meet his gaze. "I just told the guy at Best Buy to set me up with whatever he thought I needed and to put it on my AmEx card. They'll be here in a day or two to install it."

Jericho scoffed. "We don't need to pay for installation,

Freckles. Need something handy done, then I'm your man. Where do you want it?"

Atticus looked around his weirdly cozy apartment, clearly panicking. "Where would you put it?"

Jericho grinned. Atticus really did hate making decisions for himself. "I'll take care of it. Why don't you take care of dinner? Do you wanna cook? If not, we could order something."

"I could cook..." After a minute, he asked, "What should I cook?"

Jericho studied him for a long moment. "What's your favorite thing to cook? Is it something fancy? Like roast duck?"

Atticus did that thing where his gaze floated away from Jericho, like he had some shameful secret. "My favorite thing? Chicken and dumplings. My mom used to cook it for me when I was a kid. When she was lucid, anyway."

That was so not what Jericho had anticipated. "Do you have the ingredients?"

"No." Atticus looked disappointed, then hopeful. "I could have them delivered, but then dinner won't be ready for about three hours from now."

Jericho glanced at the boxes. Installing the television and whatever else was in those boxes was going to take a while. "Are you starving?"

Atticus shook his head. "No, I can wait. I'll call downstairs and ask them to run and get me what I need."

"They do your grocery shopping, too, Freckles? What kind of magical building do you live in?"

Atticus rolled his eyes. "One with concierge services."

Jericho shook his head. "You're so spoiled. Have you ever seen the inside of a grocery store?"

"In real life?" Atticus asked without a trace of humor. "No. The lighting looks so...anemic. Kind of like something out of a horror movie."

"You're adorable. I'm stealing some shorts."

"You should just bring some of your clothes here," Atticus said, then froze as if he'd proposed marriage.

Jericho didn't react, just dropped a kiss onto his lips and turned on his heel, throwing over his shoulder, "That's a good idea, Freckles. I'll do that."

Installation was not an easy task. Mostly because Atticus hated the black speakers that needed to be mounted on the walls for the sound system to work properly. When Jericho offered to just skip the sound system so he could return it, he scowled and shook his head. Jericho made a mental note to find a way to hide the speakers to fit in with Atticus's default decor. Did Atticus even know what spaces he liked?

Jericho had a hard time getting things installed properly because Atticus in the kitchen in a pair of sweatpants, pale skin and more freckles than stars in the sky on full display, was distracting. The way he moved around the kitchen with ease, chopping vegetables with a wickedly sharp knife that he wielded with precision. Atticus might not like killing, but Jericho guessed he was probably not as bad at it as his siblings implied.

Jericho had the television face down on the couch, attaching the mounting bar when he felt Atticus watching

him. He glanced up to see him leaning against the counter, arms crossed over his broad chest. Jericho's gaze drifted to toned abs and a trail of reddish-blond hair that disappeared into gray sweatpants that rode low on his hips.

"Whatcha doin', Freckles? Admiring the view?"

"It's a pretty good one," Atticus admitted.

Jericho's stomach did a somersault, but he didn't let it show. "Only pretty good?"

Before Atticus could respond, his phone erupted on the counter beside him. "Calliope."

Atticus had called when they'd woken up from their post-sex nap. Had she already found dirt on Gabe?

"Hey, Calliope," Atticus said, putting it on speaker. "Did you find something?"

"Not sure, honestly."

Atticus sighed. "Not helpful."

"I ran my usual checks, and while your boy is definitely on the take from...someone, I don't see anything specific leading to some kind of secret, corrupt organization. He's also not very good at hiding his ill-gotten gains. There's a very good chance that if the FBI doesn't get him, the IRS will. He's dropping large cash deposits on the regular, but there's no way to chase the cash."

"Is there anything at all that could tell you if he's just dirty or if he was specifically planted there to handle people like Jericho and their families when someone mysteriously goes missing?" Atticus asked.

Calliope made a 'hm' sound. "I could hack his phone, his computer. But that's going to take time. I would limit how

 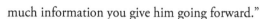

much information you give him going forward."

"Yeah, not a problem," Jericho muttered.

"I'll let you know if or when I find something."

With that, she was gone. Jericho sighed. Some part of him always felt like Gabe was…managing him. Always steering him away from looking into Mercy's case himself. But maybe he was reading too much into it. Either way, he was dirty. If he was turning a blind eye to gang activity, he was hurting people. A lot of people.

He snagged his phone from the charger beside Atticus's and dialed his brother. He answered on the third ring. "What?" he asked, clearly still sulking.

"I'm just checking in. Has anybody reported back with any information?" he asked.

Felix snorted. "I thought we answered to you and your boyfriend. Why would they come to me?"

"Felix, I don't have time for this. I know you're being territorial, but this is about Mercy. Remember? Atticus isn't…replacing you. You're my only family left, *didi*. Stop being difficult, please."

Felix heaved a sigh. "Fine. Nobody's reported back but Seven, and he said he had a weird conversation with Benny, the guy who sits outside the Dunkin' on 3rd street, but that doesn't mean much of anything. All conversations are weird with Benny. He's not all there. Always rambling about being abducted and experimented on by aliens. He's coo-coo for Cocoa Puffs."

Jericho waited for his brother to say more and, when he didn't, prompted, "Well, what was it that Benny said to

Seven that stood out?"

"Just that Benny showed him a scar."

"What kind of scar?"

Felix hesitated. "The kind that looks like somebody took his kidney."

SEVENTEEN

ATTICUS

When they went to the coffee shop the following morning, Benny wasn't there. Jericho said this was his usual haunt, that the staff often gave him the leftovers from the night before and the patrons chatted and bought him the occasional cup of coffee. They considered waiting for him, but Jericho said he was likely sleeping off a hangover under the overpass where many of the homeless made camp.

Atticus had experienced poverty, had lived in horrible conditions before Thomas had found him and decided to make him his first subject. But the rotted out trailer, where he'd spent the first eight years of his life, was nothing like the grassless stretch underneath the overpass where more than a dozen tents were all clustered together.

They weren't real tents. They were sheets and blankets tossed over heavy duty rope that spanned the length of the overpass. Some had tarps thrown over them to protect the occupants from the elements, but others didn't. A small group of people sat outside around an even smaller fire

242

trying to ward off the early morning chill of fall.

The change of seasons never seemed like some kind of cause for celebration to him. It was simply science. A thing that was inevitable. But to these people, the weather was a cause for concern, something to survive. It had been so long since Atticus had to worry about his survival it was almost like his past had happened to somebody else.

Jericho walked up to a woman with a young child who was bundled in an oversized jacket with a knit cap pulled down over their ears. "Hey, you seen Benny?"

She didn't answer him, her gaze guarded as she pulled the child closer, chucking her chin towards the tents. A man in an old Army jacket and a maroon beanie sat across from them. He looked at the two of them suspiciously. "Who wants to know?"

"My name is Jericho. I just wanted to ask him about something. I'm—We're—not here to cause any trouble."

The man stared hard at Atticus almost like he could sense he was a predator, or maybe he just didn't know why a guy like him would be hanging out under an overpass. Atticus had tried to dress down in jeans and a sweater, but his jeans cost three hundred dollars and his sweater was cashmere. Jericho had laughed, saying he just screamed money. It didn't feel like a compliment. It felt stupid and frivolous standing in this place.

Finally, the man said, "Purple tarp on the right." He flashed a knife. "Don't start nothin' and there won't be nothin'."

"Noted," Atticus assured him.

When they got to the purple tarp, Jericho called out, "Hey, Benny. You in there? It's Jericho. We met a few times at the coffee shop. You talked to my friend, Seven, yesterday. Can I talk to you for a minute?"

At first, there was silence, but then there was a rustling sound and a voice said, "Who's your people?"

Jericho and Atticus exchanged confused glances. "Our people?" Jericho asked.

"Your parents. Your folks. Who raised you?"

"Antonio and Mei Navarro," Jericho said, once more giving Atticus a *what the fuck* look.

The flap of the tent burst open, and a grizzly middle-aged man with a tuft of white hair and a missing front tooth stepped out, shielding his eyes from the sun like a vampire. Atticus could see why. The man's pupils and irises were obscured by severe untreated cataracts. There was no way he could see more than a foot in front of him. "What is it you want?" He narrowed his eyes at Atticus, looking him up and down. "You one of them doctors?"

Atticus couldn't help his surprise. "What?"

He tugged on his dirty coat with one gloved hand. "You one of them doctors from that charity? Helping Friends or something?"

"I'm not a doctor," Atticus lied, since it was clear the man didn't trust doctors.

Jericho tilted his head, stuffing his hands in his pockets. "Benny, do you remember talking to my friend Seven yesterday?"

Benny frowned as if trying to remember. "I think so."

Jericho kept his voice calm and neutral, hunching his shoulders in, either to ward off the cold or make himself seem unintimidating. "He said you had a scar on your stomach. Would you be okay showing it to us?"

Benny's spine stiffened and he looked around, even though Atticus was certain all the man saw was amorphous blobs of color. "Is this a trap?" he whispered, leaning closer.

"A trap?" Jericho echoed.

Benny nodded, eyes sweeping the area directly behind him. "Are you one of them?"

"One of who?" Atticus asked.

Benny's tone became conspiratorial. "The lizard people."

The man appeared to suffer from some kind of delusional thinking. Schizophrenia, perhaps. Paranoia for sure. Atticus shook his head. "Um, no. We're definitely not lizard people."

"That's what a lizard person would say," Benny reasoned.

He wasn't wrong. Atticus doubted any reptilian creature would tell the world they were inhuman. But Atticus didn't know how to prove he wasn't something more than human. Luckily, he didn't have to. Benny lifted his dirty blue sweater, revealing a wicked ten-inch scar that came from poorly approximated stitches. That was a hatchet job.

Jericho immediately looked to Atticus, askance. He nodded. It was most definitely a surgical scar. Was it from the same person who'd given Mercy her surgery? Hard to say. The water had left her skin far too compromised to compare the wound pattern. They needed more information.

Atticus dropped his voice to a conspiratorial whisper.

"We're not one of them but…we've seen them around. We know they've done things like this to other people. Did they do that to you? The lizard people? Did they give you this scar you told Seven about?"

Benny hesitated, once more swiveling his head around as if to make sure he wasn't being overheard. "They come at night," he rasped. "They come at night and take you to their spaceship and they do terrible things to you. Poke you with needles. Keep you in rooms with no doors."

Rooms with no doors? Atticus could have just written it off for what it seemed—a mentally ill man forgotten by the system—but something about his story rang true.

"When did they take you?" Jericho asked.

"Which time?"

Jericho gave Atticus another apprehensive look before peering back at Benny. "They've taken you more than once?"

Benny nodded. "The first time they took me, they brought me right back. But the second time they kept me for…longer."

"How long, Benny? A day? A week?"

Benny blinked. "When I went in, Bush was president. When I came back, he wasn't. That's all I know."

Jericho's gaze jerked to Atticus. That couldn't be a coincidence. What the fuck was going on? "Benny, do you remember where they took you? Abducted you?"

He turned to look off in the distance, even though Atticus knew he couldn't see whatever it was he was looking at. "I was sleeping in the alley behind Melvin's Deli. Over there." He pointed towards a tall building in the distance.

"Benny!"

The old man startled, head snapping towards the voice, raising a hand in greeting. "That's Sister Agnes. She brings us food every Saturday."

A woman with a blunt blonde bob cut and yoga pants approached them with a smile that would freeze lava. "Benny, dear, there's food over there by the fire. I don't want you to miss out."

Benny gave them one final look before returning his attention to her. "Is there bacon today?"

"Of course," she said brightly, wrapping an arm around Benny and guiding him away from them. "Excuse us, gentlemen."

As she started to walk away with Benny, Jericho called out, "What church are you affiliated with, Sister?"

"No church. I work with a local non-profit."

"Oh? Which one? My father works with many," Atticus asked.

Once more, that slippery smile slid across her unmarred face. "Helping Hearts. We provide meals and other services for the…disenfranchised."

Atticus nodded. "How nice."

"Have a blessed day," she said.

"Yeah, you too," Jericho managed.

Sister Agnes tracked them all the way out. Once they were back at the truck, Jericho turned to him. "What the fuck was that? That was weird, right?"

"Yeah, I think it's safe to say," Atticus said.

"Do you think the same people who did that to Benny

could have done it to Mercy?"

Atticus nodded. "It's possible. He said that happened to him somewhere around twelve years ago, which doesn't really make sense. That scar was from an open nephrectomy. We stopped using that technique in the nineties. Whoever did that surgery wasn't an amateur, but he certainly is practicing trench medicine. I think we need to head back to my father's place and regroup, have Calliope do some research in real time."

Jericho nodded, looking spooked. "Yeah, okay."

Atticus placed a hand on Jericho's shoulder without thought. "We're going to figure this out."

Atticus was relieved to see his father looking much more put together than the last time they'd seen him. He was still dressed fairly casually in jeans and a zip-neck cardigan, but he was clean shaven and sober. Well, sober enough. He nodded towards Jericho in a hello, escorting them down into the war room.

The twins were waiting, their clothing different but weirdly complimentary, like they'd coordinated their outfits. But that was the thing about the twins. They could speak to each other without words, could convey paragraphs with a look.

They were mirror twins, their features asymmetric. Asa's left eyebrow was slightly higher, but on Avi it was the right. Asa had a birthmark on his right hand, Avi on his left. But

when they faced each other, it was as if looking at their own reflection in the mirror. They were effectively the same person and they worked as a unit.

Thomas fell into a chair with a groan before hitting the button that connected them to Calliope.

"You've got Calliope," a chipper voice said.

"Callie, we need some information on a charity," Atticus said, earning a surprised look from both his father and Jericho.

There was the sound of heels clicking on tile and then a chair squeaking in protest.

Finally, she said, "Okay, shoot."

"It's called Helping Hearts."

"That sounds like some fake shit to me," Avi murmured.

Atticus agreed. He was about to turn his attention back to Calliope when a thought occurred to him then. A way to possibly get into Felix's good graces. He pushed the thought to the side, making a mental note to talk to Avi before he left.

There was the tell-tale sound of rapid-fire typing. "'Helping Hearts is a non-profit organization dedicated to connecting those without access to healthcare to the care they need.'" Calliope said, clearly reading it directly from a website.

"Sounds pretty innocuous," Thomas said, looking at the two of them.

"Yeah, except the woman said they provided meals to the homeless. What does that have to do with medical care?" Atticus asked.

Jericho spoke up then. "Can you pull up a list of employees or volunteers? Looking for a woman who goes by the name of Sister Agnes but who's apparently got no religious affiliations."

"Sounds shady to me," Asa said, earning a solemn nod from Avi. "What kind of psycho wants to cosplay a nun?"

"The kind that might con a clearly mentally ill man into donating a kidney and then convince him that aliens did it," Atticus said, voice grim.

"What?" Thomas asked.

"I've got my guys out there questioning people. Seven said—"

"Seven? You got a guy named Seven?" Avi asked.

"Is that pertinent to the story?" Thomas asked, leveling his dad stare at him.

"No, I guess not," Avi mumbled.

"Seven talked to a homeless man named Benny. He sits outside the coffee shop. He's crazy but harmless. Benny showed him a scar on his abdomen and told him aliens had done it when they abducted him."

"Couldn't he have done that years ago and is just conflating the two events?" Thomas asked.

"Possibly," Atticus agreed. "But there was something about the way that woman steered him away from us. I want to know who she is."

More furious typing. "Agnes Walker-Young. She's listed as the Donor Relations Manager and Eligibility Screener. Up until fifteen years ago, she was...she was the donor coordinator for the hospital."

Jericho looked at Atticus. "That can't be a fucking coincidence."

"So, what exactly does she screen for at Helping Hearts?" Avi asked.

"I'm sure she'd like the world to believe she screens for patients in need of help," Atticus said. "But I'm guessing that's not the case."

Jericho frowned. "And why did she lie to us about what the charity does?"

"She could just be out there doing her good deed for the week? Some people have a need to help others," Thomas reminded, reclining slightly in the plush office chair. "But I sincerely doubt it."

Atticus shook his head. "Yeah, she's no do-gooder. She's like us."

Thomas's brow furrowed. "Like you?"

"She's a predator. There was something missing in her eyes. We recognize each other," Atticus said.

The twins nodded. "He's right," they said in unison.

Atticus couldn't stop the surprised look on his face. He wasn't sure his brothers had ever agreed with him before. Ever.

"Yeah, I think Atticus is right," Calliope said. "It appears Ms. Agnes was terminated with cause before she started working for Helping Hands."

"Helping Hearts," the twins said.

It was eerie when they did that. Some days they were more in sync than others.

"Follow the money," Thomas reminded them. "Calliope,

can you tell us who owns the clinic?"

"Hold please," Calliope quipped. After several seconds, she said, "It's a shell corporation. If you want me to figure out who owns it, that's going to take a lot more digging than I can do on the phone with you."

Thomas grunted in disappointment.

Something occurred to Atticus. "Who's listed as the Medical Director?"

"Um…" Calliope started typing. "Dr. Joseph Reed, MD, Board Certified Psychiatrist."

"What's his story?" Jericho asked.

"Graduated from the University of Florida, did his residency at Johns Hopkins, a fellowship at George Washington University, and then went into clinical research."

Atticus sat up a little straighter. "What kind of research?"

"According to his LinkedIn profile, he worked for Braddock Pharmaceuticals researching drugs to help people with memory loss," Calliope said, then perked up. "Ooh, this is interesting. He was sanctioned by the board of medicine three times and then had his license suspended."

"Unfortunately, that doesn't mean much. There are a lot of shitty doctors out there," Atticus said.

"Well, how about this? The next job listed is for the US Military, top secret clearance. Why would the military hire a disgraced doctor?"

"Did he work anywhere after that?"

"If he did, it's not on his resume."

Jericho gave Atticus a look. "Nothing?"

"Yeah, it says he quit working for the military in 2002 and then nothing."

"It doesn't list his position at Helping Hearts?" Thomas asked.

Calliope sighed. "No, that I got from their generic-looking website page."

"So, we've got nothing," Jericho said, disappointment obvious.

"We have everything," Asa said, tone implying they were all stupid for not putting the pieces together. "Don't you see? That dude's resume screams psyops."

Psychological Operations. Military warfare. He was right. A psychiatrist with a history of shady pharmaceutical research could be just what the military needed for persuading assets to spill their secrets.

"Psychological warfare?" Jericho asked. "How?"

Asa took a swig from the energy drink sitting in front of him. "Why else would a psychiatrist be working for a drug company? Drug companies hire eggheads like Atticus. PhDs, not MDs. MDs don't usually come in until the local level. The clinical trials."

Atticus was begrudgingly impressed with his brother. It wasn't as if he thought Asa was stupid. He was a gifted architect and had designed numerous buildings that dotted their skyline. But he liked people to think of him as an idiot partier. Maybe that was just a deliberate move on his part.

"Why else would the military want to hire a psychiatrist for a position that required top level security clearance?" Avi asked.

"Calliope, can you do a blanket search for any kind of darknet site or message boards that mention Reed and the military or Reed and the drug company?"

"Yeah, give me a few hours and I'll get back to you when I have something."

Thomas disconnected Calliope and stood. The others did the same, following his lead as always. Atticus caught Jericho by the upper arm, saying, "Can you meet me at the truck? I need to talk to Avi about something really quick."

Jericho looked at him and then looked to Thomas, a hint of something flashing across his face. "Yeah, sure, Freckles. Do what you gotta do."

Atticus watched Jericho follow his father out, then turned to his brothers. "Avi, can I talk to you?" The twins exchanged long glances until Atticus said, "I hate when you two do that."

Avi sighed, closing the distance between them. "What's up?"

"I need a favor."

Avi narrowed his gaze, suspicious. "What kind of favor?"

Asa leaned in, suddenly very interested in the conversation. Atticus ignored him, directing the conversation towards Avi. "One that involves your label."

"Since when do you care about fashion?" Avi asked, gaze raking him from head to toe, implying he had no fashion sense.

"I don't care about fashion. But I care about Jericho, and his little brother, Felix, is a fashion design major. He hates me."

"Well, he's got good instincts," Asa teased.

Atticus let the snarky comment roll off him. "Would you consider taking him on as… I don't know. A paid intern? I'll pay his salary myself."

Once more, the twins exchanged meaningful looks. "You really like this guy, huh?" Asa asked.

Atticus closed his eyes, sighing deeply. "Yes. I really like this guy. And I need his brother to like me because Jericho is all he has and Felix is very…territorial."

Atticus waited for the hazing to start. But Avi just shrugged. "Yeah, I got you, big bro. Just have him call the office to set up a meeting."

Atticus couldn't hide his astonishment. "Thank you."

"It's just an internship and if his designs suck, he's going to be strictly a coffee boy."

Atticus snorted. Good luck getting Felix to be just a coffee boy. "A word of warning. He looks dainty, but he's definitely a force to be reckoned with. He's killed. More than once. He has a look that tells me he wouldn't hesitate to do it again."

"Stop, you're turning me on," Avi snarked. "I work in fashion, I know my way around feisty twinks."

"I never said he was gay."

"Is he?" Avi asked.

Atticus nodded. "Yeah. I'm pretty sure he is."

Avi gave a superior smirk. "I can handle him. But he better not fall in love with me."

Yeah, like that would be a problem for anybody.

Atticus rolled his eyes. "I'll let him know."

EIGHTEEN
JERICHO

Jericho left Atticus with his brothers, but he didn't go to the car. He followed Thomas down the hallway until he noticed Jericho followed. Whatever look he saw on Jericho's face had him glancing back down the hall before saying, "Let's talk in my office."

"Let's," Jericho said.

Thomas led Jericho across the enormous house and down another short hallway. With the exception of the desk in the corner, the room looked more like a library or study than any kind of office. Lots of dark wood, rich leather, and dusty books.

"Anybody ever read these?" Jericho asked, motioning to the shelves.

Thomas grinned, looking around at the thousands of books. "Only August. I'm almost positive he read every one of them cover to cover before he was ten. His appetite for knowledge was voracious."

Jericho glanced at the shelf to his left, wondering what

kind of child wanted to read books with titles like *The History of Palestine* and *The God Code*. A true psychopath, no doubt.

"I ran a background check on you. I also had you followed," Thomas said casually, crossing the room to the small bar against the wall, reaching for a bottle of amber liquid. It wasn't even noon yet.

Jericho made sure his tone matched Thomas's. "Find anything interesting?"

"Nothing I didn't already know. You have a brother, your father's deceased, your mother's...unwell. You have a record so clean it squeaks. Not even a speeding ticket. Given your extracurricular activities, I find that very impressive, especially when your 'crew' consists of boys barely old enough to vote. I know better than anybody that teaching a group of murderous teens how to not get caught is a full-time job."

Jericho supposed he should have been pissed that Thomas had him followed, but Atticus had already warned him there was a chance that his father would look into his life. Still, he couldn't stop himself from saying, "Yeah, but unlike your sons, my boys weren't born killers. They were made that way by life."

Thomas gave him a *fair enough* nod, gesturing for him to have a seat. Jericho almost refused but thought better of it. The couch was brown leather and supple beneath his fingers.

Thomas uncorked the crystal decanter, filling the glass with two fingers of the dark alcohol. "Not every psychopath

is born a killer. A large majority go on to be ruthless in far different ways. Corporate raiders, CEOs, defense attorneys, surgeons. But those are often the ones who come from good homes, without trauma. And even that sometimes doesn't matter. I found broken boys who needed a purpose and taught them how to utilize their evolutionary advantage to help the greater good."

Jericho snorted. The greater good. "You think the lack of empathy or remorse is a…gift? Some kind of superpower?"

Thomas poured another drink, holding it up. Jericho shook his head. It wasn't even noon. "I think that we live in a world full of dangerous predators. Who better than to eliminate them but other predators? A group of people who can kill without the burden of a conscience."

"I'm no psychopath and I sleep like a baby at night. My boys aren't conflicted. We understand that some people don't deserve the gift of breathing. You didn't need to find psychopaths to create a group of killers. You only need people whose sense of right and wrong is greater than their fear of getting caught."

"But what if you could have done what you did without having to have been radicalized by trauma? Surely, your mother's attack spurred you to act, to retaliate? How could it not?"

"But the choice was mine. Did any of your sons have a choice? At any point, did you ask if this is what they wanted, or did you just make it clear that this lifestyle came with a price tag? That they were killers first, your sons second."

Thomas faltered, then gravitated closer. Jericho couldn't

help but ask, "How could you even know they were all psychopaths?"

Thomas sat beside Jericho on the couch. "I'm a trained psychiatric professional. I know the warning signs."

"What if you got it wrong?" Jericho asked.

"I didn't."

"Not even with Aiden?"

Thomas's drink was halfway to his mouth. "Excuse me?"

Jericho shifted so he was turned towards Thomas. "Did you know one of your sons doesn't think Aiden is a psychopath? Did you know that when you adopted him?"

Jericho expected him to lie but, instead, he just said, "Aiden is a...special case."

"Because you love him?" Jericho prodded.

Thomas's pupils blew wide, studying Jericho, as if trying to discern exactly what it was he was getting at. "I love all my children," he hedged.

"Do you? Because Atticus is convinced you don't love him at all. In fact, he's almost positive nobody in this family cares if he lives or dies. He claims that doesn't bother him, but I know for a fact it does. You might have dulled his ability to feel remorse over killing scumbags who deserve it, but Atticus is no psychopath. He feels things...deeply."

Thomas looked dumbstruck. "What do you mean my son thinks I don't love him? Of course, I do. He's my first. My oldest. I'm not particularly affectionate with them because they don't like it. Too much touching or declarations of love makes them uncomfortable. I love my son even if he's incapable of loving me. And Atticus is a psychopath."

Jericho's jaw thrust forward. "You're wrong."

Thomas shook his head. "I'm not. Psychopathy is a scale. My son never had the ability to feel remorse or guilt or empathy for others. That doesn't mean he doesn't want people to feel those things for him. My son doesn't like being inconvenienced or questioned. He does have a lot of feelings about a lot of things, but that doesn't negate that he is a psychopath. Have you ever seen him express a shred of regret or even empathy for another person?"

Jericho nodded. "Yes. Me."

Thomas shook his head. "I've watched two of my sons find their partners over the last year or so. They are perfect for their significant others. They show concern for their feelings, show a shocking amount of self-awareness with how they can provide Noah and Lucas with what they need. They love their partners to the fullest extent of their capabilities. That doesn't make them any less psychopathic. If my son says he loves you, believe him. He likely means it. But you will find that when he wants something, he is ruthless about going after it and he will cut through anyone who gets in his way."

"That's not how he is with me," Jericho assured him.

Thomas took a sip, looking at Jericho from over the rim of his glass before saying, "Maybe you've just never gotten in his way."

"Even if Atticus is a psychopath, he still wants your love and respect, and he doesn't feel like he has that. So, if you were trying to be their father, you failed, and it's sad because none of you seem to realize how good a man you've raised."

"What's happening in here?"

The two turned to look at Atticus, who loomed in the doorway, his expression guarded.

"Nothing to worry about," Thomas assured him. "Your boyfriend and I were just having a chat. He's a good man. You've done well."

Atticus stood there in stunned silence for a full minute before nodding. He looked at Jericho. "We should get going."

Jericho nodded. "Good seeing you again, sir."

Thomas nodded. "You as well. I'll have Calliope call you when she has any updates."

They were almost to the office door when Thomas called out, "Jericho."

"Yeah?"

"Next time you come by, bring your family," Thomas said. "All of them."

Jericho did his best to mask his shock, just giving a nod.

Once they were back in the truck, Atticus turned on him. "What the hell was that all about?"

Jericho shrugged. "I'm not sure. I think your father was just feeling me out."

"That's the first time you've lied to me," Atticus said. "Don't do it again."

Jericho sighed. "Fine. I told your father I think he made a mistake with you. I told him that I don't think you're a psychopath and that I think it was super shitty of him to turn you into a killer."

Atticus's brows ran for his hairline. "Wow. I bet that

went over well."

"He told me I was wrong."

Atticus nodded. "I would expect nothing less. The alternative would be he was wrong, and Thomas Mulvaney is never wrong. Even when he's wrong."

This was hardly new information. Anybody who spent five minutes with Thomas could see he was used to going unquestioned. He carried himself with an air of superiority that came from being born into privilege. Still, the man seemed to genuinely care for his children, even if he never uttered the words out loud.

"He said he loves you," Jericho said.

Atticus blinked rapidly, like his brain was trying to process that information. "What?" he said, voice hoarse.

Jericho nodded, as if that would somehow make the words penetrate. "Yeah. He said he loves you and he's proud of you. That he's not affectionate because none of you seem to like it." A strange look crossed Atticus's face. "What?" Jericho questioned.

"Before August came, when it was just me and him... he was far more affectionate. Not in a creepy way like my real dad. In a...fatherly way. With each new arrival, he became less and less touchy feely. I thought he was just losing interest in us as children and saw us more as, at best, colleagues, at worst, science projects."

Jericho's heart squeezed in his chest. "That's...grim, Freckles."

"It really isn't a big deal. I'm almost forty years old. I have more than most people. I'm more than content with

my life as it is. "

"Including me?" Jericho asked, holding his breath.

Atticus hesitated, flushing like he was trying to gear himself up for something, finally saying, "Because of you."

Jericho gripped his sweater, dragging him across the seat to seal their mouths together in a kiss that left them both breathless. "Same, Freckles."

Atticus pressed their foreheads together, looking down at where Jericho still fisted his sweater, murmuring, "That's cashmere."

Jericho snorted, releasing the sweater and swiping his hand down the front to smooth away any damage. "My bad."

As Jericho turned over the engine, Atticus asked, "Why do you think my dad—Thomas—got it wrong? Why do you think I'm not a psychopath?"

"A lot of reasons. Because you felt for me after Lucas... did what he had to do. Because you worry so much about what others think about you. Because you embarrass easily, get flustered easily, you love being touched, being praised." Those were all true, but it wasn't the real reason he thought Thomas had gotten it wrong. "But mostly, I believe it because I'm pretty sure you're in love with me."

Jericho swore he could see Atticus's pulse fluttering in his throat. He flicked his tongue out to lick over his lower lip. "Pretty sure?"

Jericho shrugged. "It could just be wishful thinking."

"You want me to be in love with you?" Atticus asked, suspicious.

Jericho should have known Atticus would never put

himself out there like that. "I mean, I'd hate to think I'm in this alone."

Atticus's breath left him in a whoosh, like it had been punched from his lungs. "You…love me?"

Jericho shook his head. "Was there ever a doubt?"

Atticus made a face. "It was all doubt. I thought you just liked having sex with me."

Jericho kissed him again, his hand sliding down Atticus's chest to palm over his cock. "To be clear, Freckles. I *love* having sex with you, to the point of distraction."

A fist pounded on the window, forcing them to jump back guiltily. Asa and Avi stood outside the window, laughing. "Get a room," Asa said, voice muffled through the glass.

"Yeah, nobody wants to see that."

Atticus flipped him off. Asa pretended to catch it and put it in his pocket before returning the gesture. Then they were gone.

"I don't think you have to worry about your brothers not liking you," Jericho assured him. "That's pretty sibling-like behavior. Brothers are assholes."

"Speaking of, can we go back to your place?"

Jericho frowned. "Yeah, why?"

"I need to talk to Felix."

Jericho tried to put the pieces together as to why Atticus would deliberately put himself back in Felix's crosshairs. "Why do you want to poke that particular bear?"

Atticus looked slightly smug. "Because I've finally figured out a way to get him to like me."

Jericho snorted at Atticus's bravado. "That's a tall order,

Freckles. How exactly do you intend to melt my brother's icy heart?"

Atticus grinned, looking smug. "I'm going to bribe him."

Jericho opened his mouth, then closed it again. Felix was very emotional. And vain. And jealous. And lethal. But above all that, he was spoiled. "Well, shit. I…I think that might work. Let's go find out."

NINETEEN
ATTICUS

It was a full house at Jericho's place. There were at least eight boys crammed onto the sectional sofa at the back of the shop. They screamed at the television, gesturing wildly, nudging each other, sometimes violently. They all had their backs to Atticus, not that he'd be able to put names to faces, anyway. Some of them were total strangers.

Atticus did recognize two of them. The blue-haired boy, Arsen, and Felix, who stood out in every crowd. He sat perched on the back of the couch, wearing the same threadbare cardigan, one delicate shoulder artfully exposed. If Atticus had to guess, he'd say the way the sweater dangled was by choice. Everything Felix did seemed deliberate. He'd pulled half his thick chestnut hair off his face in a half ponytail. Very few people could pull off that look, but he did.

Jericho ignored the melee, dropping a kiss on his cheek. "See you upstairs, Freckles. Good luck." Atticus watched him ascend the stairs, admiring the way his jeans hugged

his ass.

Atticus stayed behind, watching Felix play a game that involved a dozen men in fatigues running through a barren wasteland. It only took a moment or two before Felix seemed to feel the weight of Atticus's eyes on him. He turned to glower at him with daggers in his eyes.

When Atticus didn't immediately disengage, an eerie calm settled over the boy's face, and he tilted his head in a way that would have probably unsettled somebody who didn't grow up in a house full of psychopaths. He handed the controller to the boy beside him, slipping over the back of the couch with a grace few could manage.

Felix moved like a dancer, each movement fluid and deliberate, like a snake winding closer. Beneath the oversized cardigan, he wore a cropped t-shirt with a Nike logo and a black skirt that swept to his ankles. Nothing about that outfit should have worked, yet it suited Felix perfectly.

When he was close enough to be heard over the noise, he arched one perfectly manicured brow. "Can I help you?"

Atticus leaned against the wall, crossing his arms. "I was hoping we could help each other."

Felix scrunched his face into a look of utter revulsion. "Please tell me you're not propositioning me with my brother right upstairs?"

Shock rocketed through Atticus's whole body. "What? No. Are you even old enough to drink?"

Felix pressed his lips into a thin line, giving Atticus a flat stare. "I'm old enough for a lot of things. What do you want?"

 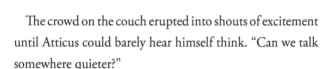

The crowd on the couch erupted into shouts of excitement until Atticus could barely hear himself think. "Can we talk somewhere quieter?"

Felix once more gave him a suspicious look, finally nodding his head towards Jericho's office. A safe choice considering there were windows to both the street and the inside of the garage.

The smell of motor oil assaulted Atticus the moment he crossed the threshold. How was the scent stronger there than in the work bay? Probably Jericho doing paperwork in a confined space. He was never quite able to get his hands completely clean. Atticus had always found the smell unappealing until it was on Jericho.

Once inside, Atticus took a seat in one of the chairs opposite what he assumed was Jericho's chair. Felix perched on the edge of the desk, just as he had the sofa. "So, what do you want?"

Atticus tried to think of how to start the conversation. "I know you don't like me."

Felix shrugged. "Okay, and?"

Atticus would have laughed if the stakes weren't so high. "Look, I like your brother—I…I think I even love him. I'm not going anywhere. I know you hate that, but it's a fact. You're territorial. I get that. I respect it. But you need to accept that I'm here to stay."

Felix sucked his teeth, making a face, then shifted to stand. "Great talk, thanks."

Atticus held up a hand. "I'm not done yet."

"Well, I am," Felix said, nose in the air.

Atticus sighed. "You have a huge advantage right now. You are in a position to negotiate, and I'm willing to do whatever it takes to make sure you stop treating me like a pariah. It's important to Jericho."

"You think you can bribe me into liking you?"

Atticus snorted. "I think I can bribe you into tolerating me. I know an opportunist when I see one."

Felix looked at him appraisingly before settling gently into the chair across from him, crossing his legs at the knee and leaning forward so his elbow rested on his thigh. "I'm listening."

"I get that you don't want to lose your brother's time or attention. I know that won't happen. Your brother loves you too much. But I thought maybe we could work out a deal. Hash some things out."

"Like?"

"Like he and I can't live here. This place is too small for all of us to live in. I would offer for you to come stay with us in my penthouse, but you would just refuse. So, here's my proposal. One day a week, Jericho is all yours. The two of you can hang out without me to distract him—"

Felix's nostrils flared and he sat up straighter, leveling those deep brown eyes—Jericho's eyes—at him. "You're giving me one whole day with my own brother. How generous," Felix said bitterly.

Atticus smirked. "You'll be too busy to see him most other days."

Felix's guarded expression slipped into confusion. "Why's that?"

"Because I've arranged for my brother to give you an internship at *Gemini*."

Felix had to know his brother was Avi Mulvaney, the owner and designer of the Gemini athletic brand. Felix went from anger to confusion to understanding in five seconds flat. "So you are bribing me?"

There was no real heat to his words, only a sudden dawning of the power he now wielded. "If this is a negotiation, allow me to counter. I get my brother three days a week and two weekends a month and the internship needs to be paid."

It wasn't bad as far as counter offers went, but he wasn't willing to concede two weekends a month without Jericho. "Two days a week, one weekend a month, and I'll make sure you're well compensated both in your internship and for whatever else might come up."

"Like what, exactly?"

Atticus shrugged. "A car? College tuition? A trip to Costa Rica? Whatever you want."

Felix eased back in his chair, pulling his sweater around him, a somewhat dreamy expression crossing his face. Atticus imagined he was now deeply entrenched in thoughts of what he might want to do with that level of funds at his disposal.

"You really love my brother?" he finally asked. His heart squeezed at the thought of Jericho. Before he could answer, the boy rolled his eyes. "Ugh, never mind. The dopey look on your face tells me enough. If you hurt him, I will literally take a butterfly knife to your testicles."

Atticus believed him. "Noted."

Felix rose, elegant all the way to the tips of his long fingers. "I'll let my brother and the others know we've reached an…understanding."

"Thank you."

With a single nod, he was gone, leaving Atticus staring after him. Putting Felix and Avi in the same building together had seemed like a good idea at the time, but now, Atticus wasn't so sure. The twins loved killing. They excelled at it. According to Jericho, Felix did as well.

Avi was an asshole. A total pain in the ass, who ran his fashion label like a military operation. Felix didn't strike Atticus as the type to take orders. He wasn't sure who he felt more sorry for. Actually, no. It was definitely Avi. Felix was going to blow through his brother's life like a pint-size wrecking ball, and Atticus couldn't help but smile.

The clash of egos would be legendary. They'd either kill each other or take over the world. Either way, it was bound to be entertaining.

Atticus laid between Jericho's jean-clad thighs, head on his belly as he threaded his fingers through his hair. Some random movie played in the background, but Atticus stared up at the skylight overhead. The sun had set, but the moon lit the clouds against an indigo sky. There was too much light pollution to see the stars but none of that mattered.

Atticus didn't care about the movie or the unruly boys downstairs or even the skylight above. All he cared about

was Jericho's touch, the heat of his skin, the soft fabric of his jeans pressing against his shoulders. It was soothing in a way he never thought possible, more relaxing than any pill.

It was strange how quickly he had come to crave Jericho's constant petting. It was…odd feeling so connected to one person, to feel totally at ease. No amount of familiarity had ever allowed him to relax his fear of embarrassment, of never being good enough for his family. But there was none of that with Jericho.

"What are you cooking me for dinner tonight, Freckles?" Jericho murmured, voice tinged with humor.

Atticus snorted. "If you want me to cook here, my guess would be something served out of a Styrofoam cup or box mac and cheese."

Jericho nudged Atticus's shoulder with his thigh. "Hey, don't knock box mac and cheese. That cheese sauce sticks to your ribs."

Atticus curled an arm around that same thigh, craning his head upwards. "Yes, because it's made of plastic and toxic chemicals."

Jericho rolled his eyes. "It is not."

Atticus sniffed delicately. "Well, it certainly smells that way."

Before Jericho could retort, Felix appeared in the open doorway, winded.

"What's up?" Jericho asked as Felix fought for breath.

"We caught that dude you were looking for trying to break in. He cut Arsen."

Jericho said, "How bad?" At the same time Atticus said,

"What dude?"

Felix looked between the two of them. "The one with the scar on his face. The enforcer guy. And Arsen's bleeding a lot. It's not deep, but it definitely needs stitches."

"Which way did he go?" Atticus asked.

Felix gave him a look like he was stupid. "He didn't go anywhere. We have him tied up downstairs. He just took a hunting knife to Arsen first. If we take him to the hospital they're going to ask questions."

Atticus nodded towards his keys on the slightly sagging dresser. "My car's still here from the other night. Under the trunk floor, there's a locker. 0323 is the code. Inside, you'll see something that looks like a tackle box. Bring it to me. I can sew him up here."

Felix gave him a look. "I thought you, like, studied rats and shit."

"I'm still a board certified physician." At Felix's dubious look, Atticus said, "Or we could just let him bleed if you want?"

Felix gave a dramatic sigh. "He's lying on the pool table."

"Where's Carlos?" Jericho asked.

Felix furrowed his brow. "Who?"

Jesus, this was turning into a 'who's on first' situation.

"The guy with the scar on his face," Jericho said, exasperated.

Understanding dawned. "Oh. Hanging from the lift. We gagged him 'cause he wouldn't stop threatening us."

Jericho rolled his eyes. "Typical."

Felix didn't respond, just turned on his heel and retreated,

presumably to grab Atticus's gear.

Jericho smacked a kiss on his cheek. "You sew up Arsen and I'll torture Carlos?" he said, as if they were divvying up household chores.

Atticus smiled. "Sure. Why not."

They descended the stairs into absolute chaos. Arsen was lying on the pool table swearing in Russian, gesturing wildly towards the guy dangling from the lift. His once white shirt was now soaked with blood. Seven was sitting cross-legged beside him on the table, holding a clean towel to the wound.

Nico and Levi were attempting to secure Carlos's legs, but he continued to kick, managing to land a blow to the side of Nico's head. "If this motherfucker kicks me one more time, I'm going to shoot him in the dick."

Levi managed to bind the man's legs with duct tape. "We need to get some information from him first." With Carlos secured by both wrists and ankles, the man began to shout at them behind his gag, flinging his body around like a fish out of water. They turned away from him, dismissing him to focus on Arsen.

Felix dropped the tackle box on the table, looking at Atticus with a quizzical expression.

"What's up?" Atticus finally asked.

"You have, like…a whole arsenal in your Volvo."

Atticus peeled the towel from Arsen's wound. It was a good gash on his abdomen, about six inches, deep enough to need stitches or staples, but not deep enough to have damaged any major organs.

Atticus flicked his gaze back to Felix. "Was there a question in there?"

"Do you kill people often enough to need a mobile kill kit?" Felix asked.

Atticus opened his tackle box. "Yes." He looked down at Arsen. "I can do this fast or I can do this pretty. Which do you prefer?"

Arsen blinked sweat from his eyes. "Fast. I'm already pretty."

Atticus snorted but reached for the surgical staples instead of the curved needle he would need to stitch him up. He grabbed a syringe, pulling up lidocaine. "This is just a local so you won't feel anything."

Arsen looked at Felix, then to Atticus. "Fancy. Usually, we just use whiskey. Is nice having an on-call doctor," he said, his accent thicker than it had been moments before.

Jericho came to stand by Atticus's side as he placed a gloved hand on the boy's belly. "How is he?"

"He'll be fine," he said, just as the boy unleashed a string of curses in Russian.

Jericho nodded, pushing the hair back off Arsen's forehead. "You did good." To Seven, he said, "Get the jumper cables, and turn up the stereo."

"I want to play with him, too," Arsen said sulkily.

Atticus pinched the edges of his incision together, deploying a staple to tack it closed before moving onto the next.

Jericho approached Carlos, using a box cutter to cut through his shirt. When the music swelled, he pulled the

gag from Carlos, who immediately shouted, "Do you know who I am?"

"So original," Atticus muttered.

"Yeah, Carlos. I know exactly who you are," Jericho said. That seemed to stop the other man in his tracks. "Carlos Perez, briefly headed the 4Loco crew before moving on to threatening and murdering people for Helping Hearts."

If Jericho was looking to rattle the guy, he'd clearly done it. He sucked his teeth. "Man, you don't know shit."

"But that's exactly why you're here, Carlos," Jericho said as Seven handed him the jumper cables, sparks flying as he tapped them together. "I have to say, I appreciate you coming to us. You saved us so much legwork. But I gotta ask, how did you find us?"

Carlos deliberately turned his eyes away from Jericho. Atticus looked down to place another staple just as the man began to make an inhuman sound. Something between a gurgle and a scream, his body convulsing as Jericho pressed the metal clips against his nipples.

"What was that?" Jericho asked. "I couldn't understand you."

"I wasn't even looking for you. I was looking for him." Carlos nodded towards Seven.

Seven's eyes went wide. "Me? Why me?"

When the man hesitated, Jericho jabbed the metal against the man's ribs, causing another garbled scream to erupt. "Fine! Fuck," Carlos cried, saliva flying as shocks still wracked his body. "Benny knew you, knew where you lived. Said you'd sent two men to talk to him but he

couldn't remember their names. But he remembered you. I found you. Followed you. Figured I could carve up you and your friends and leave a massacre big enough to stop anybody from talking."

Jericho scoffed. "You were going to murder all of them? You thought you could subdue seven men by yourself?"

Carlos looked over the sea of faces. "I thought they were children."

Jericho gave the man a malicious smile. "Thank you for your honesty."

Atticus placed another staple just as another scream ripped from the man. When Jericho pulled the cables away, Carlos slumped, breathing shallow and rapid, sweat pouring from his body, burns marring anywhere the cables touched.

"Easy, man. We can't get anything out of him if you kill him," Levi reminded.

"There's epinephrine in my bag," Atticus said.

Nico nodded. "Yeah, having our own private doctor on staff rocks. What else do you have in your magical tackle box?"

Atticus scoffed. "Pray you never need to know."

He finished closing Arsen's incision, pressing a clean bandage to the wound and taping it down. "There. Good as new."

Arsen glanced down at his dressing. "Thanks, Doc."

Atticus nodded. "Any time."

He could have gone and joined Jericho for his impromptu torture session, but he propped himself against the pool

 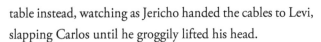
table instead, watching as Jericho handed the cables to Levi, slapping Carlos until he groggily lifted his head.

"Morning, Sunshine," Jericho said cheerily. "We're not done yet."

Carlos was drooling now but still managed to say, "Fuck you, man."

"I'm spoken for, thanks," Jericho quipped. "Nico…get the acetylene torch."

Nico's eyes went wide, but he didn't question Jericho, just walked towards the back of the shop. Carlos's head rolled towards Jericho. "Who are you fucking people?"

Jericho's smile unnerved even Atticus. "Neighborhood watch."

TWENTY
JERICHO

Jericho was doing his best to hold it together. Having the boys and Atticus in the room made it easy to remember the mission. Get whatever information they could out of Carlos regarding whatever shady shit was happening behind Helping Hearts. But all he really wanted to do was beat the man until his skull caved in. This man was responsible—at least, in part—for the kidnapping and death of his sister. He would pay for that with his life.

Nico handed Jericho the torch. When a white hot flame erupted from the end, Carlos's whole body convulsed almost against his will, his muscles curving away from the fire. The scent of piss and sour sweat permeated the space as Carlos lost control of his bladder. They never talked about that, about how a person could become so afraid he loses control of his bodily functions. It was an unfortunate byproduct of torture, expected but unpleasant nonetheless.

"Am I gonna have to use this, Carlos?" Jericho asked warily.

279

 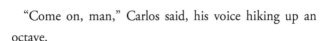

"Come on, man," Carlos said, his voice hiking up an octave.

Jericho tilted his head. "What happens next is up to you. I just need some answers."

It was odd torturing somebody with an audience. He could feel the heat of Atticus's gaze, could see Levi and Nico watching him carefully, not out of fear but a craving for knowledge, like Jericho was teaching a master class on torture.

Carlos's gaze was locked onto the torch in his hand. "Answers to what?"

"Let's start with what happened to Mercy Navarro?" Jericho asked.

"Who?" Carlos asked, seeming genuinely confused.

"The girl you tossed in the river missing a kidney?" Felix snapped.

Jericho had forgotten Felix was there. He was so quiet. It was one of his many talents. Nobody ever saw him coming. Jericho glanced over his shoulder to see Felix standing almost shoulder to shoulder with Atticus. Seeing the two of them together was like a sucker punch to his heart.

Jericho's attention returned to Carlos as a slight smirk erupted and died on the man's lips as if reliving something so great he just couldn't help the smile on his face. "Oh, her. It was a pleasure getting rid of that bitch. She was a problem from the second we snagged her."

Jericho's whole body went instantly hot, his vision becoming a deep, throbbing red at his words. He didn't remember moving, but he must have because Carlos was

screaming and there was a charred spot just beneath his ribs. The skin was already turning black.

Jericho wasn't worried about the noise. This was an industrial area. Very few people around this time of night. Anything they did here was drowned out by the music blaring at the front of the bay.

Gentle hands pried the torch from Jericho's fingers.

Jericho looked at Atticus. Whatever look was on his face had Atticus's gaze going soft. "I got this."

Jericho hesitated until Felix reached out and grabbed his arm, tugging him towards him before curling both arms around his, resting his head on his shoulder. Carlos blinked swollen eyes in their direction and Jericho got to watch the pieces fall into place.

"You're her family, huh?"

Jericho ignored the question.

Atticus advanced on the man, torch in hand. "Where did you pick her up?" he asked.

Carlos gave him a look like he was stupid. "Man, I don't fucking know. It was a decade ago."

"It was eight years ago," Felix snapped.

Carlos rolled his eyes, his lids falling shut until Atticus let the torch float close enough for the heat to revive him. "That shit all runs together. People come and go."

"Did you find her through Helping Hearts? Through Sister Agnes?"

Carlos scoffed. "That bitch. Yeah, she's the fucking recruiter. My job is just to remind people to keep fucking quiet."

Atticus moved closer. "Well, *you* better start talking or you're going to become a human candle." He looked at Levi. "Take his shoes off."

Levi hesitated for only a minute before he rushed to comply. Carlos was doing everything he could to try to wrestle his taped feet away from Levi. Nico ran to help, the two of them securing the hold on one foot.

"I'll ask again. Did you find her through Helping Hearts?"

"I can't answer that. Do you know what these people will do to me?"

Atticus sighed, clearly irritated with Carlos's noncompliance. He dropped to hunker down beside the foot held hostage between the two boys. "Want to see what an acetylene torch does to a person's toes?"

"Come on, man. Fuck. Fuck. Fuck. Don't do this." A scream ripped through him before the flame was even close enough for him to truly appreciate the severity of what was about to happen. "Alright! Alright. Fuck. Just alright."

"Tell us how it works," Jericho growled. "No more stalling."

"Fine," he said, gulping in breaths. "Agnes finds them! The subjects."

"The subjects? Research subjects?" Atticus clarified.

"For Dr. Reed?" Jericho asked.

"He runs the studies," Carlos hedged.

"What do you mean? What the fuck are these people up to?"

"Fuck this. Just light him up," Jericho snapped.

Atticus stood. "Where should I start?"

"Agnes looks for test subjects," Carlos blurted. "Helping Hearts is a front, a fake clinic that offers free healthcare to gain access to patients' medical history and run blood tests on them. She sends the information to Dr. Reed's coordinator, who determines whether they're the ideal candidate for his research."

"What the fuck is he researching that he couldn't just go through legal channels?" Atticus asked.

Carlos's lids fluttered like he was losing consciousness. Atticus slapped him hard in the face. "Lots of stuff. Mind control. Interrogation techniques. Erasing memories. Implanting memories."

"How does he decide who he's going to accept into this trial?" Atticus asked.

Carlos shook his head frantically. "Man, I don't know. I'm just the clean-up crew."

"Clean-up crew?" Lake muttered, disgusted.

Carlos's head lolled on his shoulder. "Yeah, when something goes wrong or when they need somebody silenced, they come to me."

Jericho charged forward, grabbing the man by his hair and yanking his head up. "How did my sister end up in that river?"

Carlos was fading fast. "My guess is her brain was too scrambled from the drugs and the experiments to continue using her for his research, so he scrapped her for parts."

Jericho punched the man in the face twice, finding no satisfaction as blood oozed from his mouth. "What the

fuck did you just say?"

"It's not personal. Not for Reed, anyway. That's just the way this works. Usually, he just turns them back out onto the streets lighter a kidney or a lobe of their liver. Sometimes, missing patches of skin for grafts. That's how he supplements his income. Sometimes, they don't do well after surgery. Sometimes, they get sick and die. That's where I step in."

"You're telling me that these clinics—clinics you deliberately put in poor neighborhoods—are screening centers for this piece of shit to find and kidnap research subjects and once they're too mentally incapacitated, then you sell off their internal organs?"

"It's not like that. Okay, it is like that, but Dr. Reed isn't a monster, he's just determined to continue his research, even if the Pentagon no longer finds his techniques useful. Most of his subjects live."

Seven gave a disgusted snort. "Like Benny? Who thinks aliens abducted him? Is that living?"

"He's breathing. He was homeless before we took him. It's not like we put him on the street. We just…returned him."

"So, when you took Mercy's kidney, her brain was already…" Felix started, then trailed off.

"Scrambled? Yeah. Most definitely. She would have been chasing butterflies in an institution for the rest of her life if her surgery hadn't gone wrong," Carlos said.

"Where is Dr. Reed doing these experiments? And don't you dare fucking tell me you don't know or I will make

you deep throat that torch while it's on," Jericho said, voice trembling with fury.

"The old VA hospital on MLK and Dobbs. The one that looks like an abandoned building with the ten foot chain-link fence around it with the razor wire. There are two floors below ground, some kind of tunnel system, too. Had something to do with moving VIPs to and from the hospital unseen. The government let him buy it for cheap when they let him go. It was his consolation prize."

"So, this is an off-book operation? Does he answer to somebody?" Atticus asked.

"No. He does this because he's passionate about learning all the ways he can manipulate the human mind."

"What a fucking saint," Lake muttered from where he stood against the wall with Cree.

Atticus dragged Carlos's attention back to him. "How many people are you holding down there now?"

"Like, how many patients?" Carlos asked.

Atticus looked at him like he was stupid. "Yes."

"Ten? Fifteen, maybe? I only go down there to collect my cash."

"So, you have access to the building?" Atticus asked, perking up. "Excellent. You're going to tell me how many staff members there are. What's security like? Cameras? Keycards? Where's the underground entrance?"

"Staff? I don't know for sure. Maybe three nurses on any given day. Two security guards doing alternate patrols around the perimeter. Two on either entrance of the underground entry points. But you're never getting in. You

 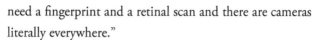

need a fingerprint and a retinal scan and there are cameras literally everywhere."

Jericho and Atticus exchanged glances. "So, we just need a finger and the eye of somebody who has access, right?" Jericho said.

They both looked at Carlos, who started shaking his head. "Oh, fuck you. Don't do that."

Jericho's smile was cold. "What's wrong, Carlos? Scared?"

"I don't want to die. I told you everything I know."

Atticus patted his face lightly. "Don't think of it as dying, think of it as being scrapped for parts."

TWENTY-ONE

ATTICUS

"Jesus, you did this?" Adam asked, voice filled with something between admiration and disbelief. Carlos's body was now slumped in a heap on the floor, exactly where he'd landed when they cut him down.

Atticus shrugged, looking around at the others. "Call it a group effort."

The group in question alternated between frantically working to clean all of Arsen's blood from the pool table and eyeing Atticus's brothers with interest and trepidation. Arsen was upstairs resting on Felix's bed. Lake and Cree had been sent to un-alive Sister Psycho with extreme prejudice, so only Felix, Levi, Nico, and Seven remained.

Not all of the Mulvaneys were in attendance either. August and Lucas were having dinner with Cricket and said it was 'too important to cancel.' Aiden was still on the other side of the country, and Archer had just flown out to Vegas that morning for another poker tournament.

So, that just left Adam, Noah, and the twins, definitely

not the crew he was hoping for but one he'd settle on just the same. He needed to get Carlos out of there sight unseen and in a vehicle that couldn't be traced back to any of them. Adam had picked up the van Atticus had used the other night from the garage and parked it in the alley behind the shop. Jericho had assured Atticus there were no cameras back there.

"Why couldn't one of your boyfriend's orphans do this?" Adam complained, earning a smack on the arm from Noah.

"Because none of us have cars, dick," Seven said, looking at Adam like he was a pompous prick. Which, to be fair, he was. All of the Mulvaneys were. If they were actually blood related, people might think their dickish behavior was hereditary. Of course, very few people ever saw them as they truly were. Publicly, they were Prince Charming and Mother Teresa all rolled into one.

Adam stared at Seven for a long moment before saying, "I like him."

Noah shook his head, smiling at Jericho. "We're happy to help," he said, as if they'd asked for help moving a sofa. Noah was a born diplomat, strangely adept at getting people to trust him.

Asa kneeled beside the body, peeling back the lid to gaze into the empty socket. "Where's his eye?"

"Over here," Nico said, jiggling the clear glass jar where the eyeball bobbed around in formaldehyde. As always, he had a lollipop in his mouth. Jericho said he'd used the candy to quit smoking and had traded one addiction for another.

"You taking souvenirs now, Gacy?" Adam asked, arching a brow at Atticus.

"We need to pass a retinal and fingerprint scanner in order to access the underground hospital," Jericho said, glowering at Adam.

All traces of friendliness slipped from Adam's face. Atticus tensed as his brother tilted his head in that way he did right before he started dropping bodies. Was this battle between them going to go on forever? What was Adam's problem with Jericho anyway?

"Do you have a tarp?" Noah asked, stepping physically between the two. "It would be really helpful if we had something to wrap him in."

Jericho stared down Adam for another minute before muttering, "I'll go look."

Noah looked to Atticus. "You know you can just take a panoramic photo of an eyeball or finger and Calliope can create a picture clear enough to fool the scanner."

"So, we don't need this?" Nico asked, sounding a bit disappointed.

"No. It's…messy," Noah managed.

Nico didn't skip a beat, rising up on his toes to jump shot the jar into the large black trash bin across the room, smiling when it hit the bottom with a satisfying thump.

"That was a great shot but you know we kind of need to take that with us," Noah said, sounding weirdly apologetic. "You can't just have some random guy's eyeball show up in your trash."

Nico's shoulders slumped, his expression contrite.

"I got it," Seven said, jogging to the bin and tying off the trash bag, pulling it free.

"Tell us about this underground hospital?" Asa asked Atticus. "Is that where that Reed guy is conducting his black book experiments?"

Levi looked from Carlos's corpse to Asa. "How did you know about that?"

Asa shrugged. "I called psyops from the jump."

"So, we just tortured this guy for fun?" Seven asked, gazing down at the corpse with interest.

Atticus sighed. "No, we tortured him because we needed to be sure what was happening and whether people were still in danger. We also needed a location."

"He also kidnapped our sister and allowed her to be held prisoner for eight years," Felix said.

Avi's gaze locked onto Felix for the first time, tracking him as he swirled around the room, wrapped in his grandma sweater, looking like a movie heroine with one arm across his trim waist and the other trailing long fingers along his collarbone. Felix seemed to live his life like it was a movie and he was the star and, as such, this whole body disposal ordeal was beneath him.

Atticus's stomach dropped as Avi's grin turned shark-like. "So, you're Jericho's brother? The fashion major, right?"

Atticus rolled his eyes, begrudgingly mumbling, "Felix, this is Avi. Avi, Felix. There, now can we get to the dead body at hand?"

They both ignored him. Avi let his gaze rove over Felix like he was naked. Atticus had to resist the urge to hide

Felix away from his perpetually horny brother.

Avi fixed Felix with a smile Atticus was sure would have dropped even the tightest of panties anywhere else. "Felix, huh? Like the cat?"

Felix's expression grew haughty, his chin jutting forward as he folded his arms across his chest. "No, Felix like Felix Mendelssohn, the German Composer."

Atticus sighed, relieved that Felix's underwear would stay where it belonged, at least for the time being.

But Avi apparently wasn't done. He stalked closer, stopping just inches from Felix, as if he wanted to drive home their size difference. If anybody else had done it, Atticus would have thought it was an intimidation tactic, but the way Avi was looking at Felix made it clear this was some kind of…mating ritual.

"I hear you'll soon be working…under me." The implication in his words had Atticus cringing. This was why Asa did most of the talking.

Felix scoffed, raking his gaze over Avi before flicking his eyes away as if he'd been weighed, measured, and found lacking in anything Felix wanted. "I'll be working *with* you. I don't work *beneath* anybody," he said, boredom bleeding into his tone.

Avi smirked. "That's okay. I'm sure you'll look just as good on top."

Felix flushed, blinking rapidly, as if processing Avi's words. Atticus was grateful Jericho was out of earshot or Avi would have had his lips ripped off and stapled to his ears.

"O-kay," Noah said, dragging everyone's attention away

from Avi and Felix. "That was both uncomfortable and highly disturbing, so kudos for that, but how about we get rid of the soon-to-be rotting corpse and figure out what we're going to do about Dr. McCreepypants and his little shop of hospital horrors? Sound good? Great."

Jericho returned with an ugly blue plastic tarp that had clearly seen better days. "Will this work?"

When nobody said anything, Jericho looked around at the Mulvaneys and his own boys, zeroing in on Avi and Felix still side-eyeing each other. "What did I miss?"

"I have no idea, but I wish I'd missed it, too," Atticus said.

Noah dropped down to his knee beside the corpse, taking the photos needed for the retinal and fingerprint scanner before Jericho and Atticus dropped Carlos onto the tarp and tied him up.

"What are you going to do with him?" Seven asked.

"Most likely take him to the meat packing plant and dump him in a vat of acid," Adam said.

Seven's brows furrowed. "Are you guys like cartoon villains? Who has access to vats of acid?"

Levi snickered.

"We have access to almost anything, really," Asa said with a shrug. "This just seems like the most efficient option if we don't want him turning up where he doesn't belong."

Nico pulled the lollipop out of his mouth. "But what do you do with the barrels?"

Asa shrugged. "After they've been…soaking long enough we seal them and toss them."

"Toss them where?" Levi asked.

"That's classified," Adam said, giving them a wide grin.

The boys quickly lost interest in the conversation. Atticus looked at Jericho, who was gazing down at the tarp like he was contemplating kicking it a few more times. He would definitely need to find a way to relax him before they went to his father's house or there was a ninety-seven percent chance he and Adam would end up in a fist fight before the meeting was over, and they just didn't have time for that.

"Meet us at Dad's tomorrow. We need to come up with an extraction and elimination plan. The numbers aren't in our favor. Especially being down Archer and Aiden, but with Jericho picking up the slack, I think the five of us can handle anything that pops up."

"Oh, fuck no," Felix snapped. "Do you really think you're going in there without me? Without us?"

Avi gave Felix a look that was somehow both suggestive and belittling as he leaned in close. "Don't worry, kitten. We've got this. I wouldn't want you to mess up your makeup."

Felix looked like he was going to literally burst into flames. "I could surgically remove your testicles without so much as smudging my eyeliner, you cretin."

If he was looking to make Avi mad, he clearly didn't know him. "God, that's hot. Just remember, kitten, in the office you have to call me Mr. Cretin. I wouldn't want anybody to think I'm playing favorites."

Felix's face screwed up into a mutinous look. "How about I call you—"

"Hi. Hello. It's me again," Noah interrupted. "Once again bringing everybody back to the task at hand." When he had everybody's attention, he continued. "We will all meet at Mulvaney headquarters at nine a.m. Jericho can decide who should be on his team for this mission. I think six on each side should be sufficient. Okay?"

There was some grumbling but, mostly, they nodded.

"Great," Noah said. "Atticus, send all pertinent details to Calliope. We need to see if we can find any available blueprints so we know what we're walking into. I'll send her the pictures so she can create the high resolution images. Any more questions? Concerns? Apologies? No? Then we should get out of here so we can drop off the corpse and get the van back where it belongs before morning."

Just like that, the small crowd dispersed. Nico and Levi went back to playing video games, and Felix shot one more glare in Avi's direction before heading up the stairs to check on Arsen.

"Do you want to sleep here or head to my place?" Atticus asked when it was just the two of them.

Jericho glanced at him, eyes dull, expression distracted. "Whatever you want to do, Freckles."

Atticus guided him towards the back where both their cars were parked, handing Jericho the keys to the Bronco. Once they were inside and had the ignition turned over, Atticus slid across the bench seat, one hand sliding up Jericho's thigh as his mouth found his jaw.

Jericho let his head fall, granting Atticus unfettered access. He took it but that wasn't the only access he was

looking for. He fumbled as he attempted to open Jericho's jeans one-handed. He quickly got the message, batting Atticus's hands out of the way to shove his jeans and underwear down his thighs. "Fuck, Freckles. You always know just what to do."

Atticus licked his palm, closing his hand around Jericho's cock, feeling it harden in his hand with each firm stroke. Jericho turned his head to capture his mouth in a kiss that didn't end. Atticus swallowed every groan, every breathy exhalation as he worked Jericho with increasing speed until he was just fucking into Atticus's fist, hand knotted in his hair to make sure Atticus couldn't pull away. As if he would.

When Jericho finally ripped his mouth away, it was only to say, "I'm gonna come."

Atticus made an approving sound against his throat as Jericho came, his hot seed coating his fingers.

After a minute, Jericho reached for Atticus's zipper. He was much smoother with the process than Atticus had been, but as soon as his cock was freed, Atticus smeared his fingers through the mess on Jericho's belly, using it to ease the slide of skin on skin as he stroked himself.

Jericho literally snarled against his ear. "Fuck, Freckles. That's so hot. You're so fucking hot. You like the feel of my cum on your skin? I do. I fucking love it. Love knowing I've marked you, inside and out. That you're just mine. Fuck, I want to watch you come. Show me."

A full-body shudder ripped through him as he came, his hand working himself until he physically couldn't take anymore. Atticus let his head fall to Jericho's shoulder. "I

 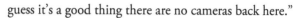

guess it's a good thing there are no cameras back here."

"If I'd have known this was going to happen, I would have installed some."

Atticus chuckled. "Let's go home. I'll make us some dinner."

Jericho gave a weak laugh. "Give me a second, Freckles. I need the blood to return to my brain before I try to drive again."

Atticus righted his clothing. "Fine, but hurry up. I'm hungry."

TWENTY-TWO

Jericho chose which boys to bring using very specific criteria. Skill set, time, health, and well, availability. Luckily, Felix made the cut, so Jericho was spared the theatrics that took place whenever his brother didn't get his way. He also chose Lake, Levi, and Seven. Nico and Cree had to work, and Arsen was still recovering.

Walking them through Thomas Mulvaney's mansion was like trying to herd a bunch of kids through Disney. There was just too much to distract them. They kept trying to wander off. Atticus seemed to find it amusing, a smirk on his face as he led them to the war room.

The Mulvaneys were already waiting. August and his husband, Lucas. Adam and Noah. The twins. Initially, Jericho couldn't tell one from the other. Now, he could tell the difference because Avi was singularly focused on Felix, winking as soon as he walked in. To his credit, Felix rolled his eyes and ignored him. But it was still disconcerting.

Jericho wasn't sure he wanted to know exactly how Felix

would fare in this 'internship.' He didn't hover over his brother because he had seen him take on people three times his size without breaking a sweat. But this was different. There was something unnerving about the way Felix made a pointed decision to ignore Avi. That wasn't Felix's style.

Jericho shook the thought away. That was a crisis for another day. This was about revenge. Revenge for Mercy. Revenge for Benny. Revenge for anybody who had ever had the misfortune of running into that bitch who called herself Sister Agnes. The bitch that was still alive.

They'd waited for her all night, but she never came back. Jericho didn't know if she was in the wind or just laying low, but he wouldn't stop until she was sharing a space in hell with Dr. Reed and all his staff members.

Atticus gestured for them all to sit, which they did, but it was clear they were sizing each other up from both sides of the table. Thomas burst through the door with not a single hair out of place, looking like he'd just injected caffeine straight into his veins. He wore dress pants and a white button-down shirt with the sleeves rolled up to the elbow, highlighting his perfect tan. He took each of them in with a smile. "Welcome, everybody," he said, like he was about to give the keynote address at KillerCon. He seemed pleased to have so many more people in the room.

Even Thomas's own children looked at him with a mixture of curiosity and trepidation.

"Damn, Daddy," Seven muttered under his breath.

Thomas didn't acknowledge what they'd all heard, but the smallest of smiles formed, then disappeared, before he

cleared his throat. The screen lit up on the wall, drawing everybody's attention.

"You there, Calliope?" Thomas called.

"Does Raggedy Ann have a cotton crotch?" Calliope chirped through the speaker.

Jericho snickered along with the others.

Lake nodded towards the speaker. "I like her."

"Oh, my God. Look at all of you. There are so many," Calliope said.

"She can see us?" Jericho asked, genuinely surprised.

Atticus shrugged. "Yeah, apparently."

"That hardly seems fair," Asa quipped. "How come you can see us but we can't see you?"

Calliope made a dismissive noise. "You're celebrities. I knew what you looked like even before I started working with Thomas."

"Still, I don't understand why we can't just meet her," Avi said.

"Because you can't. It's for her protection," Atticus said. "Drop it."

"Since when are you so concerned about Calliope?" Adam asked, narrowing his gaze at Atticus.

"I'm concerned about all of us. I don't know about you, but I wouldn't do well in prison," Atticus said, shuddering at the thought.

"We'd do great in prison," the twins said in unison.

Atticus looked them dead in the eye. "Not if you went to separate prisons."

Jericho had to bite back a smile at the stunned looks on

the twins' faces. It was clear the two had never been apart for any length of time. Jericho couldn't have ever imagined wanting that level of intimacy with another living soul before Atticus.

"Why would you even suggest that?" Asa asked, scandalized.

"Do you really think they let you pick your roommates in prison? With the amount of bodies we've dropped, they'll put us underneath the jail. Eight different jails. So, how about we just don't get caught?" Atticus asked.

August nodded. "Atticus is right. We're wasting time. Let's knock out a plan. Lucas and I have other, more important, things to do."

Lucas beamed, his hand lifting to rub August's back. "Let's do this, quick and dirty."

"Kinky," Seven snickered.

"Calliope, pull up the blueprints, please," Thomas said, a bit exasperated but in a fond way.

Schematics appeared on the screen.

"Shit, we need to get us one of those screens," Lake said.

"Okay, these blueprints are from when the hospital was first built, so there's no guarantee this is up to date, but it's all we have," Calliope cautioned.

"Noted," Thomas said.

The schematic moved, becoming a three-dimensional model. "There are two ways into the building. There's the main entrance, which requires you to enter through the hospital and take a staircase down to the sub-basement levels." A red circle appeared around the space in question.

"The other entrance requires parking in this garage"—another map appeared showing a square that Jericho assumed was the parking garage—"and taking a door that leads to a tunnel that leads to the second entry point."

"Do we have any information regarding security?" Asa asked.

"Oh, so much," Calliope quipped. "If these people are collecting data for the military, they should be court-martialed just for their shitty firewall. I've already gained access to their system. Once we get closer to go time, I'll loop the footage, so the guys in the security booth are blind. You'll still have to take out the two armed guards patrolling topside and scale some pretty intense razor wire if you want to go in the front door."

"We need two teams, clearly," Noah said, looking to Thomas as if to make sure he agreed. Thomas gave a singular nod. "I think Jericho should lead his guys and August will lead ours. Jericho will be red team for this. August will be blue."

Everybody looked at Atticus. He frowned in confusion. "What?"

"You're not going to argue that you should be lead as the oldest?" Avi asked.

Atticus rolled his eyes. "We're not children. I just want to get in and get out with all of us in one piece."

They all stared at him for a long moment before Asa nudged Avi, muttering, "That dick must be fucking magical."

Felix groaned. "Gross."

Avi feigned contrition. "Sorry, kitten."

Thomas looked back and forth between Felix and Avi, eyes narrowing. Avi immediately dropped his gaze to his hands. How did a man get seven psychopaths to respond with such deference? Were they afraid of him? Grateful? Could psychopaths be grateful?

Jericho reached beneath the table to grip Atticus's thigh, earning a startled response before his hand came to rest on top.

"We should blitz attack from both sides," Noah continued. "They'll have nowhere to go. This will give you a huge advantage, but also means people are going to fight for their lives by any means necessary. This means you need long range weapons. Guns with silencers. Blue team should breach the front since we've got more experience with large scale elimination missions. Also the patients are less likely to be closer to the front entrance. Red team will take the back and meet in the middle."

"What's the goal here?" Seven asked. "Are we shooting to kill?"

Thomas smiled at Seven. "Yes. If they aren't a patient, they need to be eliminated. You go in with faces and tattoos covered. There won't be any staff left to ID you but the patients might, and we don't want this backfiring on us."

"What about the patients?" Felix asked.

Thomas studied him. "What do you mean?"

Felix bit his lower lip, worrying it between his teeth for a few seconds before saying, "I mean, Carlos said these people have had their brains scrambled for months, even

years. Are we just going to dump them on the street?"

Lucas looked at Thomas, shaking his head. "We can't do that to them. If we dump them on the street, they'll get lost in the system. They'll end up homeless and completely helpless."

Thomas nodded slowly. "Calliope, you know who to call, don't you?"

"Yes, I'll make sure there's a team standing by to take the patients to the…place," Calliope stumbled.

"The place?" Lake asked.

"That information is need to know and none of you need to know," Thomas said, not unkindly. "There are many powerful people who help me do what I do. People who would get into a lot of trouble if their identities ever became known."

Lake dropped his gaze to his hands folded on the conference table. "Oh."

"Which brings me to another matter," Thomas said, earning the attention of all in attendance. "Jericho, it seems as if you're here to stay and, by extension, so is Felix. That invitation is being extended to all of you as well, if Jericho is willing to vouch for you."

Jericho looked at his brother, who seemed to take that information in stride. He and Atticus must have had quite a talk.

"Being part of this family comes with a lot of hazards, one being if we're ever found out and you're linked to us, none of us are ever getting out of prison. I don't think that will scare you, but these boys are barely old enough to

drive. They should know what they're getting into."

Seven scoffed. "You think jail scares us? We go where Jericho goes. We're ride or die."

Lake and Levi nodded. "What he said."

Thomas nodded. "Then it's settled. We go in tonight. After shift change. Coms stay on. Calliope will be your eyes and ears. Noah and I will be watching from here. Jericho, I would suggest picking one team member to get the patients to the garage to make the drop."

"I'll do it," Lake said without hesitation. He looked to Jericho. "If that's okay."

Jericho nodded. There was truly nobody better for the task than Lake. He was calm under pressure. He had an aura of peace around him that people responded positively to.

"Then we go in tonight."

"Red team, are you in position to breach the tunnel?"

Jericho and his boys sat dressed in all black in another of Thomas's plain white work vans. The man seemed to have an endless supply. They had balaclavas, but they were rolled up so they could still see each other's faces. It was chilly but not cold enough to want the rough cotton clinging to his face.

If they were somehow caught sitting in the middle of the nearly deserted garage, it wouldn't matter if their faces were covered, anyway.

"Red team's a go," Jericho said, making sure the round was chambered and the safety off. The others did the same.

"Blue team?" When there was no answer, Noah said again, "Uh, blue team?"

There was a sound like scraping, and then August's voice came over the line, calm but clearly irritated. "Blue team's a go."

"Everything good?" Noah asked hesitantly.

"Yeah, except your fiancé decided to drink a gallon of coffee before we left and made us stop 'cause he had to take a piss," one of the twins said.

Adam's surly voice appeared on the line. "I didn't sleep for shit last night. I had to dump a body, remember?"

"Everybody, focus," Noah said, bringing their attention back to the task at hand. "The security footage is looped for twenty minutes. Blue team, taking out security is priority one. Red team, safe patient extraction is your goal. Everybody know what they're doing?" Everybody answered in the affirmative. There was a long pause, and then suddenly Noah said, "Okay, three...two...go."

Jericho and the boys obscured their faces and poured from the van, breaching the barely visible garage door. The tunnel was short and surprisingly clean and bright. Even megalomaniac doctors seemed to worry about the safety of their workforce. Or maybe he just didn't know how many people he wanted to trust with his super secret underground lair. In truth, it was probably just untouched from the elements outside so had withstood the time since the hospital closed until Reed took it over.

Jericho felt a sliver of anticipation as they reached the end of the tunnel and held their position. They had no

idea what they were walking into. Calliope would tell them where to go moment by moment, but for now, it was a mystery what lay on the other side of the door. The hospital was in the shape of a cross with a nurses station smack in the middle.

"Red team's in place," Jericho said in a stage whisper.

"Hold for go," Noah said. "What's your position, blue team?"

"The two security guards have been neutralized topside, but Atticus is limping," August said.

"What happened?" Jericho barked, adrenaline sparking through his blood.

There was the sound of snickering through the piece in his ear. "He got caught on the razor wire and cut his leg. Don't worry, Jericho. Freckles says it's only a flesh wound," one of the twins taunted.

"Go fuck yourself," Atticus said, tone sulky.

Jericho smiled. God, he fucking loved him. He didn't love the way his brothers constantly taunted him, though. He was going to end up fighting the entire Mulvaney clan if they didn't back off of Atticus.

"I'd prefer to hear it from him. You good, Freckles?"

"I'm good. Promise," Atticus said, sounding resigned to the level of teasing he was likely to get over his small snafu.

Calliope's voice suddenly appeared in their ears. "Alright, children. My name is Calliope and I will be your tour guide for this excursion. Do what I say and everybody will make it out alive."

Calliope's voice loosened something in Jericho's chest.

She always added much needed levity to the conversation.

"We're in luck today, because there doesn't appear to be anything in the sub-basement except the generator and other various machinery, so that narrowed our playing field immensely," she said.

That was something. Jericho had been dreaming about revenge for so long, but now, he just kind of wanted it over with. He wanted Reed dead, the patients freed, and for all of them to walk away unharmed.

"Red team," Calliope said, pulling Jericho's focus. "You are in the north hallway. Just inside the door, you'll find four patient rooms, two on either side. Past those rooms, there's a nurses station. There are currently two employees sitting there and another in a break room down the east wing. You're going to need to work fast to get the patients freed. I'm releasing the locks on their rooms as soon as you enter but, remember, they may not all be lucid."

"Roger that," Jericho muttered, pointing at the boys standing beside him. They nodded in understanding.

"Blue team, you have six rooms on your end. You need to eliminate the staff at the nurses station as well as free the patients and get to the north tunnel exit. Also, not to be the bearer of bad news, but it appears Carlos was a dirty liar in addition to being a vicious killer. There aren't four guards. I currently count two armed guards at the security station at the end of the right hallway. Two standing in the break room with the other staff member, and three armed men in scrubs all carrying. I wasn't expecting the staff to be armed."

Neither was Jericho. Once more, his trepidation seemed to ratchet higher. Fuck. He was dragging his kids into a war zone. How did Thomas do this? "Head on a swivel, boys."

Jericho pulled the phone given to him by Thomas that morning, hoping the hospital hadn't somehow realized Carlos was no longer with them. It would suck if his access was revoked. Before he could put the phone to the scanner, Calliope swore in his ear. "Red team, there's a guard heading straight towards you."

No sooner had the words left her mouth than the door swung open. The guard startled, clearly not expecting to encounter five masked men brandishing guns. Jericho yanked him through the door, while the others filtered inside. The man tried to reach for his gun but Jericho shoved him hard, causing him to stumble backwards. Jericho raised his arm and fired, putting a bullet between his eyes, watching the man fall into a heap on the ground before advancing into the hall.

The boys were already trying to rouse the patients, many of whom were strapped down to their mattresses with thick leather cuffs on their wrists and ankles. It was clear they were drugged and frightened. Still, Lake, Levi, and Seven managed to get them on their feet, doing their best to keep them quiet. The hallways were longer than Jericho had imagined, but he could see blue team—and Atticus—at the end of the hall. Even with a mask on, Jericho would know him anywhere.

Sparks shot through him as Atticus made eye contact. He wished they were on the same team, but he knew he would be too distracted worrying about Atticus's safety. That was how mistakes were made.

Calliope's voice broke the spell. "Incoming."

They all froze as a man in wrinkled blue scrubs crossed directly in front of them in the hallway. His eyes were locked on his phone screen, oblivious of Felix lingering just on the other side of the wall.

For a moment, it appeared he might just walk right by, but then the man looked up from his phone, doing a double take when he saw them.

The man dropped his phone, reaching for the gun in his holster. "Hey—"

He was dead before the word even left his mouth, his forehead exploding outward, knocking him off his feet. Jericho's gaze darted up to see Adam holding the weapon that fired the shot. He gave a single nod, which Jericho returned.

There was a scream from somebody at the nurses station, and then all hell broke loose. One woman tried to run, another pulled a firearm from somewhere beneath the desk. The confident way she handled the weapon let Jericho know she was no stranger to guns. But she had too many targets. She froze, trying to assess who posed the biggest threat. She settled on August, likely noting he had guns in both hands.

Felix raised his arm and fired, hitting the woman in the neck. She crumpled to the floor, blood pumping onto the linoleum floor. The patients began to scream, forcing Lake to push them all back towards the rooms.

"Security incoming, both hallways," Calliope said, voice

urgent.

Gunfire rang out, the noise deafening in the echoing hallway. The first bullet was nowhere near any of them, but the second missed Atticus by less than a millimeter, causing Jericho's heart rate to skyrocket.

The twins were missing. They were likely securing the other patients. August gave Jericho a hard stare, then stepped into the fray, raising both guns, unloading in the direction of the guards. One hit its mark, knocking the man off his feet. The other grazed the other guard's shoulder, but he managed to duck into a room before August could finish the job.

Jericho and Adam both turned to take the east hall where four men charged down the hall, guns drawn. As soon as they were in view, more gunshots rang out, but it was hard to aim while running, so every one of them missed. Jericho took two without breaking a sweat, leaving Adam to take out the other two. One went down easy, the other ducked behind a wall.

Adam didn't chase the man. He stood stock still, arm outstretched. After a moment, the man peeked around the corner. Adam's bullet went straight through his eye. How long had these guys been training? It was as if Thomas had put a gun in their hands their first day with him.

Asa and Avi appeared, herding the frightened patients to the nurses station where all four hallways intersected, hesitating until August put a bullet in the final staff member.

"All clear," Calliope said. "Sweep the offices for stragglers."

"Where's Reed's office?" Jericho asked.

There was silence on the other end of the ear piece, then

Calliope said, "Just keep heading down the west hallway."

"Is he there?"

"I don't know, sorry. There's no camera in there."

Jericho stepped around the corner, gesturing for the others to send the terrified patients across the hall. They kept fighting them, uncertain whether they were also bad guys or maybe even a vivid hallucination.

Once they were on the other side, Lake said, "You're safe. We're going to get you out of here."

They didn't look like they understood or trusted that he was going to do either of those things, but one look at the bloody body on the floor and they became very compliant. "You're sure we have all the patients?" Jericho asked Calliope.

"Checking the cameras," she said. "Yeah. Patient rooms are empty."

"Get them topside," Jericho instructed Lake, Levi, and Felix.

They nodded, ushering the patients through the door to the tunnel.

"Look for a black transport van," Calliope said. "They're waiting to take the patients to another hospital. They won't ask questions."

Once they were gone, Jericho turned, stalking back to Reed's office. He cautiously jiggled the handle. Locked. Something about that infuriated him. Was the man seriously cowering in his office?

Jericho backed up, giving himself enough room to shock and awe the door from its hinges. When it crashed inward,

Jericho swept his gun from left to right, but it was empty. Jericho's heart squeezed. All he'd wanted was to be able to put a fucking bullet in that monster's head, to see the fear in his eyes as he realized this moment would be his last.

August's voice came over the speaker. "Left hallway secure. Targets eliminated. Rooms cleared."

When Jericho didn't respond, Seven said, "Right hallway secure. Rooms cleared."

"Patients secure and en route, awaiting further instructions," Lake said.

"Keep the van running," Noah said. "Everybody in one piece? Atticus's booboo aside."

"Yeah," Jericho said. "Red team's good."

"Blue team's good, too."

"We'll meet topside," August said, gesturing to Jericho.

The plan was for each of them to return the way they came, retrieve their vehicles, and muster back at Thomas's super-secret garage to pick up their own cars. Jericho knew what they'd done was a good thing. The patients were free, the staff was dead. But Dr. Reed and Sister Agnes were still free to set up shop and do this all over again.

Jericho made his way back down the hallway, his gun at his side, Seven following close behind. Jericho pushed the door open, taking two steps, stopping short when he saw her.

Sister Agnes, pointing a gun directly at him.

The guard's gun.

Fuck.

The woman's voice shook as much as her hands when she said, "Don't fucking move."

TWENTY-THREE

They were halfway up the staircase when Atticus heard it, the sound of a revolver cocking and a woman's voice ringing through the earpiece. The others heard it, too. Atticus froze, an icy fear tightening around his heart, constricting his breathing. What the fuck was going on? Had they not been clear? Had a nurse or doctor managed to hide themselves away? There was no way. Calliope had checked.

Then he was barreling back down the stairs, taking them two at a time, pausing only when he made it to the door that separated him from the south hallway. If he went charging in there, Jericho could die. Jesus. Jericho could die. Atticus suddenly felt like he couldn't breathe. He took a deep breath and let it out.

Behind him, he could hear the others, but he didn't wait, slowly easing the door open.

"What's happening right now?" Noah asked through the ear piece.

Jericho's voice was clear and steady. "Agnes? What are

313

you going to do? We're not here alone. That revolver has six rounds in it and there are ten of us. Put the gun down."

He was telling them what was happening without alerting her he had a hot mic.

"Fuck you. You put your gun down," Agnes snarled.

This bitch had to know she wasn't walking out of there, right? Maybe she thought she could just go back the way she came. If she thought she was cornered, she might start shooting. Who knew the state of mind she was in?

"Shit. Okay. Can anybody get behind her?" Noah asked. "Lake? Levi? Felix? Are you still in the garage?"

"That garage door's hinges are rusty and that hallway echoes like a motherfucker. She'd clock us before we were anywhere near them," Lake said.

"But maybe that would give him a chance to shoot her," Felix said, voice choked.

"No," Atticus and Jericho said at the same time.

"What? No, what?" Agnes said, her voice ratcheting up a notch.

"I'm just telling my colleagues to stay back. That's all. You're in charge."

"I'm not just going to let this bitch kill my brother," Felix said, voice raw. "I'm not going to let them kill you."

"Nobody's going to get killed," Noah said.

"That's an order," Calliope chimed in. "We're going to figure this out."

Atticus was in the hallway now, inching closer to the nurses station. The view from the left was completely obscured by the corner of the wall and Jericho's body.

Atticus went right. It wasn't much better. Seven stood closely behind Jericho.

Atticus felt, more than saw, his brothers fanning out, each of them trying to get the best shot.

"Seven, can you take a small step to your left?" Atticus asked.

Seven couldn't answer, but he slowly, carefully, swayed to one side, carefully lifting his foot and placing it an inch to the left before swaying back and repeating the movement with his opposite leg. It was imperceptible to Agnes, but it finally allowed Atticus a view of Agnes's blonde hair.

Atticus raised his gun, leveling his sight on the very top of her head, the only thing visible. Everything seemed like it was moving too slow and too fast at the same time. Fuck. Atticus couldn't lose him. Not to that bitch.

"Drop the guns," Agnes shouted over Jericho's shoulder, her voice taut like a wire close to snapping. "All of you."

She was barely hanging on. If Atticus didn't do something, she was going to snap and Jericho was going to die.

Jericho dropped his gun to the floor. "That's not going to happen, Agnes. These guys aren't my friends. They're willing to sacrifice me to get you. Just put the gun down and go. We won't follow you."

"Goddammit. I need a bigger fucking target," Atticus growled, frustration leaching into his tone.

Atticus watched Jericho's shoulders rise, heard him take a huge breath, heard him let it out, his shoulders falling. That was for Atticus. Somehow, Atticus knew that was Jericho calming him down.

"But you do have a target?" Adam asked.

Atticus shook his head. "Barely. Jericho, is there any way you could shift to your left like Seven."

Jericho gave the barest shake of his head. Fuck. Fuck. Fuck. He could see the top of her head just over Jericho's shoulder, but if he was even a hair off, he would shoot Jericho in either the shoulder or the throat. One could maim him, the other could kill him. Atticus couldn't live with himself if he was the reason Jericho died.

"Can you make the shot or not?" Asa asked.

"You know he's not a great shooter," Avi muttered.

"Both of you shut up," August snapped. "You can do this, Atticus. Even if you only graze her, it will be enough for Jericho to get the jump on her."

Atticus swallowed the lump in his throat. "But if I miss, I'll kill him."

"So, don't miss," August said, voice as calm and rational as always.

Sure. Don't miss. That seemed easy enough. Atticus, the guy who fucked up half his kills, just had to take a nearly impossible shot that could potentially kill the only person who ever loved him. "I can't do it."

"You can." Atticus snapped his head to where Adam stood. "You *won't* miss," Adam reiterated. "You've got this."

Atticus couldn't recall a single time when Adam had ever implied that Atticus was anything more than incompetent. Maybe Adam figured Atticus would hit and kill Jericho and then he wouldn't have to worry about dealing with him. That seemed too extreme even for Adam. But the

alternative was Adam saying something nice about Atticus, which seemed equally absurd.

Atticus refocused on Jericho, narrowing his vision until the only thing he saw was the top of that blonde head. He took a deep breath and let it out.

"You won't miss," Jericho said, shifting his body weight just enough to give Atticus a target. "Now."

Agnes had barely enough time to register his words. "Wha—?"

Atticus pulled the trigger, eyes going wide as a perfect hole formed between her brows. She hung there suspended like a puppet on a string before she dropped out of sight.

"What happened?" Noah shouted.

"Target eliminated," August said. "No casualties."

Atticus dropped his gun and ran to Jericho, throwing his arms around him. He didn't care if he looked weak or desperate. He just needed to touch him, feel the heat of his body, feel his breath, hear his voice. Holy fuck. Holy fuck. That was so close. Too close.

Jericho hugged him back tightly, burying his face against his neck. "And you said you were bad at killing, Freckles."

"I think my heart stopped," Atticus confessed.

Seven clapped Atticus on the back. "Nice shot, man. Can we get the fuck out of here?"

Atticus nodded. "Yeah, let's go."

Atticus stared down into the pit below, at the slew of boys

shouting and throwing Doritos at each other. There was a movie on, but none of them were really watching it. Felix had a sketch pad and was drawing something with long, sure movements. Arsen was sitting in the corner of the couch, away from the melee.

"Is it always like this?"

Jericho wrapped his arms around him from behind, hooking his chin over his shoulder to peer down at the chaos, saying fondly, "Sometimes, it's worse."

"Where did they all come from?" Atticus asked. "Do they have families of their own, or are you it?"

Jericho sighed. "Some of them have family, if you can call them that." He pointed at each of them in turn, starting with the blue-haired boy. "Arsen had a father with Russian mob ties, who drove home with his fists exactly how bad for business having a gay son was."

"Asshole," Atticus muttered.

Jericho nodded, pointing to Nico, who sat dead center of the fray, a lollipop hanging from his mouth, like always. He reminded Atticus of Adam, so cocky, so self-assured. "Nico's dad is doing twenty for money laundering, and his mother's a disaster. He shares a shitty apartment with Levi, but the walls are paper thin and most of their neighbors are either sex workers or drug dealers, which makes it hard to sleep."

Atticus scoffed. "I imagine it would be."

Atticus knew what it was like to be afraid to go to sleep at night because it wasn't safe. He hadn't thought about it in years, but seeing Benny, seeing those boys below—barely out of their teens—trying so hard to stay safe made him

think of his own fucked up past.

Jericho pointed to Cree. "Cree's adoptive parents are abusive as fuck evangelicals who treated Cree like a servant most of his life."

Finally, he pointed to Levi with his angelic face and a mop of blond curls. "And Levi's mom was an exotic dancer, so he had to be alone at night in a very dangerous neighborhood."

"So, you...adopted them," Atticus said, sounding both amused and impressed.

Jericho turned his head, kissing Atticus behind the ear. "I gave a bunch of queer kids a place to feel safe."

Atticus tilted his head, giving him better access. "And trained them to kill."

"It wasn't my intention. When I went after the men who assaulted my mom, word got around. People started coming to me, people who couldn't go to the police for fear of retaliation or being deported."

Atticus leaned back against Jericho, sighing as his hands slid up under his sweater to caress over his abdomen. "You're a good man. They held their own in the extraction."

"Better than me," Jericho said, his tone suggesting he was only half joking.

Atticus craned his head to make eye contact with Jericho. "There was no way you could have known that bitch would be there on the other side of that door."

"I dropped my guard. I should have had my gun at the ready, then I could have just fired. I would have had the element of surprise." Jericho shook his head. "Yeah, but if

you hadn't been there—"

"But I was. I'll always be there," Atticus said, knowing deep in his bones it was true. There was nobody but Jericho. Nobody. Nobody even came close.

Jericho still gazed down at the boys, his voice quiet as a confession. "Sometimes, I wonder if I fucked them up for life. I never set out to create an army of teens. I just couldn't handle everything on my own. There were too many people who needed help. At first, I tried to keep them away from the violence. They just gathered information for me, but eventually, they began to see it as a…"

"Calling?" Atticus supplied.

Jericho nodded. "It didn't happen all at once, you know? Felix was being tormented at school for acting too feminine, wearing girl clothes, whatever the fuck that means. He was miserable, cried every single day. Then he became friends with Levi, who was also out and a little too pretty for the liking of his classmates. Whenever his mom was working, he would come here so he had a safe place to sleep. They just kept showing up, looking for a safe space. I just wanted everybody to feel safe."

"You must have done something right. They're still here."

Jericho nodded. "They're all adults now—barely—but they come back here night after night, still trying to avoid their shitty lives or their shitty apartments. That's one of the hazards of being with me, Freckles. We're sort of a package deal."

Atticus turned in his arms. "I was raised in a house full of homicidal boys. This is nothing new. Where do they sleep

when they're here? Seems like cramped quarters."

"A couple of them will fight over the couch, and others will bed down in sleeping bags."

Atticus frowned. "On the concrete?"

Jericho shrugged. "I've offered to let them crash up here, but it's not really big enough."

"It doesn't seem right that they don't have a place to sleep when they're here. You should buy the place next door and turn it into a dorm or buy an apartment building somewhere safe and just let them live there."

Jericho laughed, lips dragging across Atticus's. "I do okay for myself, Freckles, but my name's not Rockefeller."

Atticus's mouth went desert dry. "But it could be Mulvaney."

Jericho's whole body went rigid for a split second, then Jericho peered up at him. "Did...did you just propose to me, Freckles?"

Atticus gave a stilted nod. "I think I did, yeah."

"Did you mean it?" Jericho asked, a tension in his tone that matched the sudden panic seizing Atticus's heart. What if he said no? What if it was too fast, too soon? Jericho had said repeatedly that he'd never let Atticus go, but that was a far cry from making it legal.

Atticus gave another stilted nod. "Yeah. Yeah, I did."

"Then, yeah, Freckles. The answer is yes."

EPILOGUE

ATTICUS

"I can't figure out if you're trying to be romantic or if you're taking me out to the woods to kill and dismember me."

Atticus scoffed. "Dismember you in these pants? They cost almost two grand." When he snuck a glance at Jericho in the passenger seat, he stared out into the inky black darkness, still looking suspicious. Atticus laughed. "Like I'd kill you on our anniversary? I'm not that sentimental."

Jericho grinned, finally looking at him then. "Aw, thanks, Freckles."

When Atticus made the turn off, Jericho's face lit up. "Are you taking us to our murder cabin?"

Atticus didn't answer, just reached out and squeezed Jericho's hand, holding it the rest of the way. When he brought the Bronco to a stop, Adam and Noah were already waiting there. Jericho frowned. "What's going on?"

Atticus turned in his seat to look at Jericho. "Well, one, I'm not just taking you to our murder cabin. I bought our murder cabin. For us." He pulled the key free from his

pocket and dangled it between them.

Jericho's brow shot up, and he gave Atticus a heated glance. "You bought me our murder cabin? I don't know, Freckles. That sounds pretty fucking sentimental."

Atticus snorted. "Please, I got it for a steal." He wrinkled his nose. "Apparently, they found bloodstains on the floor and pieces of human remains in there."

Jericho started to open the door, then quickly closed it, turning to look back at Atticus, suspicion returning. "Wait, you said one. Does that mean there's a two? And does this two have anything to do with why your brother and Noah are crashing our anniversary?"

Atticus rolled his eyes. "They're not, I promise. I just needed them to…babysit your present."

"Babysit my present?" Jericho repeated slowly.

Atticus grinned. "You'll see."

Jericho studied Atticus's face. "Did you, like, adopt a baby without telling me? I think we've already got a full house at home."

"Yes, I adopted an infant and asked my brother and his fiancé to drive it out to the middle of the woods so I could present it to you in our murder cabin as a surprise." When Jericho continued to stare, Atticus laughed. "No, you know I hate kids. I'll definitely leave that to August and Lucas."

August and Lucas were deeply entrenched in the process of in vitro fertilization. Now that Cricket had agreed to be their surrogate, they spent a lot of time hopping between doctors appointments and attorneys. Having a baby was much more complicated when there were two fathers, it

seemed. Luckily, there was a village of murderers just waiting to raise this child. Bet they wouldn't mention that in any legal documents.

No, Atticus much preferred his and Jericho's children. They were fully grown and completely self-sufficient. Well, okay, not completely, but there were no diapers or teething or schoolyard bullies.

Atticus had bought the building beside Jericho's shop and demolished the inside. Asa had redesigned the space to accommodate up to twenty people, if necessary. The zoning had been a nightmare, but it was amazing the doors money opened.

The top floor had several small but efficient rooms, the bottom was a recreation center of sorts. There were games and books, couches and chairs, pretty much anything a bunch of twenty-one year olds needed to amuse themselves.

There was a door between the two buildings that allowed them to come and go from Jericho's shop as often as they liked unseen, which Arsen loved since he could essentially roll out of bed and be at work.

"Why are we here, Freckles?"

Atticus dragged himself from his thoughts. "Because, after months of searching, I finally found you the perfect anniversary gift."

Jericho eyed him warily but slid from the Bronco, waiting for Atticus to come around the vehicle before approaching Adam and Noah. Adam nodded at Atticus and then proceeded to do some complicated handshake thing with Jericho. The two of them had their own thing now that

they'd reached some kind of understanding.

Adam was still an asshole, still spoiled and selfish, but he stopped making snide comments about Atticus's inability to kill, or the way he dressed, or, well, everything. Maybe Jericho had threatened him, but Atticus didn't think so. He also didn't question it.

"Careful with that one," Noah said, nodding towards the cabin with a grimace. "He's a spitter."

"A spitter?" Jericho echoed.

Noah nodded earnestly. "Yeah, like one of those creepy little Jurassic Park dinosaurs that spits goo at you to blind you. I put a bag over his head."

Jericho looked at Atticus in confusion. "What the hell did you get me, Freckles? A llama?"

Atticus took Jericho's hand and led him into the cabin as the others drove away. Jericho stopped short just inside the doorway, taking in the scene. There was a man tied to the chair in the center of the room, arms and legs bound, a sack over his head.

"You wanna tell me what's going on?" Jericho asked warily.

"Sure," Atticus said, voice going soft. "I found him."

Jericho frowned. "Found who?" At Atticus's heavy silence, Jericho's eyes grew wide. "Him? Him, him? Reed? You found Reed? Where?"

Atticus glared in the man's general direction. "Running some hatchet job clinic in Mexico. It was a giant pain in the ass getting him back over the border, but you'd be shocked at what the Federales are willing to do for a paycheck."

Reed was the last domino to fall. They hadn't been able to find anything linking Gabriel Velez to Reed or his hospital of horrors. As much as Atticus would have loved to get Gabe in their murder cabin, he was just a shitty cop on the take. Well, he was anyway. Now he was a shitty former cop working as a bartender.

Jericho crossed the room, yanking the hood from the man. Atticus couldn't believe that a man so…average could have caused so much chaos and destruction. He was pathetic, really. Thinning gray hair, doughy face. But there was a meanness to him. He had dead eyes. Almost reptilian. Maybe that explained the spitting.

"Who the fuck are you people?"

"The medical board," Atticus quipped. "We're here to officially revoke your license."

The man frowned in confusion. "What?"

"My name is Jericho Navarro. My sister Mercy ended up in one of your little clinics. Then she ended up dead."

Atticus watched understanding dawn. The man began to frantically shake his head, his body erupting in flop sweat. "I'm sorry for your loss, but this was for a greater good. There's much more at play than simply one person. My studies could change the way wars are fought."

Jericho punched the man in the face hard enough to rocket him backwards, blood flying from his lips.

Atticus stepped closer. "The military shut you down years ago. We thought, at first, you were just running a black book operation. But through numerous sources we learned that your tactics were deemed too cruel for the military.

How much of a fucking monster do you have to be for a super-secret military operation to decide you're too brutal?"

Jericho looked around. "Did you bring my tools, Freckles?"

"Of course." Atticus nodded towards the bag on the floor. "I even packed something extra special for the occasion."

Jericho kissed him long and deep until Atticus felt warm in his core. "Thanks."

Atticus preened, hopping up onto the table and lying back, just as he'd done when they'd interrogated Trevor. Jericho took his time, setting up his tools, pausing when he stopped at his special surprise. "Is this a hand saw?"

"August found it at the old meat packing plant. Turn the safety off and squeeze the trigger."

Jericho did as instructed and it roared to life. His eyes went wide. "It's cordless? This is amazing."

Atticus snickered. "Don't fall too in love with it. It's August's favorite toy. It's only on loan."

Jericho stared hard at the doctor, who was frantically trying to wiggle himself from his restraints. "I don't even know where to begin."

"When in doubt, start at the ears and work your way down," Atticus said, opening a granola bar and the latest Journal of the American Medical Association.

Jericho shrugged. "That's a great idea."

"Please, don't do this—" There was the sound of the saw roaring to life, and then Reed began to scream.

Atticus flipped through his journal, looking for his latest paper. "I can't believe they shoved my article all the way in the back," he said sulkily. "That was definitely a front page

article."

There was another scream and the slick sound of the man's ear falling to the floor. "Yeah, you definitely should have been front and center, Freckles."

"It's true," Atticus agreed, taking another bite of his granola bar and chewing it thoughtfully.

Atticus was halfway through the journal when the screaming finally stopped. There was blood everywhere. Luckily, Atticus had the forethought to lay down some tarps. They had to be much more careful now that they owned the place.

Atticus heard the sink turn on as Jericho washed up, pulling his shirt from over his head to let the water run over his chest. He was so hot.

When he caught Atticus watching, he grinned. "What's that look for, Freckles?"

Atticus reached down and unbuckled his jeans. "Want the third part of your present?"

Jericho crossed the room, yanking Atticus into a sitting position on the end of the table, smashing their mouths together, just like the first night they met, but this time, Atticus was a much more active participant. His dick was already hard.

"Fuck me," Atticus whispered into his mouth.

Jericho didn't break the kiss, just said, "No lube. Or did my little boy scout bring that, too?"

Atticus pushed him back enough to look him in the eye. "No. I...prepped."

"Christ, Freckles. You can't just say that shit to me."

Jericho pushed Atticus back onto the wooden table, yanking off his boots and pulling his jeans and underwear out of the way, pupils dilating as he saw Atticus's flushed erection standing at attention. Jericho freed himself, dragging Atticus forward until his ass hung off the table. He probably had fucking splinters but he really didn't fucking care. He just wanted Jericho inside him. Jericho used Atticus's jeans to practically bend him in half, his free hand probing Atticus's hole.

"Fuck, you're already wet for me. When did you do this?"

"At the restaurant."

Jericho growled, pulling his fingers free. Atticus had just enough time to recognize the blunt head of Jericho's cock pressing against him before he slammed home, burying himself to the hilt. They both groaned. "I'm not going to be gentle, Freckles."

"I didn't fucking ask you to."

Jericho's pace was relentless as he pounded into Atticus in a steady, driving rhythm that had him grazing his prostate with every third thrust until Atticus was leaking all over himself. This was his favorite Jericho. The raw, unfiltered, fresh from a kill Jericho. Atticus loved how animalistic he was. Sex was the only way to feed that need, to burn through all the adrenaline coursing through him.

"Fuck. I can't believe I was eating dinner and you were in the bathroom, pants down, fingering yourself open for me. Fuck. Did you think about me? About this? About how good it would feel when I was pounding into this slutty little hole again and again?"

"Yes. Fuck. Oh, God. Touch me."

When Jericho's hand closed around him, he couldn't help the cry that escaped.

"You're always so tight, so hot inside. I'm not going to last, but I swear I'm going to bend you over and fuck you again before we both go to sleep. Hell, I might just stay up and fuck you all night long. Would you like that, Freckles? Want me to fill you up? When we're done, maybe I'll let you fall asleep nursing my cock. You fucking love that."

Atticus flushed to the tips of his ears. He did love that. He loved falling asleep with Jericho inside him, or with him still in his mouth. Sometimes, he would just lie there with his head in his lap, Jericho's soft cock in his mouth as they watched TV and Jericho threading fingers through his hair.

Jericho loved it. He told Atticus all the time. He'd play with his hair and tell him how much he loved how needy Atticus was, how he loved that Atticus needed them to be joined in some way as often as possible.

Jericho's thrusts grew faster, his hand quickening, matching his tempo. He was so close, had been so ready since way before they'd gotten to the restaurant. Lightning shot down his spine with every twist and pull of Jericho's hand until his toes were curling. "Oh, fuck. I'm gonna come."

"Do it," Jericho rasped. "I love the way it feels when you come with me inside you."

Atticus gave a harsh shout, his cum shooting over his belly. Jericho gave a deep, throaty moan. "Holy fuck, Freckles, your hole is just spasming around me, milking every fucking drop."

Jericho's whole body went rigid as he came, working into Atticus in short aborted thrusts, his cock throbbing inside him. That would never stop being sexy. Ever. He winced when Jericho pulled free, gently lowering Atticus's legs.

"Fuck. You really know how to treat a man on his anniversary."

Jericho righted his clothing without cleaning off, then dragged Atticus into a sitting position once more, kissing him again, gentler this time.

"Seriously, Freckles. This was just what I needed to close this chapter once and for all. I'm sorry Felix didn't get his chance at him."

"I offered," Atticus said. "Felix said he didn't want to see the man. That you should just text him that it was done so Mercy could be at peace at last."

Jericho pressed their foreheads together. "I love you."

"I love you, too," Atticus said truthfully.

"What do we do with him?" Jericho said, rolling his head to look at the mess still tied to the chair. "We can't just leave him for the animals this time."

Atticus grimaced. "That's what the tarps are for. There's a boat out by the lake. We'll dump him there. I know that's not exactly the most romantic way to end the night, but…"

Jericho grinned, kissing Atticus once more. "A boat ride under the stars with you? I don't know, Freckles. Sounds like romance to me."

"Our kind of romance," Atticus said.

Jericho kissed him again softly. "We're the only ones who matter."

DEAR READER,

Thank you so much for reading *Moonstruck*, Book 3 in my Necessary Evils Series. I hope you loved reading this book as much as I loved writing it. I'm so grateful I've found people who love my quirky little psychopathic family. If you are desperate for more Jericho and Atticus, be sure to check out their bonus epilogue.

If you've read my books before, you have probably come to realize that I have an addiction to writing about the psyche and exactly how both nature and nurture often play a part in who a person becomes. I spent years working as an RN in a psychiatric hospital, and most of those years I spent with children aged anywhere from five to eighteen. It took a big toll on me and my own mental health, which is why writing these characters has become my own form of therapy. While sociopathic bodyguards and megalomaniacal cult leaders are all works of fiction, my heroes and villains are all drawn from real people who I encountered during my time as a nurse.

Writing Atticus and Jericho's story was a huge break from the major angst in many of my previous books in the series. Do Atticus and Jericho have trauma? Sure. But they've both found ways to channel that trauma. Jericho has a near pathological need to control everything, and Atticus is desperate for the world to see him as perfect. Together, they fill the voids in each other's lives without having to exorcise any personal demons. They stay just as fucked up as they were but find somebody who compliments their fuckery. My favorite kind of love story.

Coming up, I have Book 4 in the Necessary Evils Series, *Headcase*, where Asa meets his match in a cocky, calculating reporter with an agenda.

If you guys are really loving the books, please consider joining my Facebook reader group, **Onley's Oubliette**, and signing up for my newsletter where you can find my current weekly serial, *Where the Devil Don't Go*, a kinky Daddy book about an ancient demon with a pain kink and the human slave boy who just happens to be a masochist. You'll gain access to any previous chapters when you sign up. And if you really, really love my books and want to read them before anybody else, as well as gain access to things like signed paperbacks, upcoming books as I write them, and exclusive merch, consider joining my Patreon.

You can also find signed books and merch on my website throughout the year. Feel free to hit me up on my social media. I love talking to readers.

Finally, if you did love this book, (or even if you didn't. Eek!) it would be amazing if you could take a minute to review it. Reviews are like gold for authors.

Thank you again for reading.

ABOUT THE AUTHOR

ONLEY JAMES is the pen name of YA author, Martina McAtee, who lives in Central Florida with her children, her pitbull, her weiner dog, and an ever-growing collection of shady looking cats. She splits her time between writing YA LGBT paranormal romances and writing adult m/m romances.

When not at her desk, you can find her mainlining Starbucks refreshers, whining about how much she has to do, and avoiding the things she has to do by binge-watching unhealthy amounts of television in one sitting. She loves ghost stories, true crime documentaries, obsessively scrolling social media, and writing kinky, snarky books about men who fall in love with other men.

Find her online at:
WWW.ONLEYJAMES.COM